I0779809

From Before

From Before

Jess J. Blooms

Copyright © 2025 Jess J. Blooms All rights reserved

The characters and events portrayed in this book are fictitious. Any similarity to real persons, living or dead, is coincidental and not intended by the author.

No part of this book may be reproduced, or stored in a retrieval system, or transmitted in any form or by any means, electronic, mechanical, photocopying, recording, or otherwise, without express written permission of the publisher.

ISBN: 9798292644972
Imprint: Independently published

Cover design by: Jess J. Blooms
Library of Congress Control Number: 2018675309
Printed in the United States of America

To the risk-takers, wish-makers, and those

that had to heal after heart-breakers.

Content Warnings:

Abuse, Domestic Violence, Marijuana, Guns, Stalking, Alcohol

PRESENT DAY
AGE 25

CHAPTER 1

"Shit!" The yelp comes out of me as I jerk back, wincing.

Abby's smiling at me as I continue to take in our surroundings.

Air mattress. Floor. Empty house.

Oh, right…

Despite it being the fourth morning in a row of waking up like this, I wake up confused every time. Quickly packing up all of your things and moving has a way of throwing you off.

"Were you watching me sleep?" my best friend actually looks offended by my question.

"No! I woke up and looked at you to see if you were awake. And then you opened your eyes".

Her shoulder-length, straight blond hair is all over her face and she pushes it out of the way as she sits up to nervously say "I had a very strange dream last night".

We are stark contrasts of each other when I put my long, wavy brown hair in a bun as I sit up, interested in what she's about to say. Before telling me her dream, she mutters to herself "It felt so real…" and then directs her eyes to me "I had a dream you and Silas were still together".

She says it in a way like she's just as

surprised as I am and I give her a little scoff before questioning "Silas, like my dead ex-boyfriend?".

Abby replies "That wasn't confirmed… just that he's missing".

I flinch at her reminder and mutter "…he better be dead" and see that her eyes went wide in surprise but also holding in laughter at my menacing tone.

I try to sound less aggressive, not wanting her to regret telling me her dream "Obviously I don't wish death on anyone. But… I'd prefer that over having a boyfriend of two years that just disappeared on me for no reason".

Not knowing what to say that, she continues "We were the age we are now and it was like an older version of him, how weird is that?".

Shrugging, I try to be even more passive than I was a moment ago "Definitely weird… are you hungry?".

She smiles and I'm happy that my distraction worked as we get up and I cook us breakfast in my almost-empty kitchen. I make food and distracted conversation as my thoughts go further and further back in time.

While we share lighthearted conversation, I can't stop the incoming flashes of forest-green eyes. Or the glimpses that follow of a wide, perfectly-dimpled grin.

I can feel myself slipping into memories again, so I shake my head and let out a quick breath as I presume my morning routine. I don't have the time to think about useless, painful memories right now... which is why I don't tell Abby about the dream that I had last night.

This was our fourth night at my new house and we have one more night before I drop her off at the airport in the late-morning. I've put my friend through some hard labor of helping me pack up my life, move it a state over and unpack everything.

So, I thank her the only way she will really receive: food. She's rejected all other forms of payment so if I'm not making her food on my limited supplies, then I've been treating her to restaurants nearby.

It's a win-win because it gives me an excuse to check out my new city and I get to thank her for leaving her fiancé, Tyler, for a week. Not to mention, taking the time off of work. They've been dating since college so she usually gets excited about having a week of space, but I'm sure she would have preferred an actual vacation.

She does a little dance in her chair as I bring plates of toast, eggs and fruit down to the small table in front of my kitchen. "Okay we just have to finish unpacking the pod today and then I think we are good to go" I bring my glass of juice in and she does the same to clink glasses.

A questioning look comes over her face to ask "You have me for one more full day, are you sure there's nothing else you need help with?".

Thinking for a moment, I rattle of a few last-minute things that would be easier to do as a duo and then finish with "and obviously we deserve a really nice dinner tonight".

Abby smiles inquisitively "You don't have to keep shoving food at me, I'm happy to be here for you".

"I know, but it was also last minute and you had to use your PTO for this" I reply.

The entire process of buying the house and moving was only a few weeks so there was a lot of last-minute coordinating.

Her voice has a little edge to it as she clarifies "Hazel, you had to move fast because you got a suspiciously amazing deal on this house… and I'll do anything to help you be as far away as possible from Brandon".

Abby finishes with an eye roll and I can tell she worked herself up so I try to de-escalate "Well, if we didn't take any stops, it would have taken us nine hours to get here so I think we definitely got enough distance".

Her blue eyes take on a comically threatening look when she says "I hope so… or I'm buying you a gun".

I laugh in surprise and take a huge bite of food, realizing we haven't eaten because we once again got too distracted while talking.

Abby soon realizes the same thing and begins shoveling food into her mouth. The rest of the quick meal is used to plan the day out before we both go upstairs and get ready for the day.

We quickly divide to the different bathrooms, washing up and then changing into our ratty moving clothes. We meet downstairs and make a list of where to start. The house has two bedrooms, two bathrooms, and a garage that will be used for my business's workspace.

I left the heavy furniture at home with my

parents so we don't have a lot of heavy things to move around. The couch, bed and mattress that I ordered will be delivered after Abby leaves so we really only have to move smaller things which is easy to divide between us.

I'm on the shorter side, so Abby loves the opportunity to show off. She puts the mason jars and coffee mugs on the higher shelves while I crouch to put the crackpot and air fryer in the bottom cabinet. We work while a fun playlist blasts from my Bluetooth speaker and end up making mimosas which has become a daily pattern for us.

Once we decide most of the house is unpacked, we wander into my bare backyard- trying to visualize what it will look like.

I don't have any outdoor furniture besides a small set for two that will need to be replaced eventually. I'd love to get everything I need at once, but I will have to slowly buy and replace so I don't spend all of my money in one go.

There's a nice-sized backyard, small front porch, and a small balcony outside of my bedroom on the second story. So, I will definitely be patrolling through the wealthy neighborhoods looking for any throw-away's that I can salvage.

The front yard has a one-car driveway leading to the garage and large patches of grass on either side that connect along sides of the house to the backyard. I have a neighbor along my back-fence and a neighbor on the right side who I haven't seen yet.

On the left side, there is about 20 feet of dense shrubs and trees giving me privacy until the next property starts. As we go to walk back inside, I think I hear a noise from the yard next to mine that I share with the next-door neighbor.

Pausing, I stop to listen but don't notice anything so I walk a little faster inside and double-check that I locked both locks on the backdoor. Ever since leaving Brandon, I've been on edge trying to convince myself that I'm not being watched. But I can't help feeling the paranoia every time I'm outside of my home.

CHAPTER 2

At dinner, we clink glasses of white wine when Abby suddenly gets a little misty-eyed "Congratulations, Hazel! I know it wasn't the best circumstances that led to you being here... but everything happens for a reason and I think you will find out why that is soon enough".

I nod "I couldn't have done it without you- if I ever complain about maid of honor duties just remind me of this and I will shut up immediately" ... and now my eyes are misty. We spend dinner making plans of when we will see each other next and promising to have regular phone calls.

Neither of us can seem to get rid of the sad undertone of being far from each other for the first time in almost ten years. The last night of having Abby over goes by too fast, but we get to stay up a little later since her flight is in the late-morning and the airport isn't too far away.

One of the first things we bought when we got here was a new TV. I knew we would want to watch our dumb shows in our down time together, and I wouldn't have been able to fit one in my car for the drive here.

So, we watch reality shows until our blinks get slower and slower and we fall asleep to the standard scripted fights we love. I toss and turn more than usual, suddenly much more aware of how lonely it will be when Abby leaves and I have no one near me.

When she wakes up, I don't tell her about my dreams that I can't seem to get rid of. Instead, I ask "Want to sit in the grass and sip some coffee in the sunshine?". She looks at me curiously for a second likes she's caught on to my act, before smiling the same way back "Of course I do!".

Laying out a large outdoor blanket, we make a little breakfast picnic with Nespresso cappuccinos and pastries, soft music playing in the background to complete our sunny start to the day. After about twenty minutes, we hear my side neighbor's back door slide open and purposeful, booted footsteps.

We look at each other in excitement as we hear a hose turn on and bushes being sprayed in the farthest part of his backyard. The steps sound like a man's but that's all I can tell and I might not even be correct. I was hoping for a woman around my age so I can have an immediate friend (I know, wishful thinking), but after hearing the footsteps I can't help but hope it's a cute single guy.

I haven't seen many signs of life next door- if it wasn't for the dark green jeep that's parked on the street out front, I would have thought it was a model home. Abby and I look back at each other and both silently stand up to see if we can see through the cracks in the shared fence.

I don't see anything but I hear the back door slide open and close so I look at Abby to see if she sees more since she has a greater height advantage.

She waits a minute and then whispers "I didn't get a good look but he's tall, in good shape and has dark hair". She looks as excited as if it was her neighbor and she didn't have Tyler waiting for her back home.

Even though my new neighbor is inside his house and can't hear us, Abby still whispers "I think he's around our age!". She looks so excited that I don't want to ruin the moment by saying we don't know if he's single so I just make an excited looking face and sit back down.

Abby is back and sitting on the blanket, but she looks like she's thinking about something while staring at the house. "What are you thinking?" I ask.

She's still looking away when she answers, "Maybe if you do become friends with your neighbor, you can ask why there's so much security for this house".

I realize she's staring at the motion lights surrounding the house. She's not exaggerating, there's an additional lock on every door and window so there is no way to get in from the outside. I think it over, debating if it's normal to have that much security or if it's excessive.

I think for a moment, "If we become friends I'll ask about the previous owners- the nice part is that it's all the same things I would have bought anyways".

Abby nods "All that's left is your doorbell camera. You got it today, right? Let's go set it up!" and she gets up and helps me up.

It takes us less than an hour to install the

doorbell and learn how to use the app with our show playing in the background. We get ready for the day and while I shower, Abby packs her things up and leaves them by the door. We have time to go to a breakfast place before the airport so Abby finds one nearby as we bring her things out to the car and get inside.

I noticed Abby staring at the vacant house across the street "It's definitely a family neighborhood, hopefully whoever moves in is younger so you can have a neighbor friend".

I reverse my car out of the driveway as she adds "But the neighbor that you share a fence with is the most important one so I hope you guys get along".

I toss a quick look at the neighbor's house before putting the car in 'drive' and going forward, noticing their front door shutting at the same time. Abby's flight is at 1 p.m., so we figure 11 a.m. is plenty of time to drop her off. So, after we eat breakfast, we park in the airport's parking lot.

We walk in together and I walk her to the security line trying to hold my emotions at bay "Thank you again, Abby. I'm going to miss you so much but I'll see you soon". I feel my tears starting so I give her a tight hug that she reciprocates.

I hear her sniffle "Love you! Don't forget about me!".

I roll my eyes at that, knowing I never could and as I walk away, I say loudly "Love you too! Tell Tyler 'hi' for me and that he's invited next time!".

I walk the ten minutes back to my car but

once I'm inside it feels so crushingly silent that I don't feel ready to go back home yet. I can only hope that once all of my things are settled in, the silence will be a peace to me and not a reminder of my loneliness.

Not in a rush to go back to the house, I take my time running errands and spend a few hours reading a book at a coffee shop, just enjoying the background commotion of other people. I manage to waste enough time to make it until 6 pm when it begins to get dark and I promise myself a movie and an early night.

Pulling into my driveway, I see movement over in the neighbor's yard and since it's dark, I'm able to finally get a long look without looking like a creep. It's too dark to make out details, but I do see a tall, muscular man walking gracefully with a few boxes in hand.

He's bringing them from his garage into his jeep but walking quickly. When I step out of the car and shut my door, he makes a clumsy step and looks at me before turning away. Feeling caught, I yell "Hello!" and wait for him to acknowledge me- but disappointment sets in when he doesn't react. He keeps walking to his car and setting his handful down in the backseat.

Maybe he didn't hear me? Too embarrassed to try again, I quickly walk inside and hope that isn't how the rest of our time living next to each other is. It isn't long before I hear his car speed away and I sigh in relief that he's probably just busy and didn't notice.

CHAPTER 3

The next week goes by surprisingly fast. Once the mattress, bed and couch got delivered, I was able to get fully unpacked and decorate the house how I wanted. I tentatively plan when I will paint and get more decor done later down the road, prioritizing everything around my bank account.

One of the selling points of the house was the large park nearby with great running trails, so I head over almost every morning to run a few miles to start the day. Feeling motivated, I've also slowly set my workspace up in the garage to start my business back up next week.

What started as a side-hustle, became a full-time job that I can fully operate out of my home with just a few machines I have amassed over the years. Creating custom embroidered and printed merchandise in individual and bulk orders has somehow led to a semi-comfortable income.

I began just making random custom items for loved ones but, fortunately, word of mouth spread over the years and once a few businesses liked my products, I was able to fully dedicate myself. Other companies can do it cheaper, so I make up for it by being able to do more customized items- even hand-sewing if necessary- to set my products apart.

With the sky looking like it will be dusk in an hour or so, I get dressed in my running clothes and head to the park that's a short walk over.

I've been an avid runner for a few years but I'm never too confident about my surroundings. Despite the safe area this neighborhood seems to be, I still have my running vest with a whistle, gel pepper spray and a pocket knife in easy-to-grab places. I also run with a taser since this park has less people in the evenings and no place is perfect.

I used to feel ridiculous having this many self-defense weapons, but it's worth it just for the peace of mind to run alone. With the intent to run five miles, I begin a podcast to get lost in, to make the steps go by easier. I want to get back to the house before it's actually dark out so this gives me motivation to stick to the time frame I had in mind.

The podcast I'm listening to is about self-growth and new beginnings- this isn't a talk I'm normally very interested in, which is probably why my mind keeps snagging on irrelevant thoughts. I haven't heard from Brandon since I broke up with him over a quick, short text- which made me relieved at first but the silence has made me increasingly nervous since he's probably the most dramatic person I've ever met.

Also, I haven't seen my neighbor since the first time I actually saw him. I'm in and out of the house a lot so I feel like I would have seen him by now. And why do I keep having dreams about Silas?

The run is easy with my thoughts being preoccupied between men, my business, and the house that seems a little too good to be true. Even though it is a historic home, it has many newly added features that I would have added myself.

Not just the security either, the bedroom has an outdoor balcony that was added right before I bought it- the realtor explaining that the seller thought that I might like one. I mean they were right; I was always jealous that my parents have such a nice outdoor space right by their room. I wanted to have one just like theirs when I had my own home, but the former home-owner knowing that is just a little weird.

Also, I noticed my neighbor- who has a very similar historic home- also has a new-looking balcony on their second story. Did we have the same sellers? I think I'm focusing on unimportant details but that doesn't make it any easier to stop thinking about.

These random, overlapping thoughts mix with the podcast playing in the background and before I know it, I've ran four miles so I just push through the last one and walk back home, looking forward to a hot shower. When I get back to my driveway, the sun is officially setting and I see my neighbor walking out to his car.

He hasn't looked in my direction so I stare shamelessly and with an even better look now, I can see that he has tattoos completely covering his hands and arms.

Basically, everything showing besides his face has artwork all over it, but I don't get close enough to see what the images are. I feel a sudden, quick strike of familiarity when I look at him but I can't think of why since I know he is a stranger.

Forcing myself to stop staring at his tattoos, I move to his outfit.

He has a plain white t-shirt on, with black jeans and boots- nothing fancy but completely highlights his tall, muscular frame. He looks over at me and quickly looks away. It's hard to make out his face because he has a baseball cap on, just like every other time I've seen him.

Nervous that he caught me staring and a little energized after a run, I take my earbud out of my ear and say "Hey! I'm Hazel by the way". Doing my best impression of a golden retriever, hoping that this attempt will go over less horribly than it did last time.

Even though he was clearly walking to his car, he quickly turns around, back to his house but slightly turns his head to say "nice to meet you" and hurries inside. I stand there like an idiot as I watch him walk inside, and then I look around in hopes someone else saw the exchange so we can look at each other like "weird, right?" but of course, I'm alone so I just head inside.

A few hours later, I hear his car door open and close a few times before his car drives off around the same time it did last week. When I looked through the camera app, I watched him for a second as he took the same medium-sized boxes out to his car.

I'm not sure what weekly commitment would need that, but at least I know some of his routine so it can be easier to ignore him. I can tell he's good looking from the few glances I got; how can a handsome guy be that shy and awkward?

I know that's an asshole way to think, but usually the tall, muscular men I've met are obnoxious or just plain loud. Or maybe he thinks he's too hot and doesn't need to be polite… Either way, that was awkward.

Every time I remember it, I cringe to myself. My annoying personality made a grown man haul ass inside to get away from me. I consider that he might have some sort of trauma- he's huge, maybe he was in the military or something?

Either way, I plan on leaving him alone. I don't even want to look in his direction- nothing that would risk a moment that uncomfortable every again. It's probably better that he's a little off, or rude, I don't want to have a crush on my neighbor. I'm new to the area and the last thing that will improve my life right now is shitting where I eat.

The bummer is, he had really nice hair.

Like that medium, dark-brown hair that I would have loved running my fingers through. If I could tell he has nice hair while wearing a hat, I can only imagine what it looks like underneath. I'm woken up several hours later when I hear the same doors shut, and then the front door to his house being closed just like last week.

I'm actually grateful for the interruptions to my sleep, and the dreams that I can't seem to get rid of since my first night here. The dreams that would feel more like nightmares, despite the comfort when I'm actually in them, living them.

Being wrapped in familiar, strong arms and combing my nails through soft, thick hair. The dreams are never specific scenarios like I usually have, instead they are a kaleidoscope of images and feelings. Despite how nice they are while it happens, I somehow always wake in a panic and feel even less rested in the morning- having to make it up with naps later.

They keep going back to the same memories and fantasies from years ago, rather than my most recent breakup- Brandon. Maybe it's the lack of a resolution with a missing person rather than a situation that is already resolved… at least for me it is.

I wake up in bed the next morning, deleting the notifications that I missed a call from an unknown number and head down to start my morning. I've received a few calls from unknown numbers but on principle, I don't answer calls from people I don't know. I never got that many before, but I am noticing more and more and I can't help but to think that they have something to do with Brandon.

After I have my breakfast and coffee, I head to my garage where I stare at the piles upon piles of items: tables, machines and endless boxes of plain merchandise, ready to be customized. I begin to set the tables up and get the equipment out of boxes before I set up the shelves.

After a few hours, I've finally got it organized enough to begin working- and after some time off I'm actually excited to get back to it.

I spend another hour or so replying to emails and scheduling when to make and ship the orders. Once I am almost done, I hear my phone ringing and see it's from an unknown number. As usual, I ignore it and let it ring to completion, feeling relieved when it's done. A moment later, it begins ringing again so I pick it up just in case it is important.

Not saying anything, I just press 'answer' and listen for a voice. There isn't a voice, but there is a noise in the background like a phone in a car driving with the windows down. After a few seconds, I hang up because it sounds more like an accidental call than anything else.

As ridiculous as it is, I can't help but spend the rest of the day a little on edge. There are only a few hours left of the day so I have dinner while watching a movie… and then I decide to watch the sequel.

I quickly head upstairs to get ready for bed and once I'm clean and comfy, I head back down to get cozy on the couch and turn the lights off. I drift off to sleep halfway through the second movie, enjoying being lulled to sleep with the noises in the background.

My sleep isn't deep, I hear the movie go to credits before another movie auto-plays and I drift back off to slightly deeper sleep. It's still dark when I bolt up in my sleep- hearing a huge crashing noise right in front of my house.

Without even thinking, I run over to the window and peak out through the blinds- it's still the middle of the night.

Since I can't see much in the dark, I open the app on my phone to see it through the night-vision feature on my doorbell camera. My fingers are shaky but I concentrate and zoom in a little. It's definitely a crashed car, right in front of my house.

I think about just calling 911 and leaving the situation alone but once I see one person on the ground and another leaning over them, I run out in my bare feet. Since it's a Saturday night, it's most likely a drunk driver so I keep that in mind as I observe the situation from afar before coming closer. There's a man passed out on the ground, with glass from the driver's side window all around him and the man that was standing, is now crouched over him.

I hesitantly walk closer and see the man isn't just observing him, he's gripping the man on the ground by his shirt collar, shaking him but I still can't make his words out so I walk faster until I'm a few feet away. I catch the tail end of the man's growled threats before he quickly stands back up as I approach. I don't stand too close, not wanting my feet to touch shards of glass.

But I watch the furious man begin to turn and as my eyes adjust to the darkness, I realize it's my neighbor- and he's too quick as he walks away from the man on the ground… who I realize is Brandon.

CHAPTER 4

He's passed out on the ground, on the sidewalk in front of his car and it looks like a small explosion happened. Not just the scene around him, but his face is already swelling, along with quite a bit of blood on the ground. Not understanding what's happening but scared by seeing Brandon, I back up and try to understand what I thought was a car accident.

"Go back inside, the cops are on the way" a loud, demanding voice yells. But when I turn to look, my neighbor is already walking up his porch steps and opening his door.

"What happened?" I try to ask him, but he shuts the door instead of answering (or even looking back) and now instead of worrying about Brandon I'm worrying about how he definitely hates me now.

Knowing that the cops are on the way and probably not far, I sit on the porch and keep an eye on Brandon to make sure he doesn't get up. It's only another minute before a cop car shows up, and two men calmly get out despite the scene in front of them. The older one walks towards me, while the young cop goes over to Brandon and checks his vitals. "We heard there's been a drunk driver?" I don't know if that's what my neighbor thought, but I decide honesty is the best policy.

"I'm not sure, I woke up to a crash and saw him like that." the older one stares at me, waiting for more, so I add without thinking "That's my abusive ex, so… I guess he knows where I live now. I just moved here… away from him". The cop looks at me a second longer, analyzing me. He's older like my dad so I hope he takes pity and believes me and gets Brandon as far away as possible.

I don't mention my neighbor, deciding he will just hate me more if the cops go over to his house and ask him questions. I have no idea why my neighbor was that aggressive with Brandon since he doesn't know him. A normal person would assume he needed help- unless he's very passionate about neighborhood safety?

The gray-haired cop is standing next to me, taking notes when I add "It looks like he's drunk and was driving and maybe crashed or something? I was scared to get too close to check because he's been violent in the past". He nods and walks over to his partner who has still not managed to wake Brandon up, but I watch them quietly consult with each other before they come back up to me.

They ask more specific questions like Brandon's address, if he could have any other reason for being in this area, or if we have spoken recently. I tell them the truth and they promise me that they are going to get him checked out, and then ask him some questions. "We may come back or call you for further information. I noticed you have a doorbell camera. Any chance that it recorded everything?".

I briefly look back at the camera to give myself a chance to think "I just moved in and haven't upgraded to the recording version- I'm sorry". It's true, and I plan on changing that as soon as possible.

They both look around at the scene and the younger officer uses a gentle tone "No need to apologize, go back to sleep if you can- the sun will be up soon".

They take it from there as I go back inside and overhear the car getting towed, and a paramedic taking Brandon away to give him a real check-up. I make a note to sweep the glass up in the morning and then make sure everything is locked again, upgrade my doorbell description to include recording, and go back to trying to sleep on the couch.

I don't know why I prefer sleeping here tonight, I think it's an animal instinct to be closer to the exits, or maybe to hear things better. I can't believe that Brandon is here- and that he found me. That didn't take long at all. What was he planning on doing? I haven't heard from him this whole time but he's going to show up in the middle of the night. Also, how did my neighbor get involved?

It looked like he broke the glass and pulled Brandon out, but obviously he wasn't rescuing him. The neighbor doesn't seem like he cares about other's business at all and why would he care enough to risk an arrest for himself? I don't feel comfortable going to his house and asking about what happened because he has been so weird this entire time, but I still want to thank him so I put it in my mind to think of a non–confrontational "thank you" in the morning.

Somehow, I am actually able to sleep after an hour of repetitive thoughts and questions and around 9 AM I'm awake and feeling semi-rested. Once I have a full mug of coffee and I'm fully conscious, I realize what I need to do. I go to the oven and click the "pre-heat" option, and get ingredients out.

I need to thank my neighbor some way, since he might have saved me from Brandon and the only way I can think of is my grandmother's chocolate chip cookies. They've been a hit with everyone in my life- and if he's anything like Silas, he's going to love them. Silas made me especially confident with these cookies- treating them like they were the best in the entire world.

I made them for Brandon once but he was so normal about it, he just said thank you and ate one, leaving the rest out. Because of the pedestal Silas put them on, I was expecting the same reaction from Brandon but maybe he was the more normal one in that scenario.

When the cookies cool down after baking, I set 12 of them in a cute, small bakery box with a twine string in a bow and an attached note to the box saying *"Thanks for the help! P.s. Please let me know if you see him around again- He's my ex and is not handling the breakup well"*. I put my number underneath so he can let me know if he sees him again and I go to sweep the glass off the sidewalk.

It takes me about 10 minutes to make sure it's all cleaned up and I spend the time looking over at my neighbor's porch every few minutes and when I go back inside, the box is still untouched on the porch. To be fair, it's only been 10 minutes but it takes everything in me not to go outside every 20 minutes to see if they are finally inside.

After a few hours, I go to the mailbox to pretend to look for mail but really, I want to check my neighbor's porch and confirm that the cookies are finally gone. They're finally gone- and I also notice that there's a new security camera pointed at the same spot Brandon's car was so if anyone goes near my front yard, the neighbor will also know.

CHAPTER 5

A few days go by with no updates on Brandon, but the officer who was here the other day called me with some hopeful news. He told me that they gave Brandon a warning to not come near me or my house again, and that they will have him on record for any future indiscretions.

When I asked whether he had an explanation, the officer reluctantly told me that Brandon wouldn't say anything. I put a note in my planner to request a restraining order since that's pretty much all I can do in this situation.

I flinch at every loud noise and when I shower, I'm mostly listening for any noise I might be able to catch of someone getting into the house somehow. Now that I have confirmation that he knows where I live, I have no peace. I now know it's possible for him to show up at any time and do anything.

About a week after the incident, I get a letter in the mail from Brandon. It's a long rambling letter about how sorry he is that I found him passed out in my yard and called the cops on him. He didn't apologize for showing up, instead he said that if my "asshole neighbor" didn't attack him, he was going to try to leave a few presents and wish me luck.

I don't believe him at all, and I also don't

respond- I don't want to stoke the fires. Instead, I save the letter and take pictures of it for evidence as proof of contact and try my best to forget about it. As if he knew when I got the letter, he texted me the next day.

"*Your neighbor won't always be home to assault me, I hope you'll let me talk to you next time*".

I read it for what it is- a threat. I screenshot it and ignore it, but I don't block him. I want to know anytime he's trying to contact me. But now I also know for sure that me getting rid of Brandon isn't going to be as easy as just moving away and hoping he forgets.

He's right, my neighbor won't always be home. I lie low for a week just out of fear but after that, I get back to my routine of running at the park. Torn in two, part of me wants to hide forever in my new fortress- the other half not wanting Brandon to control my life when we aren't even together.

When I told Abby, she freaked out and said I should buy a gun and I'm sure my parents would say the same if I told them. Which, I didn't. I don't want to immediately scare them after moving. After my run today, I wandered a little farther on the other side of the park and ended up at a cafe and bookstore called "Cabookccino"- I stared at the title for several seconds, trying to decide how I felt about the funky name and then I made my way inside.

The entire space is small with the cafe towards the front, and books throughout the back. They made a little reading nook for people to read or work from their laptops with mitch-matching chairs and an old loveseat. I'm not sure why, but this place is mostly empty besides some quick cafe customers.

After I buy two books and a latte, I take the most comfortable looking chair and try to get lost for a little while. After an hour goes by, I've drank my coffee, lots of water and had a pastry while getting absorbed in my book. A woman my age sits down a few chairs away- we're the only ones in the sitting area and I notice her pull out a familiar book.

I quickly look her over and decide to take a risk "Hey! Sorry to bug you but I just need to run to the restroom- can you watch my stuff?".

She smiles, "Of course! I'll guard it with my life" and confidently nods. I thank her before speed walking to the bathroom.

Once I'm back, I thank her and sit back down, re-opening my book- "By the way, I noticed what book you're reading- it's so good! I hope you love it!".

Her face lights up "I do love it- But I can't wait for her step-brother to die!" I decide not to tell her that he doesn't die until the third book in the series. Instead, I ask if she's heard how there's going to be a movie made out of the series. She has, so we spend a few minutes discussing the perfect cast. And then the topics snowball from there.

We spend the next two hours talking about books, movies, how I ended up here and how she's from here but left and moved back after hating a city she thought she was going to love. Carly lives nearby and when she found out that I'm new to the area, she exclaimed "Oh! I get to be your first friend here! Feel free to say no but if you want my number,

I am happy to meet up and talk about books and boys anytime!".

We laugh and then trade numbers and talk about getting coffee next week at the park and walking around since its close and between both of our houses. She lives with two roommates who sound fun and I secretly hope I like them as much as I like her because I could definitely use a friend with all I've got going on right now.

At this point, I was starving and itchy from sitting in the cafe for so long so I tell Carly that I'm headed back home but we should hang out soon. She excitedly replies "Yes! Sometime next week. Text me or I'll text you- Bye, Hazel!". I walk out with a dorky smile on my face that I can't contain. I'm so excited that I made a friend. It will take me awhile to count her as an actual friend and be able to trust her, but even having plans to hang out makes me happy.

We meet up a few days later when she texts me for a last-minute invite to get coffee together. She picks a different cafe than where we meet and it's also close, so I know I will be here again. I appreciate her warmth- a hug when I walk in, and straight to real conversation when we get our orders and sit at a table.

We do the same as before- drink coffee and talk with quickly changing subjects and then go for a walk around the area so she can point out some other fun local businesses. When we part, I ask if she wants to get drinks next week at a bar I keep seeing and she quickly agrees. We meet up about once a week for coffee or drinks for the next few weeks and I spend the rest of my time getting orders out, leaving my card at local businesses, and getting the house in order.

The fear of Brandon fades with the weeks that pass when I don't hear from him, and as Carly invites me to more events with her friend group, I begin to enjoy my new life here. Since the incident with Brandon, I've only seen my neighbor in glances here and there- of course it's mostly on weekends at night when he continues his routine of loading and unloading a couple of boxes.

Somehow, even those few times of seeing him were odd. One time, I was upstairs and I heard him going to his car, so with the lights off I peeked through the curtains, to see if I could get a better view of him- I just wanted to see what he looked like. I moved the old curtains an inch aside in the guest room and peeked through, squinting through the darkness to see if I could see his face.

I switched the weight from my right leg to my left, causing an old floorboard to slightly squeak. I ignored it thinking it didn't matter, but he turned and looked right at the window like he could hear it so I quickly moved away. I felt the shame and awkwardness of being caught but also assumed there's no way he could have known I was spying, so I went to bed.

I hated that my heart was still beating fast for way too long after he looked at my window. The longer we live by each other, the more I understand why no one visits him. Also, he never said anything about my cookies.

CHAPTER 6

Almost every night, I dream about Silas. Never anything specific, no actual story lines- just flashes of images of the dark-haired boy I used to know better than anyone. The only reason I can think this is happening is this situation with Brandon dug up old trauma that I don't think I'll ever recover from.

I would never admit this to anyone, but I secretly get excited to go to sleep, just to have more time with him. The dreams have made me think about Silas more than Brandon- probably because they are actually enjoyable.

I spent tonight bar-hopping with Carly and her roommates, Amanda and Jenna. As we drank, danced and laughed more as the night went on, I noticed my thoughts went more and more to my dreams. When I can tell they are beginning to affect my mood, I decide to hug them goodbye and start my short walk home. I've sobered up in the past hour and feel safe with the short walk, the streetlights, and the pocketknife in my hand.

I have a little giggle when my hands feel the cool metal, laughing at myself hiding a knife- it just feels so dramatic. But after everything that's gone on… and a few drinks- it feels good to feel weightless. I'm sure I could use a knife if I have to, but I try to focus more on the great night out that I just had rather than imagining stabbing someone.

I'm also excited because tonight, I invited Carly and her group of friends over to my house in two weeks for a barbecue and I can't wait to host new friends. The guys in the group aren't very attractive to me, but I liked them enough to trust them at my house and the girls I've met are all sweet.

I want to make a few friends and I want to keep hanging out with Carly so I'm impatient to have people over and actually be a host in my home for the first time. I walk up to my house thinking of what food I will make and what I will ask others to bring when I stop at my mailbox to get the mail on the way in.

It's right in between my yard and the neighbors, and the last time I saw Brandon was when he was in this same spot. In a little bit of paranoia, I open my knife as I open my mailbox and I actually have a lot of letters- I can already tell that most of it is junk mail.

Locking my mailbox door, I move the knife's handle to my inner elbow to hold and use both my hands to quickly scan my mail, looking for anything from Brandon. I'm so focused on looking for any unwanted mail, that I don't hear my neighbor's car door shut and I jump, losing my grip on the mail….and my knife.

The knife falls and hits my shoe before clattering on the ground, causing me to yelp in pain. Hoping no one heard me, I bend down to grab the knife and clutch my foot for a second. I'm wearing sneakers, so they didn't have a very thick layer between my foot and the blade- but better than if I was wearing sandals.

I can tell that it isn't a serious cut, but the sharp point still hurt and I can definitely feel a little blood. I hear my neighbor quickly running over and he sounds more worried than I would expect "Shit- are you okay?". I'm embarrassed so I just stay crouched over, putting pressure on the knuckles of my big toe "I'm fine! Sorry about that".

I don't know why I'm apologizing, but I feel like I'm just constantly annoying him. He's crouching down next to me and I see his tattooed hands come into my vision as his hand examines my shoe for holes, I guess. I look up to confirm I really am okay when I take a close up look at him.

He's looking down, in focus of an injury that doesn't warrant this much of a reaction from him and I study his perfect nose, his perfect lips and a five o' clock shadow. Then he looks up to examine my face, like he's still making sure I'm really okay. And that's when I really see him.

The familiar evergreen eyes, his panicked scrunched eyebrows, and hair that I used to run my fingers through when it was longer.

"Silas?"

The whole world goes silent.

A few seconds slip by of us staring at each other until he confirms quietly "yes".

There is a little nervousness in his eyes, waiting for my reaction- but I don't say anything. I bolt up, leaving my mail splattered on the ground

and I walk to my house in a blur, letting myself
inside and locking the door.

5 YEARS BEFORE
AGE 20

CHAPTER 7

"Hazel, do you have any questions about your assignment?" Mrs. Green asks from the front and I politely tell her "No, thank you" while I concentrate on looking like I'm focused and not spacing out like usual.

I love my photography class and I really like Mrs. Green but I can only make it so long before I feel my attention waning. This is why I hate being in the front row- she knows every time I'm not paying attention for longer than ten seconds. I was sick the first day everyone took their seats and now everyone has their assumed seats so I'm stuck here for the rest of the semester.

I have 30 minutes left of photography class, and we are using the time to start our first official project: a three-page essay on our favorite photographer, due at the end of the week. It's a solo project and thank God for that because I don't know anyone in this class. I blame the fact that it's early on in the semester but I know it' really because I always just want to get in and out of the class as quickly as possible.

Even though my business major is not photography related, I need this class and a few more "fun" electives to be able to graduate in 2 years. Since it's the spring semester, I only have to finish the next few months before summer and I already feel angsty to be done, even if this class is (sort of) fun.

My sophomore year hasn't been interesting to say the least but that's fine with me- I can't wait to get it over with. Is it sad for a college student to think that? A lot of my friends think of this as their most exciting years, but I really hope that happens after graduating college. When I'm not having nightmares of missing homework and having a curfew at 20 years old.

I'm not saying all I do is think about school, I do get out and have fun, but I don't want to get too distracted and waste my time and my (and my parents) money to be here. I still live with them since it's only a 20-minute drive so I am also trying to save money with my part-time job at the university bookstore. I've been in college for two years and I haven't even dated anyone because I know that will be a distraction.

My parents are paying for most of my college because they make enough money to not qualify for any financial assistance. But they make a few thousand over the maximum allowed for assistance so I know it's not easy for them... And I'm distracted again. Thinking about money, thinking about my parents, thinking about work.

Luckily, Mrs. Green has decided to not call me out again. She announces that the rest of the class is for silent reading time so we can do research on photographers for our homework. I flip through the old and oversized book until I find some photography that I like and choose my photographer. After a couple of minutes of reading in my textbook about Walker Evans, I get distracted by a loud cackling laugh on the opposite side of the room.

My head already turns before I can stop myself and then I make eye contact with Silas Ashwood, who had his head back and laughing at whatever his friend, Ben, was saying, but is now upright and looking back at me.

He doesn't look annoyed but looks like he's analyzing if he was being too loud- which he obviously was, because a few others are looking at him too. I panic at the fact that we are still staring at each other so I give an awkward smile which Silas notices and gives back a genuine one, then I look away.

I think to myself okay... that wasn't too bad. I thought by now I would be less awkward with cute guys but I don't know if I'll ever be how I imagine myself in daydreams: confident, chill, unbothered.

I know of Silas because we had a class together last semester in a lecture hall. And not that we ever talked, but I would pick up his name here and there since he was a row behind and always had people coming over to talk to him.

Guys, girls- didn't matter. People were always coming up to him at the beginning and end of each class. And even though he never seemed like he was dating anyone (or wanting to) he did seem to know half the school. For example, it seems like him and Ben go way back, but I wouldn't be surprised if they're new friends since a lot of Silas's interactions look like whoever he is talking to is a longtime friend.

I'm not exactly sure why that many people know him, and I'm not sure why I never see him dating anyone but I know exactly why so many girls seem like they want to date him. He's tall (almost a foot taller than me) and in great shape (semi-athletic but mostly lanky) and the amazing black-brown hair that is almost too long and reaching his eyes.

Speaking of eyes, they're dark-green like evergreen trees and almond shaped. It's not often you see men with absolutely beautiful eyes but they truly are stunning. He could absolutely play into his looks more but he seems unaware with his almost-constant band-tees and ripped jeans.

I think he's around the same age as me because he still looks pretty young besides his height and confidence that somehow also lacks arrogance. I have a lot to learn from him and confidence. I've been working on not mumbling when I talk, and maintaining a normal minimum of eye contact when talking to people I don't know that well.

Working part-time and being in college has helped me be more comfortable talking to people but I'm sure if someone like Silas and I ever had a conversation he would find me dull and awkward, giving up before he actually got to know me. I've been 20 years old for a few months now and besides my personality, I still feel like a teenager in my looks as well.

I've accepted that I'll always be short, but I am still fighting off my few extra pounds of baby fat and don't put in as much effort in hair and makeup like a lot of the girls around me. I'd like to say it's for some noble or confident reason and how I'm not like other girls but really, I just discovered how much extra sleep I got and I wasn't willing to compromise.

I have hazel eyes (I know, I know) and light brown curly hair that loves to double in size with the slightest hint of humidity. I consider looking back at him out of curiosity but thank the universe when Mrs. Green announces "Okay everyone, don't forget your assignment is due Friday. Have a great night!".

The class rushes out as I pack my things in my bag, thinking about what I'll watch on TV tonight when I hear a voice in front of me.

"Hey… sorry if I was being obnoxious".

I quickly look, and it's Silas standing in front of my desk, looking amused at almost scaring me, then adds "I'm Silas, by the way".

He's by himself, so I guess Ben left already. Seeing him up close and straight on, he's so good looking that it takes me a minute to gather my thoughts. Just as he starts to tilt his head in confusion, I rush out "It's fine- I needed something to wake me up".

He waits for another second before smiling "Well, even though you didn't tell me your name, Hazel" I open my mouth to apologize when he keeps going "It was nice meeting you. I'll see you around". There's a little smirk on his face, and I can tell he's trying to figure me out as he backs up a foot and turns to leave.

I just smile and watch as he strolls out- wanting to wait a few seconds to make sure he's definitely gone. A cute guy finally talks to me and seems nice- and I was so awkward and uninviting. I'm sure he'll never try again- and I deserve that. I walk out of class feeling like an idiot but also thrilled that we've met... and that he knows my name.

CHAPTER 8

Like any other Monday, I stop at Abigail's work, The Early Bird Cafe, for a coffee and a chat- if it's not too busy. As soon as I see her, I can't help but immediately blurt out that a cute guy named Silas talked to me. She listens in rapt attention until another customer comes in and she begrudgingly makes them a flat white.

As soon as she's done, she rushes back over to the counter I'm sitting at and begins asking a thousand questions- What's his major? Does he have a girlfriend? Does he live around here? I have no answers for her and she gets exasperated before insisting that I try to talk to him in our next class on Wednesday.

"And say what to him? 'hi, remember me? I was super awkward the other day but I'd like to be your friend? '".

She thinks for a second before sighing "I'm sure there's something you could say to him".

"I'd prefer it to be an organic conversation- like I get hit by a car and he comes to my aid." at least I could think of something to talk about then.

Also, she's no one to talk. She had her boyfriend, Tyler, in the friend-zone for two years before he finally couldn't hold in his feelings anymore and blurted it all out one day. When I remind her of that, she becomes stubborn "You know why he liked me so much? I initiated the friendship! I sat by him and started conversations with his shy ass until he finally caved".

"Well, I'm the Tyler in this situation. If anyone dates me, they will need to be an annoying Abby and initiate. That's why we are friends, remember? You also forced your friendship on me as well". Sophomore year, high school- I couldn't get away from her and before I knew it, we were best friends. I get another (free) coffee to go, before saying I'll text her later.

When I get home, I don't tell my parents. I used to tell my mom about any boy I talked to, but since nothing ever happened with them, I would be embarrassed when she excitedly brought them back up. Instead, I quickly help with dinner before spending the rest of my night holed up in my room, working on homework.

The next day goes by with nothing interesting, so before I know it, I'm back in Mrs. Green's class on Wednesday. I turned in my assignment early, so I walk in feeling pretty good about my day so far. Without wasting time, she announces that on Friday we will have an in-class partner assignment: taking pictures of each other to learn about portraits.

My hand grips my pencil as I listen, panicking about a partner exercise. I quickly debate skipping class on Friday but I know I'll be here and that I'll just have to see what happens. After an hour-long PowerPoint going over portrait-taking, class is finally over. On the way out of class, I see

Silas and Ben walking out of class talking- before Ben rolls his eyes, and then says something with a smile to Silas and walks out.

On his way out he looks at me with a smile and a little speculation and I get so distracted by that, that I don't notice Silas making his way over to me. He's already smiling at a some inside joke Ben and him are having, when he stops at my desk "Hazel… how's it going?".

What the hell is happening. "Hey, Silas! Good… how are you?" I'm a little too enthusiastic so I try to dial it down a little bit but he doesn't seem bothered by it. He puts a hand on my desk as he leans on it and I get distracted by the faint smile lines bracketing his lips.

I notice some other students looking at us as they walk out and I hate that my first concern is that Silas is messing with me. But I can't think of any other reason for his random interest in me. "I'm alright. I wanted to ask you a question- Ben can't make it to class on Friday so I was hoping you could be my partner". He didn't phrase it like a question so I wait for him to add one on but he just stares at me until I stammer out "Okay, sure".

Silas has a smile that's almost a smirk as he murmurs "Sweet, see you Friday", making quick little taps with his fingers on his way past my desk and out the door. The next two days are consumed by the anxiety of not only being partners with Silas on a project, but also taking photos of each other. Photos that are close and intimate enough to be portraits and photos that I will have to awkwardly pose for.

"Omg! Just pretend he's ugly and have fun! and tell me everything after!" Abby texts back after I couldn't take mentally spiraling by myself anymore. By the time it's Friday, I've calmed down a bit and I take my time getting ready- aiming to look as good as possible without looking like I tried too hard.

The forecast of rain today makes it easy to decide on knee-high moto boots, soft leggings, and an emerald green wool sweater. I slept with my long hair in braids so my hair has soft waves and my makeup is very light and natural since I hardly ever wear it anyways.

Even if Silas wasn't my partner, I'd be putting in more effort than normal since someone will be taking my pictures. At least that's what I keep telling myself when I'm driving to school Friday morning.

CHAPTER 9

I have two classes before my photography class so my hair has become a tad more poofy but, my minimal makeup still looks fresh. So, by the time I'm sitting in photography class, I feel pretty good about what's to come.

I get to class a few minutes early to collect myself and right before class is about to start, Silas walks straight over to the empty chair next to me rather than his usual seat.

Once he sits down, he quickly eyes me up and down before smiling "This is going to be easy" and before I can reply, he nods at Mrs. Green who's starting class. She explains that we need to take portraits with our phones today before she can trust us with expensive cameras for the next project, we get our assignment.

We need to take three photos of each other in different lighting and angles, and then edit them using any app we want. Then, we email them to her with a paragraph for each picture on how they meet the requirements and any editing done and why. With one last direction- we need to send each other the photos we took- she sends us outside for natural lighting.

As everyone gets up and walks toward the door to head outside for natural lighting, I can't help but to blurt out a question that's been bothering me. "So, why couldn't Ben make it today?" hoping it sounds like a casual question since he was so vague before.

He looks over at me with a little confusion before he casually answers "I think he had an appointment or something" and holds the door open for me.

In a quick change of subject, Silas stops walking and asks "Do you want to go first?" and I stop in my place to face him. I think it over as we stare at each other, his smile slowly growing before I clarify "I can take your pictures first".

He doesn't move, but keeps the smile on his face as he asks "Okay… how do you want me?" and I feel my face go red at the thought of how I really want him. I direct him over to a brick wall that comes up to my shoulders and he leans his hip against it.

I think it over before pointing to the wall "hop on" and he looks at me questioningly. I tap the top of the wall twice and say "Sit on the wall, I'll tell you how to pose".

Without question, he easily lifts himself up to sit on the wall. I tell him to put his hands on either side of him and lean forward, looking down at the camera. As he does it, I take several quick photos so I can have a few from each pose to choose from and then go to the next pose- a simple, close-up portrait. We fly through that pose since I was too nervous to be that close to him for too long.

On the third pose, I get stuck on ideas. Silas

confidently says "I got this" and as I see him walk off, I begin to look around at the other students and poses they are doing. Some are getting really

creative and I think I might get the worst grade due to lack of creativity.

Suddenly, more and more classmates are quickly looking at me and then behind me in shock and then excitement. Quickly turning my head, I see Silas on the wall again. This time, he's balancing himself upside-down on his hands, looking like he has all the time in the world.

Too quickly, my eyes fly down to the piece of his torso being revealed from the shirt falling downwards. I hurry to take a few photos and he effortlessly hops back down on to the ground with a big grin. I feel my eyes bulging out and stammer out "y-you… wha… oh my god!!" he only steps closer and laughs at my near heart attack even though I really thought I was going to see him crack his head open.

He's smug as he says "Your turn" and as I puzzle over if he means doing a handstand, he takes his phone and holds it up. I nod and sigh "okay…" as he eyes me up and down with a very serious face in deep concentration.

He gently grabs me by my shoulders and rotates me so the sun breaking through the clouds is directly in front of me and stays close to me to move my arms and hands how he wants. He steps back a few feet and tells me to smile and I keep the smile on my face until he moves only a few inches from my face and tells me to stare into the camera.

His face is at my level as he concentrates on

getting what looks like a close-up picture. Silas doesn't move as his hand with the phone goes to his side, and he keeps looking at me in concentration. I begin to awkwardly look away and then back, and he blinks several times before quickly bringing his phone back up "turn around".

He has no hesitation so I listen and turn and follow his directions when he says "Wrap your arms around yourself and look back at me". His voice is a little husky but I ignore it and look at him- and then his camera. He's a few feet farther than before and holding his camera vertically and then horizontally, trying different angles.

"Okay, go stand on the wall".

I quickly turn around to stare at him, mouth open but then almost yell "I can't get up on that thing! It's as high as my shoulders!". I could try, but I don't want to risk completely embarrassing myself.

He walks with me towards the wall saying "Yes you can, Hazel. Just try." but I stubbornly stare at him and quickly shake my head.

He laughs for a quick second so I think I'm getting out of it but before I know it, he's lifting me up by the hips and setting me on top of the thick wall. I don't even have time to make a squeal in shock so I just stare at him with wide eyes.

He's looking up at me with his hands on his hips, his hair's a mess and almost going into his eyes as he exclaims "See? I told you that you can do it!". He looks so surprisingly proud that I don't argue that he actually did it, I just smile at him "Okay… so now what?".

Just like before, he quickly gets up on the

wall and sits a few feet away from me, with his legs dangling like mine. "Sit there like that, but just look over at the camera". When I do it, he scoots closer for a second to move my head how he wants and moving my hair as I hear him murmuring "Stay… just like that".

Before moving away again and clicking the phone's buttons a few times. I see him look the picture over and smile but rather than show it to me, he hops back down and before I have a chance to do the same, he comes back over and grabs my waist- setting me on the ground.

I feel myself stare at him in surprise but he just smiles and quietly says "good job" before walking back inside with me. For some reason, we go back to Silas's table instead of where I was sitting.

Mrs. Green gives a quick explanation of the remainder of the assignment- "Don't over edit" - "It's due by class Monday" - "Don't be a creep and save the pictures". Then, she gives us the last 5 minutes of class to figure out logistics of sending photos to each other.

"What's your number?" I hear Silas ask me, but I get distracted by a girl in front of us who overheard and looked back at me quickly and then Silas in surprise. I'm clearly not the only one paying way too much attention to the cute guy on my right… and now there's an awkward silence.

I follow her gaze back to Silas and he adds, a little impatiently "or do you prefer email?".

"What? No, sorry I got distracted. Text is fine" I reply, before he hands me his phone with a gentle smile. I try to not overthink that he went immediately to the option of us having each other's number rather than a professional email.

I hand him back his phone, and he immediately starts typing on it. My phone buzzes and when I go to look at it, it's a text from a new number "*Silas :)*" and I save it before putting my phone away.

Trying to shake off how awkward I've been, I stand with my things and smile "Bye, Silas! See you next week!".

He looks surprised and stands up quickly "One sec, I'll walk with you to our cars" before grabbing his things and walking next to me.

Once we leave the classroom, Silas looks at me with a mischievous smile "So, I actually had ulterior motives walking with you". I wonder if he would ask to retake his pictures but he doesn't seem that vain so I just give him a questioning look and wait for him to go on. Suddenly, he looks a little nervous which I haven't seen on him.

"If you're free tomorrow night, do you want to come watch me play shitty music and then get food after?" I stumble for a second.

Is this a date? The next stupid question comes out before I think of anything else "What kind of food?".

His reply is a little chuckle followed with a grimace "Diner food… but it's good, I swear. And it's across the street from the venue… and I'm paying". I think that means it's a date, then.

I pretend to think it over as we get near my car "Okay… can you text me the time and place?".

Once we get to my car, I turn to him as he

stands over me with his hands on his backpack straps. "Sure thing… See you tomorrow, Hazey".

He starts to walk away with a smile and I reply "Bye, Si" enjoying the rhyme- and he looks like he does too with his surprised smile lighting up his face.

When I get in and close my car door I exhale a deep breath, savoring the fact that today actually went pretty well. When I get home, my parents are on the couch watching a dramatic show together so I make a smoothie and watch it with them since this is my family's version of quality time.

I go upstairs and send in my photography assignment, but I don't delete the photos. Once I'm ready for sleep, I feel my phone buzz and it's Silas replying to the photos I just sent him, with his own photos he took of me. "*This one's my favorite*" is the next text I see pop-up, and it's one I didn't notice he took. I have a shy smile, and I'm looking away- but the lighting is good and I actually like the way I look in it.

I reply with an outtake of one I took of him earlier, when he was doing a handstand. He has a wild grin and he's upside down so it looks a little crazy, but he looks free- and since that's what I want to feel like, I'm drawn to it.

"*Then this one's mine*" once I send my message, I get a quick reply "*I hope it's not just because my shirt came all the way up?*".

I just reply "*goodnight*" and put my phone down, and then pick it back up immediately realizing I never texted Abby.

"*Sooo... how did it go??*" I would way rather tell her in person so I reply "*Pretty good- let's meet up this weekend so I can tell you about it in person*" and we coordinate the time and place that fits our schedules and we say goodnight.

I know I am too wired to be sleepy anytime soon so I take out my secret stash of joints, and smoke half of one by my window. My parents wouldn't really care that I smoke weed since they've only focused on scaring me of hard drugs but I still feel weird talking to them about it so I just do it once in awhile and casually.

Once I begin to feel it, I put everything away and put on a comfort movie on my laptop to fall asleep to.

CHAPTER 10

I wake up the next morning and go right to my phone to look at our texts, assuring myself that it's all really happening.

"The Black Cat Lounge, 8pm" was all his text said so I don't have a lot of information.

It's 9 a.m. so I have 11 hours before I need to be there. So, I have 10.5 hours before I need to leave my house, and 8 hours before I need to start getting ready. I workout, finish up a few assignments, and have lunch with my parents before I take a nap and begin to get ready.

During lunch, I told my parents that I'm going out tonight and they gave each other a suspicious glance before my mom said "As long as you're safe and back before 1 a.m., then have fun". I know they want to ask, but they've been better about my boundaries lately so I decide I'll wait until tomorrow to tell them anything.

If tonight goes horribly, then I'd prefer to avoid them being curious about a boy. As I shower, I plan how I'll do my hair- straight, and how I'll do my makeup- light cat-eye and berry-pink lip stain.

Once I get out and make both of those plans happen, I look at the clock realizing I have an hour before I need to leave. I put my outfit together last night so I put on my faux-leather leggings, sheer white button-up and a black bralette underneath before checking in the mirror that it looks as cute as I was imagining.

Putting on my platform sneakers, followed by my black over-sized jean jacket and mini leather purse, I head downstairs for a snack since I haven't eaten in a few hours. Luckily, my parents aren't home- they go on weekly "date-nights"- so I have the house to myself and I enjoy the silence for 20 minutes while eating some fruit and crackers with cheese.

Locking the door, I head outside to my car and after 30 minutes, I'm at The Black Cat Lounge with a few minutes to spare. Since I'm early, I only have to wait in line for a couple of minutes before making my way inside. It's not a fancy venue- definitely for smaller bands- there's not a curtain or anything to hide behind for the performers.

There's a stage and then a hallway going to the back room and right when I find a good spot I see a few people in the back area milling around getting ready. After a moment, I see Silas pop his head out and quickly look around like he's already done it a few times with no results- and then he sees me.

His smile is shameless as it transforms his face and he walks over to me, a few people following him with their heads. I can't stop the smile that I feel take over my face as he comes over yelling "Hey!" over the background music and wraps me in a big hug. I reciprocate but since we haven't hugged before I savor the feeling of my face in his lean pecs.

Stepping back to give me a once-over, he

leans down to say in my ear "You're like a dream come true- can I get you a drink?". The rush of the compliment quickly turns to anxiety when I realize he doesn't know my age.

Nervously, I answer "I'm 20, so a water is fine" on my tiptoes so he can hear me- hoping that doesn't kill the night that I'm not old enough to go into a bar or drink.

Leaning down again, he assures me "Me too. Privileges of being in the band" and I quickly look to see his wicked smile and laugh.

"Okay, fine- just get me whatever you're having, please" I'm surprised how confident I sound when I really only said that because I don't know that many drink names. He nods before looking down at my lips and then quickly turning and wandering off, his head just a little over everyone else.

Within minutes, he's back with a drink in each hand "Sorry- I hope you like vodka red bulls" and extends one for me to grab, which I do.

Taking a sip, I make a grossed-out face before swirling the glass to mix the vodka at the top with the red bull a little more. He chuckles before tapping his glass to mine, and taking a large gulp- with a slight squint after. I realize I forgot to thank him, and once I do, he replies with a shrug "It's the least I could do for how you're about to spend the next two hours of your life" before taking another sip and adding "I have to go to the back soon, are you still down to get food after?".

He waits with concern like he's nervous I changed my mind but I nod and answer "Of course!

I've been curious about this diner food you mentioned". He's looking down at me with an enamored grin when he gently lifts my hair, looking at it as it falls through his fingertips when he murmurs how soft it is. He begins to get a call on his phone and once he looks at it, he ignores it but says quickly "Got to go- see you after!" and winks at me before walking back through the crowd the way he came.

A few people are looking at my curiously and I can't get the smile off my face as I feel real, actual butterflies for the first time in my life, taking flight and fluttering from my stomach, into my heart and then into my brain. I notice the lights begin to get low and people start cheering so I put my phone in my purse and cheer along with everyone. I'm not sure if Silas's band is going on now or later so I look in concentration as the band begins to walk out.

Taking a big gulp of my drink, I know that Silas isn't in this band, and I also realize I don't know what instrument he even plays… or if he's going to sing. This band is also college kids, and they immediately start playing a loud, thrashy song that seems to get everyone hyped up.

As people being to push a little to get more up front, I let them go ahead so I can finish my drink and throw it out, standing comfortably behind everyone. Now that I have a small buzz, I'm less self-conscious of my awkward swaying and tapping to the music.

Before I know it, the band announces their last song- which is also their loudest. Most people seem to know this song and the three and a half minutes fly by as everyone jumps around and sings along. Once it finishes, the lead singer announces into the mic "Now, please welcome Appetite! You've probably heard their newest song "After You" on the radio- so put your hands together for the live version!" which everyone goes insane to and starts cheering.

I attempt to inch forward but the crowd in front of me has only gotten more compact in the last minute so I'm almost all the way to the back, standing on my tiptoes trying to see Silas.

First, I see Ben walk over to a bass. Oh, they actually do know each other pretty well, then. Then, I see two more guys who I don't know go over to a guitar and then the mic. Finally, I see Silas as he walks straight to the drum set and starts hitting the floor toms loudly- quieting everyone. Once it's quiet, the singer begins to shout into the mic and the music gets loud again.

This band is even louder than the first one and I notice Ben and the guitarist moving as much as they can with while playing their instruments, and the singer jumping into the crowd and jumping back up. Focusing back on Silas, he's just hitting his drums as hard as he can with a smile on his face.

Their fun and energetic show goes for a few more songs that I can tell most of the people here know, and I realize that this band is a slightly bigger deal than I thought they were. The band gets quiet again as the singer says into the mic "This next song is called 'After You'" but he gets interrupted when people begin to cheer over him for a second before he carries on "if you know the words, sing along!"

and then more, loud cheers.

After listening to it for a few seconds, I realize that I know this song. It's a little bit of a happier, upbeat song that I heard at Abigail's job last week when working on some homework and I spent time trying to find it before giving up. I begin to bounce on my feet a little more and as I look at Silas again, I see that he's looking right back at me with a big, dimpled smile before looking back at his drums.

I notice most of the audience mouthing along to the words so I realize a lot of people are here to check out a small band with a song they've heard on the local radio. They play one more song before the singer announces "Here is our last song of the night. Thank you guys so much for coming and we will see you next time!" which is met with more loud cheers. Their last song is slow and angsty, taking awhile to build up to a chorus that has the singer shouting into the mic.

When I look around, I notice everyone either already knows the words, or is very focused on the song. Once it ends, the cheers are so loud that all the singer can do is put his hands up and bow, as the others do the same and walk off the stage, towards the back. It's a little after 11 and I wait by the exit sign as people mill out of the venue- I'm not sure where I'm supposed to meet Silas but I keep my phone in hand in case he tries to call.

After a minute, I look outside- thinking that I actually missed him and he's outside waiting for me- when I feel a hand on my shoulder. Before I can turn, I hear his voice in my ear "let's get out of here" and I turn to see Silas, looking really content with his arm around me. He let's go to grab my hand and pull me to a different exit door towards the back that not as many people are using. As we quickly walk out, he gives people a smile as a greeting when they wave to him before he continues with the same, fast pace.

Once we get towards the door, he sees the small crowd of people outside who all seem to know the bands and each other before he says low in my ear "Let's hurry through before we get stuck socializing with everyone".

I nod in concentration and chuckle before we walk outside, even faster than before. As we walk out, I notice Ben and his other band mates giving him a knowing smile, but the others standing around look excited to see him. He quickly smiles at everyone but just keeps walking with me even faster until we get to the street.

Once we look both ways and see that there are no cars for the next 30 seconds, he tightens his grip on my hand and gives me a smile before leading me in a jog across the four-lane street. I can't help the little giggle that bursts out at running, and when I look over at Silas, he looks exactly how I feel.

Earlier when he was playing drums, he looked happy and confident- but now, here with me, he looks excited and free… and almost boyish. Like despite how amazing the last hour was, he couldn't wait to get out.

CHAPTER 11

We get inside the diner and make eye contact with the hostess, Silas politely says "For 2, please" and we get seated at a table towards the back with our menus. We still haven't let go of each other's hands until we reach the table and have to sit down but before our hands separate, Silas squeezes my hand twice and then let's go to sit across from me.

"Get anything you want, it all tastes amazing" he says as he sets down his menu to the side, obviously already knowing what he wants.

I briefly meet his eyes to ask "Really? Usually diner food is sub-par" he smiles and replies "I may be exaggerating a little… I'm usually a little stoned when I come here" a small laugh follows from us both.

"So, you eat here often?" I ask, which he answers after a second of thinking.

"Sometimes I come here after shows to eat and work on any last-minute homework assignments. They're 24 hours so that makes it pretty easy for me to come here when I get done late".

When the waitress comes with our waters

and asks for our food orders, I order boneless buffalo wings in hopes that they will be a less messy option in comparison to their delicious, better bone-in version.

Silas orders a full breakfast plate with eggs, bacon, hashbrowns and pancakes. Once the waitress walks away, he notices my shocked expression "What?". I open my mouth to say something but I remember how hard he was hitting the drums and close my mouth with a shrug and a smile. I remember the song at the end and ask him "What's the name of the last song you guys played?".

"'Let Me In'... You liked it?".

"I loved it! I'm going to add it to my playlist now before I forget" and I quickly take out my phone to add it in. He looks happy at the compliment and smiles before saying "Thanks for coming by the way, I hope you had an okay time".

I think it over and reply "I really did. Although I will admit I am having more fun now- there was so many people bumping into me, I was getting annoyed- I know, I know- It's a concert so of course there is, but that doesn't make it less annoying".

He laughs as I over-explain and then adds "I'm enjoying it more now too". Just then, our waitress comes back with condiments for our incoming food. We thank her and turn back to each other and make small talk until our food comes out a few moments later. I put the smallest nugget in my mouth and decide he definitely was exaggerating on the food being amazing but it's good enough for me to enjoy it.

"Woah… this food tastes different sober" Silas says in a surprised voice and I hear my loud burst of surprised laughter which he joins in a second later. The waitress comes back a minute later to check on us and asks how the food is, which we both say "good" to and shrug at each other when she walks away.

I ask him about the band and how long he's been playing and if he wants to keep doing it- I can tell he gets this question asked a lot because his response seems practiced "I've been playing with them for a few years but for fun, I don't see it as a career'.

'I know people do it, but my dad always tells me to have a hobby for fun and a career for financial stability. I don't always follow his advice but I think that's fair". I briefly remember how I casually dated a guy who wanted to be a professional reiki master and I smile at Silas in agreement. He continues "He owns a real estate company and I'm planning on interning for him after graduating, I'm already his part-time assistant right now so it would be an easy transition".

"That's amazing! I'm happy for you because not everyone gets that. I have no idea what I'll do once I graduate". I end with a chuckle, unconcerned since I still have time to figure it out.

"Thanks, Haze. You have no idea what you will do... but in the meantime, what's your major?".

"I'm just getting a business degree. If I want to get more specific, I will. But since I have no idea, I think that's at least a good enough degree to have to get my foot in some doors… at least I hope so."

Between bites of food, we go back and forth for another hour about ourselves: current, past, family, friends, and other random topics that come to mind. When we get the bill, Silas quickly snatches it and puts some cash down, "Either way, I'll pay. But is this a date?".

Instead of giving a normal answer, my first thoughts spill out "You tell me! I didn't know if you would think of this as a date, you're friends with everyone".

He shakes his head and laughs "Not everyone, but I also don't take any of those friends on dates".

I just stare at him with a slightly confused smile, wondering why he's randomly interested in taking me on a date now. He must read my mind because he leans in like he's sharing a secret "I thought you were cute since the last class we had together but I finally had a reason to ask you out".

I stare at him in shock for a brief moment before responding "I didn't even know that you noticed me".

He looks over my face for a second and then says "I didn't want to look like a creep but I definitely noticed you. Sometimes you wore a plain baseball hat and I don't know why but I thought it was the cutest thing, and then sometimes when you were getting focused on taking notes you would turn it backward… it was hard not to focus on that".

I've never been speechless before but… I have no idea what to say because at first, I thought he was just trying to be nice but I know that he's talking about me. Well… if we are admitting things,

I may as well blurt out "You have a black jean jacket with Sherpa lining and I think it's the best item of clothing I've ever seen".

I say it so fast and urgent I could feel how badly I needed to get that out. So could Silas, because he laughs so hard for a second that he's silent with his head down, just shoulders shaking but getting out "Thank you. I'll wear it to the next show if you come".

"If I'm free, I will. But I'll have to bring my friend Abby and her boyfriend, Tyler". I look off for a second and continue "She's going to be mad when I see her tomorrow and tell her about a show that I didn't invite her to".

At least, until I tell her why and who I was seeing. Silas warmly smiles "Bring them whenever- just give me a heads up so I can set tickets aside for everyone".

There's a pregnant pause before Silas adds "If I just asked you to hang out without an excuse would you have said yes?".

I answer too quickly "yes." so he smiles and asks "Do you want to hang out... without an excuse? Like a more official date?".

He sounds kind of nervous which surprised me but also makes me happy that he's not as impenetrable as I thought. We're both leaning in on both sides of the table and my voice comes out quieter than I expected as I ask him "when?" and his voice comes out even softer "tomorrow?".

This whole conversation feels too good to be true but I quickly calculate my morning shift at the bookstore, lunch with Abby and nod

"Tomorrow it is, then. I'm free after 4pm".

I know it's going to be a long day, but I can already tell it will be worth it. With only 20 minutes left, Silas spends the time asking me about my favorite things like my favorite food, flowers and things to do until we have to walk to our cars. Just like the way in, he grabs my hand as soon as we stand from our table and doesn't drop it until we get to my car.

We walk in a peaceful silence, enjoying the warm night as we walk across the parking lot and across the street. I look up at him once, and he quickly notices and he gives me a huge, uninhibited smile that my face too soon matches right back up at him.

Our two cars are the only ones left in the small parking lot, and when we get to my car, I let go of his hand to set my purse and jacket into the passenger seat and stand back up to face Silas, who's casually leaning on my car.

I step a little closer to him, unsure of how to end tonight and start to say "Thanks again for-" but he interrupts me with his hands on my hips, pulling me to him quickly- so quickly, that I put my hands on his arms to catch myself. With my head at his shoulders, my neck is at an angle looking completely up at him. He's looking down at me with glimmering eyes and a small smile, calculating what to do next but he just stares at me.

He's looking my face all over, almost like an inspection but not looking for flaws, just taking in every detail. I start to feel shy until one of his hands comes up to gently comb my hair out of my face, and then gently cup my jaw with soft swipes of his thumb. My thoughts stop and I go on my tiptoes to close the gap between us which he completes with a kiss- and then suddenly, the easy dynamic we've had all night changes.

What felt like an excited, nervous energy earlier is now frantic, animalistic one. When my hands slide up his arms to his neck, he groans and flips around so my back is against the car. His hands and tongue use the right amount of pressure and I feel his hand slide down to my thigh to hold me, and gets us even closer.

My brain is off as I'm lost in our wandering hands and noises escaping both of us when Silas pulls his lips away to kiss my neck, working up to my ear and panting "How soon do you have to go?".

That brings me back. I answer "Five minutes ago" and he releases my leg slowly and regretfully.

Taking a small step back, he leans in a little to take a deep look in my eyes. My eyes flutter a little as he uses both hands to comb my hair back as he whispers "Goodnight, Hazel. I'll see you tomorrow, think of me tonight".

I take a deep breath, collecting my thoughts and walk to the driver's side "Night, Silas. Back at you".

He's walked over to his car and laughs out a scoff "I think that's all that I'll be thinking about until I see you tomorrow. Text me when you get home, please". When I get home, 5 minutes before curfew, the house is silent from my parents sleeping.

I get inside and text Silas *"home safe and sound :) see you soon"*.

I get my makeup off and change into a big tee and get nestled in bed, getting comfortable. I hear my phone vibrate, so I check and it's a quick reply from Silas *"can't wait"*.

CHAPTER 12

The next morning at 8, I clock in at the bookstore and glide through the short shift until I clock out at 12- not even the rudest customers can get the smile off of my face. Once that's over, I go to meet Abby at our favorite brunch spot where she's quick to react to my most recent life update.

"You did WHAT last night?!" she's mad that I didn't invite her, so I try to smooth it over.

"I wanted to tell you after the fact so that I could tell you confidently everything went well…. okay, better than well".

She thinks my answer over and goes to the next topic immediately "And you have another date in a few hours? Oh my god, Hazel".

I'm not sure why she looks just as nervous and excited as I feel but I try to tell her every detail I can remember while she doesn't even look like she's breathing. Finally, after I get tired of hearing my own voice, I quickly change subjects "So anyways, what have you been up to?". I'm sure our waitress thinks I'm a narcissist since every time she walks by, it's me talking.

"Who gives a fuck about me?! So, was he a good kisser?".

I laugh but reply anyways "First of all, I do. And yes, of course he is… I just don't understand how it's like 0-100 since that photography assignment".

We never even talked until this last week and now we are making out and going on dates? "Well… it sounds like he had his eye on you for awhile. Maybe he just couldn't find a way to initiate conversation".

I shrug in agreement and promise her "I already told him that I'm bringing you and Tyler to the next show" which makes her finally content enough to change the subject. I get home at two and immediately get to work: Shower, blowout, and a clean makeup look that still manages to take me longer than I expect.

He said he's surprising me so I don't know what to wear and decide to have two options. I pack a semi-nice outfit in a bag in case our plans are fancier than I expect- a dark green sundress with wedges. I decide to dress casual- dark, ripped skinny jeans with a black, soft, off-shoulder sweater and leather sandals.

The weather is all over the place right now, so I also grab a jacket on the way out of my bedroom. I walk downstairs and see my parents in the living room looking over bills together when they look up and make equally surprised expressions. It's funny how couples who have been together for so long begin to become copies of each other.

I can't help the smile on my face and I can tell they are about to ask so without breaking my stride I tell them "I'm going on a date! I'll tell you more when I get back but I promise. I know it's a Sunday so I'll be back before 10 p.m.! Love you!" I slip the last part out as I shut the front door. This isn't an unusual way for me to leave the house, but I don't go on dates often.

They are pretty good about boundaries and trusting me so I'm lucky that as long as I'm being safe, they usually only ask out of curiosity. Especially because Silas is in his small, black SUV, in my driveway… with his window down. I also notice my favorite flowers- dahlias- in the passenger seat. I pray my parents aren't peeking out of the windows but I don't look back in confirmation.

I notice Silas smiling behind me, toward the windows and giving a small wave so I just groan and get in his car, setting the bouquet on my lap. "Your parents seem nice, should I go in to meet them?".

"No!" it comes out too fast but I just want to go on the date and make sure it's even worth it for them to meet before going through that whole process.

He gives me a confused smile before nodding "alright, alright- next time then" and pulls out of the driveway and getting on to the main street. Since he's paying attention to the road, I take a brief second to slightly turn in his direction and admire him. He has on a thin, dark-gray hoodie (with the sleeves rolled up) and faded black jeans with sneakers. I'm relieved that he isn't dressed too fancy since I'm also wearing jeans but the way his clothes naturally suit his lean, muscular frame is making it hard not to stare.

I guess I stared too long because Silas looks at me out of the corner of his eye and then does a quick double-take, taking me fully in for two seconds before looking back at the road "shit, you look nice".

It's a compliment but he sounds a little dismayed so I just say "thanks?", not knowing how I'm supposed to react to that.

He quickly explains "it's just when I was planning today, I went with 'fun' over fancy based on what you told me about yourself last night. Anyways, I probably should have said that earlier".

Silas quickly looks me over again "and I'm sorry if you over-dressed, but you look amazing" it comes out in a rush and I can tell he's nervous. I laugh as relief washes over me, I'm more confused about our plans today but I'd also rather look over-dressed for a date rather than under-dressed.

"I think it would take a lot for me to be annoyed today" I confidently say, as I lean over and kiss him on the cheek before getting settled with my purse and bag in between my feet. He looks over in surprised before a small smile takes over and he focuses back on driving. I play it off like it's not a big deal but inside I'm so proud of myself, I made the first move and it went well.

After a second, I see him look at the bag by my feet with the second outfit before slightly bending over and grabbing it to set it in the backseat, giving me more leg room.

"Are you going to spend the night?" when I look at him in shock, he nods his head to my bag. I explain how I wasn't sure how fancy today was going to be so I wanted to have all my options covered. "So you brought a more casual outfit in case this was another diner-date?" he has humor in his eyes when they flash over to me for a second.

"Actually, this is the casual outfit- the one in the bag is a dress in case we go somewhere that jeans wouldn't fit with" he looks over at me in surprise "I've never seen you in a dress".

"Yeah, I don't really see the point in dressing nice for school. Besides, I can't concentrate if I'm uncomfortable" I explain and look over at him.

More to himself than me, he says "Probably a good thing… or I wouldn't have been able to concentrate".

I laugh and lightly smack his shoulder "Wait, what are we even doing today?".

He gives me a quick smile before saying "You're going to find out in less than 5 minutes. Think you can wait that long?".

I scrunch my nose before replying, "Not really…".

He chuckles and says, "You know good things come to those that wait". I think for a minute and reply "You'll soon find that patience isn't a skill I have developed yet".

Which he replies back with "I'm pretty frustrating, so you might learn patience sooner than you would like". A moment later, we pull into the driveway of a small building with a sign saying the name of the place: "Gather & Splatter".

I repeat the name out loud and give Silas a questioning look and he leans in to say "I hope you're ready to have fun" before smirking and getting out to quickly walk around and open the door for me. I hold my questions until we are inside and then I realize what this is.

It's a splatter room. We are guided into a room just for us and given white jumpsuits, a huge blank canvas on a wall covered in paint, and given instructions on the many different squeeze-bottles of paint. He helps me put my hair into the supplied shower cap and I help him do the same.

We put the oversized white jumpsuits on over our outfits and Silas pulls out his phone "We should take a before and after picture of us" so he puts his arm around me, pulling me in and we smile for the camera.

Once his phone is away, I ask "Have you ever done this?". He says "No, you're my first" with a smile that doesn't look completely innocent. He grabs a bottle as well and then gestures to my hand with the paint "Want to do the honors?".

I looked at canvas and back at him "There's no goal here, right? Just squirt it on the canvas?" he looks like he's trying to not say a joke but says "Yeah I think it's supposed to be abstract".

So, I squirt the bottle of bright red so there's a streak running along the top of the canvas. He quickly joins in with a navy blue and right away we get lost in concentration picking colors, where and how to put it. After a few quiet minutes of concentration, we look at each other and he starts to laugh so I nervously ask "What?".

He chuckles "I don't know how you got that much paint on your face" and then I take a brush and flick it towards his face "like that" I say with a smirk. He gets an evil look on his face as he goes to grab me, but I dodge out of his arms and run around the paint-supply table. He grabs me from behind around the waist and grabs a squirt bottle filled with yellow paint and I try to struggle out of his grip as he points it towards my face.

My laughter stops as I panic and try to calmly say "You wouldn't actually spray paint in my face… close range… would you?".

He sets the paint down and turns me around and looks apologetic as he says "Of course not. Dinner would be so awkward". His eyes flicker between my eyes and then he slowly looks over my face as he gets a serious, contemplative look on his face and leans in, wipes paint off my lips, and kisses me.

It was a quick, sweet kiss but as he pulls away, I pull him back with my hand on the back of his head and his immediate smile reassures me that I didn't just embarrass myself. He tilts his head so our lips can do more than just peck and when I feel a little of his tongue, I match it with my own. I gently bite his lip as I pull away and ask "How much more time do we have to paint?" I laugh because he's just staring at my lips in a daze.

He finally answers "Probably just enough time to put our final touches on it and go to dinner". We take our 'after' photo, with paint all over us and just-kissed lips before cleaning up, taking off our jumpsuits and making it out with a minute to spare. I make a pit stop in the bathroom to change into my dinner outfit of a dress and wedges as he coordinates with the front desk of when he will pick up the painting. Silas is waiting in front of the bathroom when I get out and he looks me up and down.

He gets a mischievous look… and then he looks behind me into the bathroom like he's considering pushing me back and locking us in. He leans into my ear and says in a low voice "Unfortunately, the restaurant has a strict reservation time policy- let's get out of here" while holding his hand out for me which I happily take.

Once we get back out to Silas's car, he holds the car door open for me as I sit down and grabs the seat belt "It's a little tricky sometimes- let me help you". And before I can react, he's fully leaning over me, clearly making an excuse to be as close as possible and I start to giggle when he clicks it in and looks at me. He's only inches away when he says with a serious face "Safety first" and kisses the tip of my nose and stands back up, closing the door and walking over to the driver's side.

I had no idea Silas was like this in class he seems so aloof that I couldn't even imagine him flirting- but now I can't remember any other side of him. As we get on the road, he puts his hand on my bare knee like he's done it a thousand times and I just smile at the window, enjoying the content silence that takes over the car.

The restaurant is a modern sushi restaurant with upscale, fresh revolving sushi. We hold hands on the walk from the car like we've done this a thousand times and before Silas lets go, he squeezes my hand twice. When our waiter leads us to our table, Silas lets me pick my seat first and then sits across from me. After we get our drinks and pick out a few plates I try to find a way to ask my questions before giving up and just going for it.

"So, Silas…".

He has a quick one-sided smile before replying "So, Hazel…". I snort and continue on "You're cute, tall, not a loser, in a band".

His reply his fast "and you're hot, kinda short, also not a loser, and not in a band… Should I be nervous with where this is going?".

I laugh at his discomfort and continue on "I guess I'm just wondering why I never see you date anyone… and why you asked me out?". I hate asking questions like that because I don't know how to ask that without sounding insecure or fishing for compliments, but I also have been wondering this for two straight days and need to know.

He briefly smiles and then contemplates for a second before saying "Hm… I guess I just don't like when girls come up to me first. Maybe that sounds out-of-touch but it's just because I feel like that also means that they would be the type to be calling or texting me all the time and… I like the chase a little bit".

He looks like he has more to say so I just nod for him to go on "And you are always in your own little world that it made me curious about you. Like is it just because you're shy? It seemed like you were always trying to concentrate but then failed because of daydreaming. It made me wonder what you think about. And then when we talked, your face lit up so I knew that there was more to you than just a quiet girl who sits by herself".

I look down to hide my smile and take a bite of sushi as he adds on "And it worked out. I saw you in that dress today and I was thinking 'why didn't I go up to her sooner?'".

I jokingly say "Yeah? The dress is what did it for you?".

His eyes take on a mischievous sparkle as he smoothly takes my free hand and leans in "Hazel, I've been enjoying getting to know you since we met".

He's blushing a little and says "Is this a good time to ask you out on a second date?" I look at his twinkling eyes as I lean in, quickly saying "Yes… next weekend?".

CHAPTER 13

After dinner, Silas drives us to a little pavilion by a park. It's a little after 8pm and we each get ice cream cones before they close and walk hand in hand on the thin path leading to the park.

I look up at him, smile, and say "You're pretty good at this for someone who says they don't date a lot". He looks slightly startled out of his happy thoughts and lets out a short laugh.

"I've gone on a few dates but nothing serious. And no pressure but you're the only girl I'm talking to" a shy look takes over "I'm a college student so I can't afford to court more than one girl.

Especially if they like sushi that shits expensive". I'm so caught off-guard by his honesty that I have to stop walking to bend over and laugh for a second, I remember his eyebrows going up when he got the check for dinner, but he wouldn't let me see the price. I start to laugh harder than I have all week, I'm partially flattered by his admission but also enjoying his honesty.

"Well thank you for spending that college-kid money on me, it went to a good cause".

"Are you going to make me ask you if you're talking to anyone else? You could be living the good life eating sushi every night this week" he looks at me with mock-suspicion before looking back at the path.

"That would be smart but who has the time for that? Just you… for now" He elbows me as we do another lap.

We talk for another 4 laps before Silas guides me over to a bench and sits down, looking up to me as he pats the seat next to him. I surprise us both by sitting on his right thigh to semi-sit on his lap so I can look up to talk to him, he doesn't seem to mind as he slightly readjusts to fit us better.

He's big, warm and smells amazing- I just want to nuzzle my face in his chest and take a big breath but instead I just smile up at him and I notice he's not looking back at me.

He's looking down at my legs with half-lidded eyes so I look down to see what got his attention. My dress rode up when I sat on his lap so my entire thighs are exposed. I know that if I try to adjust the dress it will just make it awkward, so I just try to not move so he can't see my panties.

He slowly looks back up at me with a hunger in his dilated eyes that I couldn't have imagined without seeing it for proof. In a low and deep voice I can barely make out, Silas says "Please wear this around me more often" before he tilts his head down and we kiss with a fervor I've only seen in movies. If this was daytime in the park, I would be much shyer about making out in public, but since we've been here, I've noticed that there's no one around so I kiss him back with equal intensity.

We hastily alternate between using our tongues, lips and teeth to communicate as our hands start to navigate as well. I have no control of my hand as it slowly goes up his chest, up his neck and into his hair, massaging and pulling, bringing out noises from him I could only dream about. As his breath increases, his hand on my knee trails up my outer thigh, under my dress and along my panties before gliding along the hem to my inner thigh where he gently trails down back to my knee.

Needing more pressure, I hastily get up- Silas looking confused, then relieved- as I sit back down to straddle him. Wasting no time, his hands go on my hips to press me down on him and I groan at the pressure that feels better but also only makes me want more.

I quickly look around to make sure that the park is still empty, and since we are in a small area with privacy from the trees, I'm not as nervous since it would be easy to hear someone along the gravel. I lose concentration as he licks his way from my collar bone to my ear, stopping every few inches to suck and bite.

I have no logical thoughts as I tug him as close as possible by his hair as he moans, gripping my ass hard enough to give me a light bruise. I move my hand lower down his stomach towards his zipper, feeling the ripples of abs on my way down, not really thinking about what I want to do next, when I hear my phone starting to ring. I pull back to look at Silas and he looks dazed, but I can tell he hears it too.

With one hand, he leans over and hands me my purse which I grab and look for my phone. Once I find it, I see it's my mom and that it's almost 10 p.m. I know that if I tried to talk to my mom right now my voice would sound different and that she would probably know exactly what was going on.

So, I just text her "*On my way back now*" instead while Silas patiently waits beneath me, his dark green eyes looking up blankly as he gets his thoughts together. His squeezing has turned into gentle thumb swipes as he says "Is it time to take you back already?".

I try to hide the embarrassment in my voice as I say "unfortunately" and then get up.

I pat my dress down and finger-comb my hair to try to look a little bit like the woman who left the house a few hours ago as he takes a few calming breathes and then stands up. I suddenly feel a little shy which Silas notices as he moves to stand in front of me, cradling my jaw in his hand "I'm still having so much fun with you. That was probably good timing though".

Before I get a chance to question his meaning, he kisses my forehead and leads me out of the park. He puts his arm around my shoulders as we walk out and every so often, he kisses my forehead, or cheek, or hair. Every smile up at him is met with a smile back at me as though we've accomplished something important and we are proud of ourselves.

There's a weird, comfortable certainty in our actions and glances like we aren't on our first date but our 10th and I can tell even with my lack of relationship experience that we are moving a little fast but I don't feel scared or nervous. We get to his car and have about a 10-minute ride home so I will get there a little late but I think my mom will forgive me if I tell her that this is going somewhere and she gets to hear the details of the date.

My mom usually gets excited by talking like teenagers so she relaxes with the parental rules a little. Rather than his hand on my knee, Silas confidently has his hand in my mid-thigh on the way to my house, which I entwine the fingers of my left hand with. We don't say much as Silas's playlist is on at a low volume and admittedly, I am getting a little tired since it's been a long day. When he pulls up in front of the house, I'm relieved to see the house lights aren't on.

Hopefully my parents are in bed and won't hear me, or at least won't question me as I try to get to bed. He leaves the car on but puts it in park to get out as he walks me up to the porch. We are standing in front of the door when Silas says "Thank you for today, I had fun".

I hug him to enjoy the height and feel of his body one last time for the night and say "Thanks, I did too. So next weekend?".

"Yes, but I'll also see you in class… right?" I nod and he gently cups my face in his hands to kiss my forehead, then my lips, and then both of my cheeks. I laugh- mentalizing the cross pattern he made, and he smiles for the same reason.

"Night, Hazey" we kiss one last time.

I say "Night, Si" before we part and I head inside as he jogs back to his car.

CHAPTER 14

I get inside expecting silence- but I hear familiar low chatter in the backyard. So, I go to the backyard to say 'hi' to my parents since they probably know I'm late anyways. Even though it's Sunday and my parents have work the next day, they are on the patio-set talking with hot tea mugs in front of them.

Since they like to drink sleep-inducing tea before bed, I know they are planning on heading up soon so this shouldn't take long. I open the door, not knowing if they will be annoyed with me or not, so I nervously say "Hiii… I'm back".

My mom has a look like she knows exactly what I've been up to and remembers those days fondly. My dad looks oblivious but I can tell he's in a relaxed mood since he says "Well… you at least owe us a summary of the night. How'd it go? Do you like him?" and so I tell them about last night and tonight (without the making out details). Since I hardly ever talk about guys, my parents seem more and more happy that there might be someone.

My mom looks like she can't take anymore as she blurts out "So when do we get to meet him?!" and my dad just nods his head once as back up. Strangely, I don't think Silas would mind- if anything he seems like he's ready for any relationship step but maybe I am getting ahead of myself.

"Maybe next time he picks me up, I can ask him to come say 'hi' first?" that seems to satisfy them and I say goodnight as I head upstairs.

My parents and I have always been open with each other and I think about how Silas talked about his parents like they are a little colder and not friends to him like mine are to me. They sound nice enough but I am a little nervous to meet them since I am so used to being so open with mine.

Financially, we are different levels of middle class- I'm lower middle class- clearance sections, working since high school, Olive Garden for special occasions. Silas isn't a spoiled son- but he definitely went on annual international family vacations and doesn't hear his parents' discussing bills. When I get into my room, I mutter "shit" when I remember I was going to call Abby.

Since it's before 11, she's probably still awake since she has a late morning tomorrow, so I call her.

"You're calling late" and before I can say sorry, thinking I've woken her up, she says "That means the date went well!! Right?! Tell me about it!".

And because she's my best friend, I tell her everything (including the making out). She doesn't care where the spinning art place was, or what street the sushi place was on- but she does care about us kissing in the park and our more personal conversations of the night.

I tell her as much as I can before I'm exhausted and I ask her about her day and weekend with Tyler before getting off the phone to go to sleep. The next morning, I wake up to a text from Silas that he sent after I went to sleep.

"*I don't know how I'm supposed to sleep after a kiss like that- but I hope you're sleeping well and I'm looking forward to seeing you tomorrow :)*".

After waking up for a few minutes I text back "*I hope you're not offended that I was able to sleep, but that might explain why I had the dream that I did last night*".

Once I'm in my Monday morning lecture, he replies *"ooo please tell me- better yet, please show me"* I don't want to tell him the truth which was the dream continued where we left off in the park if my mom never called me so I just say *"maybe one day I will :)"*.

Even though we have class later today, our texting conversation doesn't stop, and even after our class together we keep our texts going. I wasn't as nervous to see him after our date as I would think I'd be- I'm pretty confident that he really likes me.

He walks in and comes over to say hi before going to his desk and sitting next to Ben, who also smiles at me. On our way out, Silas and Ben walk with me to my car and Silas makes effort for Ben and I to know more about each other before he gives me a kiss on the cheek goodbye.

On Wednesday, Silas and I grabbed some coffee and walked for a little, holding hands before we went to our different jobs. Things are evolving really rapidly and it feels official- especially when he meets my parents- and that Saturday I hang out with him and his band after their show.

Abby and Tyler also join us this time and I can tell they are both observing us, zoning in when

Silas puts his arm around me or kisses the side of my head. Tyler and Silas bond over video games and seem to really like each other and Abby keeps flashing me big, impressed eyes.

When Silas drops me off at home, he pulls farther ahead so his car is out of view from my parents and turns his car off, turning to me. Torn between being nervous and assuming he wants to make out, I just look at him questioningly. He unbuckles his seat belt to lean over me, his hand cupping my jaw, kissing me.

When I begin to kiss him back, he pulls away only slightly so our foreheads are connecting, along with our noses as he whispers "be my girlfriend".

I decide to make this easy and whisper back "okay" as I connect my lips with his again for a slow, sweet kiss that seals our relationship.

And for the next two years, that was our relationship. Excitement, joy, growth. We were always surrounded by friends, family and adventures. Late nights out, early mornings, laughing, kissing, making love, fucking- it was everything that a first-love relationship should be.

We learned about ourselves as much as each other, we became experts on each other, spoke our own language and always communicated- even if it hurt. We had the type of relationship where we always talked about our feelings or if we were upset about something. No secret passwords, no deleted browser histories, no cheating, temptations or lies. Once we both passed the photography class, we started our two-year love story with a summer that was for the books.

We became friends with each other's friends, went on road trips and spent time with each other's families. My parents quickly loved Silas's easy-going nature and it didn't take long for them to accept him over anytime and made no problem when he slept over. My curfew got later and later until it disappeared because they trusted him so much. We both bonded over not having siblings, so both sides of our parents enjoyed having someone of the opposite gender over.

His parents were usually busy with their real estate and golf-club social obligations so the sparse times I spent with them were polite and nice enough for me to be comfortable. His mom, Sharon, was happy to have another feminine presence in the house so we were able to bond over "girly" things like skincare and yoga.

Sharon was born in Brazil, but moved to the US as a child. I quickly realized that's who Silas got his golden skin and amazing hair from. His height and eyes were definitely from his dad, Brock, whose parents immigrated from Scandinavia before he was born. Brock, was more serious and reserved but I always felt like we had our own special connection.

Brock has a dry humor that a lot of people overlook in conversation but I always caught his little quick jokes. If I wasn't laughing, I usually had something to say that would catch him off guard and make him laugh right back. Sometimes we would go back and forth so much that it felt like a competition, While Silas and Sharon would watch with confused smiles. Silas would find it funny and join in for a bit but Brock and I always would take it too far, and sometimes the jokes got ridiculously dark.

His parents wanted more kids but had a hard time getting pregnant after Silas, whereas my parents were happy with one kid so they had more time for each other- I think that's why his parents that seemed so rigid opened up to me like they did. We would take turns spending the night at each other's houses for half the week and using the other half to be productive since we both had two more years of school to focus on for graduation. Along with our part-time jobs, his band, and plans with friends- we were always busy.

I only got busier when Silas got me a vinyl cutting machine one year for Christmas. It was a random (but expensive) gift that I wasn't expecting at all but when I looked at him with a happy and curious expression, he just shrugged and said "Because you're crafty… and maybe you could make the band some shirts we can sell and pay you for?".

The machine didn't just make vinyl for shirts; it made stickers and permanent vinyl for decals. I have a lot to be grateful to Silas for but that machine is probably the biggest reason because once I made shirts for his band that sold, other bands noticed and had me do theirs as well. My little, fun business turned into a real, full-time job.

By the time I graduated college I was making more money than an entry level job would with sales from bands, my online shop and my different partnerships with local businesses. I don't know if I would have ever found it if he didn't think of that first and it's something that let me quit my job at the bookstore. Hazel's Creations became my career because of Silas believed that I could turn a craft into a full-time business.

Now, because of that, I have my own schedule, a comfortable income and something of my very own.

CHAPTER 15

Because of my income and Silas's job with his dad, we were able to plan on getting a nice downtown apartment together once we graduated college. Even though we were both young and new, it felt right. It was actually Silas who suggested we live together- I pushed back in the beginning. I was nervous that he would want to be young and independent- but he insisted he didn't care about that- he knew he wanted to be together.

I remember how exciting it felt to look at different apartments and having serious discussions about how we envisioned decorating our first place together. Regardless of how everything turned out, I will always look back on that time with happiness for my old self.

The first Saturday after graduation, we had our first scheduled appointments at various apartments for us to tour, starting at 9 AM. I called him at 7am since the plan was to meet up early and get breakfast before driving over to the first apartment but he didn't answer. He had a show the night before so I assumed he just needed to sleep a little more even though it was very rare he wouldn't hear his phone in the morning.

I sent a good morning text and got ready to

give him more time to sleep. Then, I called him at 8 while eating toast since we no longer had time to eat breakfast together. No answer and his phone's voicemail box was full so I couldn't leave a voicemail- instead I texted him.

"*Hey! Wake up and call me!!!*" I debated just touring the apartments by myself but didn't see the point since he would want to see them.

At 9, I called the apartments to reschedule the tours and tried calling again, this time I was concerned that something serious happened. I sent several texts which all said 'delivered', not 'read' and I didn't even know where to start.

First, I texted Ben since I knew he was with him last night and let him know I hadn't heard from him and it only took him a few minutes to reply "*I drove with some other guys at the show to a party last night, the last time I saw him he was standing outside the venue, talking to a few other guys in the other bands*".

He sent a follow up text "*I don't live far, I can stop by his house if you want?*".

I replied "*No thank you, I'm about to call his parents now. But can you please ask around for him? He's never been out of reach and I'm really scared now*".

A minute later, "*I'm on it! I'm sure he's okay*".

I called Sharon's number first "Hello, Mrs. Ashwood! Is Silas home?".

"Hi, Hazel- he isn't here. I assumed he was with you." she sounded a little concerned but nothing too bad yet.

I quickly reply "No, I haven't talked to him since last night... we were supposed to look at apartments today and I'm getting nervous something happened".

"Well let's give it a little more time. He could have just been too tired to drive home last night" I heard the blinds opening as she murmured to herself "wait… his car is out front". We leave off with the agreement that I will keep asking around and that she will call Brock while searching the house and yard.

I call Ben, not wasting time when he answers "Hey his mom hasn't seen him either. Do you know anyone who he was talking to? Maybe you can ask them. Or maybe if there's someone who worked at the bar that you know who might be willing to share their camera footage".

"Jesus, Hazel- you're freaking me out. I just knew the guys he was talking to were in another band, but let me see if I can get any contact info. I'll call you back".

When we get off the phone, I text Silas again "*Silas, we are freaking out. Call as soon as you can. I'm debating on calling 911. Please, I'm scared*". His texts were still unread and by the evening, his phone was dead and my calls would go straight to voicemail. I spent the rest of that Saturday calling his friends, bandmates, anyone who even barely knew him.

He's 6 feet tall and muscular so I couldn't imagine him being kidnapped… but I was considering everything at that point. By Sunday, we called the cops. My parents put posters everywhere, and his parents called any connections they had that could help. The police said that since he's 22, he could have just ran away. They didn't have any reason to consider anything sinister since there was no evidence of foul play.

The cameras at the venue were checked but they were missing the area where the band members were standing around, only showing the front and rear entrances instead of the side of the building which was what we needed- and the parking lot. I never once considered that he might have left- because if he didn't want to be with me, he could have just broken up with me.

For the first couple of weeks, it felt so tangible that all I could think about was finding him and so I hardly did anything but look him up and call around for him. His parents tried to track his cell phone but it didn't move after The Black Cat and then it was off so we had very little to look at.

I couldn't imagine him leaving by choice even if there was a "good reason"- he had his important documents and passport at home, and his bank showed no usage. The gravity of what might have happened began to sink in.

The Black Cat was definitely the sketchiest venue around and the worst-case scenarios began to rise to the surface of my mind.

When I joined him in turning 21, we got small matching heart tattoos on our right butt cheeks. It seemed so funny at the time but I began to imagine having to identify him by that tattoo.

But what could have happened? Would someone actually kidnap him? His car was at home which meant he drove back but it didn't seem like he ever made it inside. His wallet was gone but there was no money taken out so all he really had was his driver's license and maybe a little cash.

I couldn't fathom that Silas would ever leave by his own free will. Even if someone was after him for something, he couldn't just start his whole life over with just a driver's license- and even if he could, couldn't he still let us know somehow? He didn't even have a car, so how would he be able to get around? As the weeks turned to months, it really began to sink in to everyone that he might never come back.

I stubbornly watched as our friends began to use his name in a past-tense until I had to be honest with myself that we would have heard something by now. His parents began to mourn their son sooner than anyone else in his life, which always upset me. Shouldn't they be the last ones that give up hope?

I'd like to think my parents would wait longer than anyone before giving up- but maybe they just had a parental instinct that caused them to accept that Silas was gone for good. Their acceptance, though odd, was also what led them to be there for me, to comfort me. I felt like I should have been comforting his parents but they were always assuring me that he was in good place which was also surprising because I never knew them to be religious in any way.

As I began to accept that Silas was really gone, I began to change into a person that I didn't recognize. I never moved out of my parents' house, became withdrawn and serious, and only really cared about growing my business- loving a tangible thing to focus on. I still would look him up to see if any news articles came up but I spent less and less time looking for him.

I didn't try to go out and date or travel like I always wanted to do and my friends didn't really see me that often.

Finally, they and my family had enough. Six months after Silas disappeared, Abby came over and she and my parents took turns saying how I'm not a bad person for living my life and enjoying my youth. That Silas would want me to enjoy my life and not sit around like an empty-shelled widow waiting for something. I didn't say anything so I just sat, listened and occasionally nodded because they all had a look that they were genuinely scared.

I felt so guilty for making them that concerned to basically force an intervention but I gave it a night to think over, and in the morning, I made my first appointment for therapy. Having a good therapist helped me a lot and I also pushed myself to have a fuller life. I stopped working 60-hour weeks, limiting myself to 40 hours as I began to slowly fill my life with other things.

I started with daily walks just to get some movement and clear my head, but I started adding more and more intensity until I was able to run marathons. Therapy really helped but having a goal and something to focus on was something that really helped me accept my life the way it was.

Abby would ride her bike with me and we would listen to podcasts together. She would always keep me busy with plans so I'll always be grateful to my best friend for doing whatever she could to get me to my new normal. I made more time for my parents who were amazing at avoiding the subject at all costs and made more time for the three of us to hang out.

But mostly, I was grateful to have my own income so I never, ever had to rely on anyone ever again.

CHAPTER 16

It was about a year after the disappearance that Abby finally asked "So… have you thought about dating again?". She must be a mind reader because even though I was too scared to say those thoughts out loud, I definitely began to think more and more about it. I was 23 and surrounded by couples and even my own parents' happy marriage began to make me feel isolated.

I felt like an old widow who gave up and I wanted to remember the joy and excitement of dating while I was still young. I knew that hardly anyone could match up to the standards that Silas set, but I was also content kissing a few frogs. I didn't have the expectation of meeting my soulmate since I already had him and knew how that turned out.

Abby introduced me to a few guys through Tyler who were…alright. But none of them really made me curious about a second date. I even went on a few dating apps to try that experience and even though most of them weren't amazing, I was still happy to have the experience.

For six months, I rejected a few, kissed a few, slept with even less, and then… I met Brandon. As a believer in fate and divine intervention, there would be few better ways for me to meet a potential boyfriend than by me locking myself out of my car and a cute locksmith being the man who answered the call.

He worked for himself and it just so happened he needed new company shirts made. That was a good excuse for us to begin our near constant communication. We started out pretty innocent and casual, going on the stereotypical dates of fancy restaurants or movie theaters.

He's five years older and lived by himself in an apartment, so I would usually go to his place- understandably, going to my place and seeing my parents was a little weird for him. The fact that Brandon is older was one of the main reasons I was so attracted to him. He was settled, stable and knew what he wanted- me. He had short dark blond hair and bright blue eyes that gave him a more boyish innocent look.

He was taller than me but not 6 feet tall like Silas was so it was hard to not compare when our hugs put my face at his neck instead of his chest. He was the exact opposite of Silas, and maybe that was my attraction to him. Not only in looks but personality too- where Silas was lighthearted and laid-back, Brandon was intense and passionate.

With Brandon, it wasn't love at first sight or anything, it started out professional and slowly morphed into affection, then attraction, and then a relationship. When I dated Silas, we had an instant attraction and immediately started dating but I knew how rare that was- and that it would be silly to expect that every time.

Maybe I no longer would feel that intense

attraction and chemistry with someone, but at least I would be in control of myself. It took Brandon and I six months to develop a relationship from strangers. Even then, I thought he was handsome- but I never craved him like I did Silas, like I couldn't get enough of him to the point of wanting to absolutely drown in him. But I liked that.

I liked that I didn't feel that much of an intense connection because if this ended the same way -me, alone, heartbroken- then it wouldn't hurt as bad. No amount of therapy could help me let my walls down and let someone in that much. As we dated longer, Brandon wanted us to move in together (I think mostly so I would have more independence from my parents) but I wasn't ready.

I could tell that the people around me still needed to warm up to him and it wasn't very clear that it was ever going to happen. Abby was polite but since I know her so well, I knew she tolerated him for my sake but didn't like him. She would ask hinting questions like "So, do you think you guys will be long-term?" and "What is he like when you two are alone?".

I couldn't tell why she was so uneasy around him and why my parents seemed to always be observing him so closely… but, then I started to see what they did. Brandon was controlling. He would find a way to make it sound sweet or concerned but he nearly always needed to know what I was doing, where at, and with who.

Even if it was mundane things like getting coffee with my mom. At first, the constant attention was flattering, to be honest. I loved the reassurance that he seemed so obsessed that he could never just up and disappear but after a few months that's exactly what I wanted him to do.

Once I noticed that the undertone was more angry than loving I began to notice more and more, and I began to resist more. And resisting only made him more toxic. When I saw his name on my phone for a text alert or call, I began to feel impatient and annoyed. I knew it was no longer an excited boyfriend wanting to talk to me, it was a supervisor making sure I was being controlled.

He was so good at covering it up by paying for everything, or buying me gifts and just love bombing me in general. I was weakened enough to see it as someone really loving me. I always made it clear that I wanted to move slowly. I told him from the beginning that I wasn't looking for anything serious right away. That if anything happened, it would be because it turned into a relationship, naturally and mutually.

Whenever I reminded him of that he would say in an almost whiny voice "I just love you so much" and would try to make me feel bad for "pushing him away" when really, I just had boundaries. I don't know if he really genuinely thought that we were soulmates and "meant to be" but he was so confident that I thought maybe I was the one that was off.

Maybe I was just damaged and unable to feel like before and Brandon was right? I didn't trust my gut feelings like I used to. When Silas disappeared, I thought to myself over and over "If he was dead, I would know. I would just feel it".

But, if he wasn't dead, he's had a long time to come back to everyone that loves and cares about him, so that's the only conceivable option.

Brandon and I's first few months were… nice. That's all I can really think of when I think of that time. They weren't passionate or consuming, but steady and consistent. There was no nervousness or excitement; it was more like finding peace in the calm and happiness that someone was there and not just going to "wow" me and then disappear.

Actually, my favorite thing about Brandon was how boring he was. He didn't want to go out and explore or go on trips, he just wanted me at his apartment where we would replicate living together in our own little world. Because he was so separated from my life, it was easy for me to just forget about any stresses in my life and just go to his place and watch TV.

I still spent a lot of time with my friends and family but I usually tried to socialize without him, although it didn't feel like that since he was always in my phone. The only time he wasn't boring, was when he was upset. He did a pretty good job of hiding it in the beginning but after a few months when I would maintain my boundaries he started losing more and more control over his emotions.

I didn't really think too much about it because I figured we were more of a short-term thing. I think that's because I was hoping it wouldn't go on for very long. The guy I want to keep, disappears- and the guy who I want to leave, won't.

CHAPTER 17

He only hurt me a few times. The first time was a few months in when I was at his house. My phone kept getting notifications- nothing insidious but some of my friends would send double or triple texts and it was just adding up. Brandon put my phone on top of a cupboard where I couldn't reach it so after a minute, I got the step ladder and grabbed it.

At this point, I wasn't scared of him so I showed him my phone and said "Do not. EVER. Grab my stuff again. You have no right to my things". He pushed me against the wall hard enough that my head got a lump, holding me there by cupping my jaw in his hand.

I heard him grit out "I have every right to you when you're here. Stop being so fucking distracted. You're here to spend time with me, aren't you?".

With that, he quickly let go and walked away. Hoping to de-escalate, but also wanting to make a point, I said "I own a business, Brandon. Some of those are messages from customers".

"I own a business too! I put my phone aside when you're here".

I had angry tears in my eyes as I said "I wasn't looking at my phone! It was just receiving notifications" and started grabbing my things to leave quickly.

He started panicking and looking sad "You're not leaving, are you? Don't go, it's just a dumb fight- those are normal with couples".

"Hitting my head into a wall over my phone and trying to keep it out of my reach are not normal!". And then something happened that I hadn't seen before: he started crying. sobbing. I've never seen the men in my life cry before- and I would never judge a man for that, but it also made me feel like something must be really wrong. He must really love me, he must really feel bad.

Like an idiot, I started comforting him when I should have been comforted. He told me how his dad had anger issues, and how he'll start going to therapy, anything to keep me from leaving. And I forgave him. I actually forgave him and slept with him in his bed that night and stayed with him.

I didn't tell anyone about it, thinking it was a learning moment for us, it was a one-time thing, he felt too bad there's no way he could ever do that again. It happened more and more as time went on and he got more comfortable in my life.

I started finding reasons to not be in his apartment and tried to think of a way to break up with him without him hurting me or my family. It was never anything "horrible", just bruises from him grabbing my wrist too tight, or marks from getting pinched when he was annoyed. He would tell me how he was older so I should just listen to him because he knew better.

He threw tantrums like a child but expected

to speak to me with authority and for me to bow down. I started to hate him. I started to fantasize about hurting him in a way that I didn't know my brain was capable of. I hoped he would get into a car accident, get food poisoning- anything.

Because none of my evidence was "enough", I never called the cops. And I still never told anyone. Everyone looked so concerned when Silas disappeared that I was just tired of people worrying about me or pitying me. I wanted to handle this problem by myself and the only thing I could think of was to remove myself from his life.

I figured if I started coming over less and being more boring when we talked that he would eventually get tired of it and move on. But then he would notice immediately. It almost made it worse because then he would call more, or stop by with flowers more, or making an effort with my family and friends more.

I think he did the last one more so it would be harder to get rid of him. I don't think he realized that none of the people in my life really cared for him- they saw through his BS way before I did. He had a lot of insecurities about me and I think that was what he couldn't accept.

He hated that I liked living with my parents, he hated that I had friends that I liked to hang out with, and he always tried to paint Silas in a bad light and how he's "probably living in Mexico with a bunch of chicks by now".

Right after saying that, he would talk himself up, saying how passionate he was, how he's never liked anyone the way he likes me- but I knew it was all BS. Once I saw through him, I never saw him the same way again. The rose-colored glasses were broken and there I was, stuck with someone I hated. Abby knew something was wrong but I made it clear that anything Brandon-related was off-topic because I didn't want to hear it.

My parents were obviously not fans of him but I covered all my bruises so they never thought anything was going on. I was good at hiding it from everyone- until one day I was caught off guard at a grocery store, shopping with Brandon. There was an old, faded hand-shaped bruise on my wrist that (compared to before) looked almost healed so I had a short-sleeve shirt on.

Brandon and I were walking around the produce section so we could cook dinner at his house that night when I saw Brock, Silas's dad. He saw me at the same time so he walked over to us. When he saw me, he had a genuinely joyous smile like he was happy to see me.

Then, he looked at Brandon and looked unimpressed and skeptical... but was trying his best to be polite. He called me by his nickname for me "Hey, Witch Hazel. Long time no see. How are you?". He nodded at Brandon while I gave my standard polite response and then I see Brock's face as he looks down at my wrist and noticed the bruise.

For a brief moment, his face looks murderous and he turns red but he covers it up quickly as we politely chat a bit more before he hugs me, and nods at Brandon before going back to his cart. "Why was that random guy acting like your dad or something?".

"Because for awhile, he was my other dad" and I went to grab some oranges to change the subject.

When he asked about it later, I said it was an old teacher I had because I hated mentioning Silas around Brandon. "Oh, did you guys flirt or something? I could see him being a pedo" and I didn't have anything to say. Brock was never inappropriate, or anything negative, he always treated me like a daughter.

Losing him along with Silas almost hurt just as much, because I lost family members along with the love of my life. I stayed in touch with Silas's family for awhile before it just dwindled out- what else was there to talk about? It was mostly us just checking up on each other intermittently.

Although, every Christmas and birthday I would get an anonymous gift on my doorstep and I always knew it was from them because it was the same wrapping paper they had used previous years. The grocery store incident didn't come up again with Brandon thank God. About a week after that, I heard my phone ringing and assumed it was Brandon (again) but weirdly enough, it said Brock's name- so I immediately answered.

"Hey, Hazey! When I ran into you the other day it reminded me about this property my colleague was telling me about that I think you should look into. I remember a few years ago you were talking about historic homes and it has your name written all over it".

Brock owns a company selling luxury real estate, so I already know whatever he has, I can't afford. So, I say "Wow thank you for thinking of me! I have been saving up... but honestly, I'd need 10 more years of saving to have a down payment for one of your houses".

We both laugh for a moment and I wonder why Brock is sounding like such a salesman but I don't know how to address that so I just wait a second for his reply. "Well… honestly, that's why I thought of you. It's such an insane deal that I don't want to see it slip away and it's a historic home, which I know you love".

"Well, what's wrong with it to be a deal?".

He's quiet for a moment and then says "Well that's the one bad thing… it's a state away. In a nice neighborhood and city but it's just not in the same overpriced city like this one". I think about it for a second… I have been saving for years for a down payment on a house, and getting away from Brandon would be nice.

On the other hand, I wasn't planning on moving that far from my parents. So, I say "Well, can you send me the information? I can at least look at it… Thank you for thinking of me!".

"Of course, I always want the best for you. The house is old, but it has been fixed up a lot so don't let the age scare you". I tell Brock that I trust his judgment so he tells me a bit more about the house. "I'm going to send you my buddy Sebastian's info who is the agent over there. Give him a call but please also feel free to reach out to me at any time, for anything Hazel. I still think of you as a daughter". I tearfully say goodbye and we get off the phone.

A moment later, I call Sebastian who I can immediately tell that I am going to love. He's genuine, honest and clearly into men- making it more comfortable for me to spend almost an hour on the phone with him getting the information needed for me to take this potential house seriously. While on the phone, he sent me a link to the house listing- we went over every detail together since I had about a thousand questions.

It's a beautiful historic home, in a nice quiet suburban neighborhood, close to the city and downtown area. Sebastian doesn't list any negatives which makes me nervous that it's too good to be true, but I honestly trust Brock and his judgment. But still, to ease my nerves I end up clarifying "I only have one concern, why is the house so cheap? If it's been restored and is in good shape, why isn't it expensive? It's in a good area too".

After a pause, Sebastian explained "We just have a very motivated seller who had to move quickly. It's had a recent inspection and everything is either new or as good as new. I totally understand your concern, so why don't you make a trip here soon to see it yourself? I think that would help put your mind at ease. But I want to emphasize the word soon because this is a miracle deal that won't last long".

Two days later, my dad and I flew up to see the house. My dad worked construction and helped build houses throughout college so he was very insistent on seeing everything himself and making sure I was safe. We met Sebastian in person, who went above and beyond- starting by picking us up at the airport and walking the house with us.

He patiently answered every question- which between my dad and I was a lot. We only stayed two nights- one day to see the house and go over banking details, and the second day to tour the area and see if it was a good place to live besides the house. Again, everything seemed too good to be true- the house was a tenth the cost that it should have been and the area was perfect for someone like me.

We couldn't believe the house didn't have any other interested buyers but we saw no reason for this to be a bad idea. It had parks nearby, cute cafes within walking distance and was a quiet area. When we got back home, we took my mom out to dinner to tell her everything. She looked excited but also like she was trying to not cry.

Then, I signed on the house- the seller agreed to pay for closing costs, Sebastian's commission and included all new appliances. I couldn't think of any reason to make a seller that motivated- especially after so many repairs they made on the house.

Sebastian didn't have a reason for the seller making the house an almost charitable donation- but, two weeks later, Abby and I were on our way. I didn't tell Brandon about any of this until I was already packed and on my way out so the two weeks before moving was spent coordinating with Abby, making holiday plans with my family, and saying my goodbyes to everyone else.

The day before moving, I stopped by Silas's parents with a gift basket. When Sharon opened the door and saw me, her face lit up in a smile and called Brock over. I was able to hug them and give them a tiny token of appreciation.

"I couldn't think of a good enough way to really say thank you but I hope some snacks and goodies help"- I couldn't help the awkward chuckle that escaped my mouth. They set the basket down inside and stepped out to give me long hugs.

Sharon spoke first with a motherly expression "Hazel, you deserve this fresh start and so much more. I'm so grateful to Silas for making you a part of our lives".

I hope they didn't see the tears in my eyes but when I try to say something, anything back, Brock spoke up as well "And you better be cool about it when we want to come visit you".

I laughed through my tears and said as genuinely as possible, "Anytime. You both are welcome in my life anytime" and then I went home and had dinner with my parents for the last time in the foreseeable future.

I fell asleep that night envisioning what this next chapter of my life looked like. A fresh start, a home that is all mine, and -most importantly- no Brandon. As sad as I was to leave my loved ones and restart my life from scratch, I also couldn't wait to be there and decorate my home. On the morning over, Abby got dropped off by Tyler and we left as early as possible. It's less than a days' drive, but we had fun stopping at certain points of interest.

We also stayed at a nice hotel less than two hours away from my new house to enjoy some relaxing girl time by the pool. On the drive, I opened up and told Abby everything about Brandon and how I was planning on sending a breakup text when we got to the hotel so I would be far enough to not feel scared or stressed about it.

Unfortunately, she wasn't as surprised as I thought she would be, but she was still just as angry at him and also a little upset at me for not telling her even though she understood. Sitting poolside with mimosas, we huddled over my phone and edited each other's versions of a breakup text with a violent narcissist, trying to not piss him off.

Finally, we agreed on: "*Brandon, I have moved away and will no longer be in your life. I think you know why but I need a restart and I can't be with a controlling man. All the best, Hazel*".

I worried that he might try to take out some sort of revenge on my parents but they bought cameras and an alarm system after I told them a little bit about me breaking up with Brandon. I knew he didn't really have that much interest in them, but I figured we couldn't be too careful.

Abby sighed, finished her mimosa in a huge gulp and said "Well, that's done. Let me know if he replies but, in the meantime, I'm going to look up if any crimes happened at your new home- It's too good of a deal!". I laughed and then laid back in my chair.

Did I feel a little lame for breaking up with someone over a short text? Yes, but he hurt me multiple times so… fuck him. All I wanted now was to go to shop for house things, enjoy my time with Abby, and focus on growing my business.

I just had my small sedan that was as packed

as much as it could be without getting pulled over. I daydreamed over the fact that I will never run into anyone from my hometown again. I would never run into anyone that I used to know, asking if I ever heard from Silas or found out what happened to him. I tried to focus on important things like updating my mailing address but my mind kept going to the dumb, fun things like how I want to landscape the front yard.

I didn't know what was next in my life but I couldn't help this overall feeling that it was going to be… good. Hard, maybe- but good nonetheless. Brandon never replied but I took that as a good sign.

PRESENT DAY
AGE 25

CHAPTER 18

Silas is alive.

The moment I get inside and lock my door, I slide down to the floor as the tears trail down my face. Sobs rack my body for a few minutes before I'm able to catch my breath and attempt to get my thoughts in order. I don't know where to start.

The surprise of seeing him, the shock of knowing he's been alive this entire time, the need to know what he's doing here next to me. I keep seeing his face, staring back with an attempted control that doesn't hide his emotions as much as he would probably like.

Why does he look so different? What happened to him? He's somehow taller now, with a build that doesn't make sense outside of a professional football player. He was never someone that cared about the gym, or looked like he spent his days lifting weights.

I can see the facial features of the boy I loved, under the years of anger, despair and exhaustion. He's still as handsome as ever, but only someone that knew the old him would notice the dark circles that weren't there before. I check the camera app on my phone and he's no longer there, and neither is his car.

I call Abby and tell her what just happened and she begins to interrupt, unable to hold in her questions "Silas? Like your ex, Silas?" when I confirm it several times, she goes quiet and I don't blame her for not knowing what to say.

Thinking over the moment I add "The craziest part is when he said 'yeah' he didn't sepilogueeem surprised or embarrassed. More like he was waiting for me to guess… I almost feel like he was relieved. But I just can't figure out for what".

Abby is starting to sound madder than I am when she asks "Are you going to ask where the hell he has been? Should I come stay with you for a bit?".

"It's okay, girl. But thank you… I think I'm just going to avoid him and keep focusing on my life. I mean, he beat Brandon unconscious so I don't think he's wants to hurt me or anything- But I just can't figure out why or how he's my neighbor".

She sighs "Well, that's probably the easy part, isn't his dad the reason you're in that house?".

It all starts dawning on me- "Oh my god… this house was 'such a good deal' what the fuck?! I can't believe I trusted him, I feel like such an idiot".

Abby takes a few seconds but then timidly says "Honestly, Haze- Brock really does care for you like a daughter, I don't think he would do something to hurt you. I think maybe he was thinking he was helping you… I don't know, why but I think we can trust him". I can tell she's not trying to upset me so I nod even though she can't see me.

Then, I say "You're probably right, but I have a million questions. I think I'm going to go and lay down in bed, this is a lot".

"Okay babe, but call anytime- I'm always here. Please keep me updated". We say bye and once I'm off the phone, I get ready for going to sleep but lie in bed for a few hours until I finally drift off.

Once I'm asleep, I stay asleep- because for the first time in months, Silas doesn't appear in my dreams. A week goes by and I don't see Silas, so I focus on work and try to avoid being in my yard as much as possible to avoid running into him.

Even more fortunate, I still have not heard from or seen Brandon since I last saw him unconscious in my driveway. I'm hoping that since the weather has started to get colder, it's making him not want to travel to an even colder area or to risk sliding on the roads since the surrounding area is much more rugged.

Since it's the beginning of winter, the mornings start with light ice covering my yard and it warms up in the late-morning, going into a usually sunny afternoon, and a chilly night. I woke up early today to beat the lines at the post office and drop a few boxes of merch off but as I'm walking to my car, I slip on a sheet of ice and go flying to the ground, landing on my ass and elbows before I even realize what's happened.

Luckily, I didn't have anything heavy in this box but it still hurt to land on the hard ground and it takes me a minute to get back up, fighting tears from the pain in my elbows and hip. On instinct, I look around to see if anyone just watched my embarrassing moment, when I make eye contact with Silas who's in his front yard and looks like he's mid-step of walking over to me.

The moment he sees my face when I look at him makes him clench his jaw, turn around and go back inside. I'm already standing back up and loading the box into my car when I hear his door shut. Once I get the last box in, I head to the post office, and then run a few errands to further avoid running into Silas again.

I finally got to see him in daylight and after all these years wondering if he was really dead, or even okay, I can see what an idiot I was. He looks great- healthy, strong, and his face over the years is so much more defined and mature looking- he's still the most attractive person I've ever seen.

In college, he was attractive for his lanky and youthful looks with the swishy hair and big smile. Now, he's a whole other person. He's huge- big shoulders, tall- but also has shorter hair with the tousled locks and serious emerald green eyes makes him a fantasy as much as it makes him a threat. It's not just his physical differences that I noticed though.

Silas has preternatural calculations to his movements- like he's forcing himself to move slower as well as hyper-aware of everything around him. I could just say he's much more graceful, but something about him is almost animalistic and it counters anything about him veering towards "gentle".

I catch myself almost passing a stop sign on the way to my house, distracted by the similarities and differences of Silas, but I catch it last minute and make the full stop, and park in my driveway less than 5 minutes later. When I get out of the car, I notice that my feet feel little rocks under my shoe and when I look down in confusion, I see that its ice salt, poured all around my driveway and in front of both of our houses.

When I check the video from my doorbell recording, I see that that's what he went inside for. Right after I left, he quickly came back outside and poured it everywhere before going back inside. If it was anyone else, I would have went over and immediately thanked him, but seeing Silas do that just made me more upset for some reason.

I don't want him to be nice to me. As soon as I'm back inside, I text Carly to see if she wants to meet at a nearby bar for a few drinks to which she quickly accepts. I decided I deserve a little break and when she quickly accepts, I immediately get ready and walk the mile over to our favorite local bar.

We talk about everything but my personal life, which I avoid at every turn. I don't even want to think about Silas or Brandon or anything else and I'm scared that if I start to talk, I won't stop. And I don't really want to tell a new friend about such drama. Carly has a morning shoot, so she just nurses her two glasses of wine over the two hours.

I have two strong drinks and then when I notice I start laughing a little too loud, I start to drink water. I hate the beginning of a new friendship where you don't know where the fine line is with someone, and so you are constantly trying to see if what you do or say bothers or offends them. So far Carly is crazier than I am, so I don't think me being more drunk than her would bother her.

But I also feel a little embarrassed when I can tell she's giggling at my drunkenness- even if it isn't in a judgmental way, more like she's enjoying me enjoying myself.

CHAPTER 19

After we pay our tabs, Carly offers to drop me off and I accept the offer since walking home with more than a buzz does actually make me nervous- especially with how weird my life is right now. Once she pulls up in front of my house, she sees Silas, who is installing more motion-control lights in the front of his yard.

She blows out a quiet whistle, whispering "damn… your neighbor is HOT!" and to my horror, Silas quickly looks up, right at her. His eyes flick over to me with a little light in them like he's trying not to laugh before he turns around and keeps working on them.

Oh my god. I think he heard her.

I don't even think she noticed his reaction so she's going from staring at him to looking at me in excitement. In my paranoia of thinking Silas heard Carly, I casually say "Eh. He's alright. Once you see him closer up you notice his face is ugly. Anyways thanks for meeting me with short notice!" and I hop out. I wave as we say goodbye to each other and quickly go over the barbecue I'm hosting next week.

She waits until I am inside before driving off and I am so grateful for a friend who is cautious despite not even knowing that I have a reason to be.

As I walk up my driveway, I notice Silas is further down installing another light and looks like he's watching me.

After a second of eye contact, I turn back and decide to test his hearing and whisper "Fuck you".

I feel a chuckle coming on because being that immature always makes me laugh- but I'm caught off guard by him asking "What was that?".

I hear the confusion and surprise in his voice, but I also hear the challenge in it as well. I quickly turn around, and since he can apparently hear me well, I don't raise my voice when I look at him and say "I said 'fuck you'. Congrats on your hearing getting better" and walk back inside.

As mad as I am, I also start laughing at the surprise on his face and how I apparently made him speechless. He didn't look mad- he almost looked innocent and confused. Which, if I didn't hate him would have made me feel a little guilty. I celebrate having a good day with a bubble bath and meal prepping for the next few days before settling in for the evening.

As I begin to get ready for bed, I think about how different he is. It's been three years so I'm sure I seem a lot different to him as well. When I thought about him all these years, he was this laidback, happy, carefree boy.

Now all I see is a serious, angry and lonely man. If he looked any more different, I could easily think he was a different person all together. I actually don't blame myself for taking so long to recognize him. Did he have brain damage or amnesia which started a personality shift? Why doesn't he seem more awkward or surprised by me? Why doesn't he seem more guilty and embarrassed that he's caught? Does that mean he faked his disappearance?

I try to convince myself that I don't need to know his reasons, because no reason would be good enough for me anyways. All that matters is that he left and didn't come back. I don't see him the next day when I'm running errands, but on the following day, I get a text from an unknown number saying *"I hope we can talk soon"*.

I remember when I gave my number to Silas after the Brandon incident so I can't really tell for sure who it is based on such a short text.

"Who is this?" I reply back and only a few seconds later comes the reply.

"Who else could it be?" It's definitely Brandon then, only he could be that self-absorbed.

"I don't have time for games, have a nice night" and as soon as that message is received, I start to get an incoming call- which I ignore and hope that's it for the night.

Now, another text *"So I need to make another trip?"*. I really don't know in this situation if ignoring the messages are better or if I should try to de-escalate.

Hoping that a mature message will inspire him to do the same, I just reply with *"Look Brandon, the breakup wasn't personal. I needed a fresh start and I couldn't get that with you being controlling. Please just accept it and move on. There's 8 billion people out there, don't put so much energy into one person"*.

He calls again. I ignore it again. Then, I message him with *"Please only communicate through text so I can have documentation of our conversations"* which the only reply I get is *"Fuck you"*. Funny how those two words the other night gave me such catharsis and humor in a shitty moment, and now they bring me the exact opposite.

On one hand, I feel like I just made the situation worse, but on the other hand I can tell that no matter what I said or did, he would still be coming to the same conclusions that he is now.

So, at the end of the day, I don't think that conversation changed anything. Two days go by with no Brandon or Silas, when I get a package in the mail that I wasn't expecting. It has no sender address so my paranoid thoughts go to every option- a bomb, a body part, an actual present.

Stupidly, I open the box because my curiosity will almost always beat my fear. It's a medium-sized, new teddy bear that I have to admit is very cute. Its brown with big ears and the softest thing I've ever felt, I spend a few moments touching the soft fur and looking it over before I notice the only other thing inside the box: a note.

"I know you will never forgive me but please know how sorry I am and how hard I am going to work to prove it to you". I'm going to fucking kill him.

CHAPTER 20

I slam my door on the way out, and march over to Silas's house with the box in hand and pound on the door. He has a doorbell but I don't want to ring it, I want to pound on his door as hard as I can and if he doesn't answer, I'm going to start kicking it. It only takes a few seconds before his door flies open.

Without gauging his reaction, I throw the box with the teddy bear at his feet and say "If you try to contact me again, I am going to file a restraining order" and turn to leave.

"Well, that will be difficult since we're neighbors" he says to the back of my head and when I tu

rn around to yell something -anything- he adds "Also, that's not from me".

He bends down to pick it up and starts inspecting it like it's a map instead of a stuffed animal and I begin to feel a smidge of embarrassment at my confidence and anger. He notices the note and looks it over with just as much scrutiny and looks back at the bear with such intensity that I actually laugh a little. What is he looking for?

"Hazel, this is a camera".

I almost say "and I'm a bike" but before I

can get anything out, I notice him pointing to the bear's eyes. "Are you sure? How do you know?".

Too easily, Silas rips the head off the bear and there's a few little wires connecting it. He hands me the head and says "Look at the right eye, you can see it" and he's right, I do.

While I look it over more, I hear him swear and quietly say "I'm assuming it's from your ex then". I look up and quickly nod before looking back down at it, grateful that it was immediately found out... rather than being in my house watching me for who knows how long.

"Has he sent you anything else?" I can hear the concern in his voice and that he's trying to have a calm facade.

I angrily mumble "Just some texts. Sorry for disturbing you... bye" and I turn to leave again.

Before I move a single step, Silas impatiently says "Hazel, look..." and I can see him trying to figure out how to say what he's needs to.

Before he can say anything, I nearly growl "Please, don't. I'm serious when I say I don't want to talk to you".

I'm not used to my voice sounding this angry but it's no match for him, who chuckles before saying "My, how you've changed".

"Yeah, years of time will do that to a person. Seems like I'm not the only one... I liked it better when I didn't know if you were dead or not. Bye, Silas" I walk back to my house with the bear in my hand and throw it in the trash bin and when I hear footsteps behind me, I rush inside.

Before I can slam the door in Silas's face,

he shoves the door open and steps inside, shutting and locking the door behind him.

"Listen" he says in a voice that is commanding, yet gentle but before he can continue, I yell "Get the fuck out, I'm calling the cops!".

I walk towards him to push him despite being half his size. He just puts his arms up and chuckles "You're going to call the cops on me? For what, intruding?".

"YES! Because you are!" and now I'm so frustrated I feel like crying. He walks forward causing me to back up and it only takes two steps before my back is against the wall and he is toe to toe with me.

Even in this moment, I can't help but marvel how this is not the boy I once loved. He's turned into this confident asshole and it makes me hate him more. He starts to say "If you would just listen to me for a sec-" but I slap him in the face with my right hand before he can get out another word. I guess I learned a few bad habits from Brandon after all.

He grabs the wrist of my right arm and holds it against the wall "I deserve that". I nod before trying to hit him with my left hand which he intercepts immediately and holds that wrist against the wall too. Quietly, he says "I would have deserved that, too" and moves his head closer to mine, eyes going surprisingly soft.

Calmly, he says "I know saying sorry is an understatement so I won't start. But, even if you never talk to me again, we both know Brandon isn't going to stop. So, whether you like it or not, whether we talk or not- I am going to do what I can to keep you safe".

I can tell he's not done so I remain silent as he adds "but I need your help keeping you safe… Especially some nights when I'm gone. It probably won't be for much longer but until then, you need to tell me when he attempts making any sort of contact with you". I'm partially focused on his words but I'm distracted by his eyes that I somehow remembered perfectly in my dreams.

The genuine concern in his eyes when, until now, it didn't seem like he gave a shit about me. Before I lose my steam, I say "I don't want you protecting me at all, you haven't been the last three years". I don't understand the brief flash of hurt in his eyes as he slightly loosens his hold on my wrists and he moves his thumbs a little in gentle swipes along the sensitive skin there.

"That's not true. Regardless of your hate for me, I will give you your space. But you need to know that I am here when he comes back. Because I promise you, he will be back". He slowly moves his mouth to my ear and quietly says "Now, can I let you go so we can talk calmly? Or are you going to keep slapping me?".

I think about it for several seconds, debating my options before finally conceding "Let me go", so he does. He calmly walks over to my dining room table and holds the chair open and gestures with his other arm for me to sit, which surprising even myself- I do.

He sits down across from me, looking over my face with a sad intensity and leans in "Regardless of how much you hate me- and have every right to- you need to know that I'm going to keep you safe.

Whether you like it or not. I know that this entire situation is confusing and uncomfortable but that's the least of my worries".

"Silas, I don't even know you anymore. We're strangers now- I can't trust you and I can't believe anything you say anyways". He has the audacity to look extremely hurt over this but, after a moment, he calms his face and quietly reaches to the back of his waistband and pulls out a gun.

I jump out of my chair and back up with my hands in front of me. I open my mouth- to say what, I don't know- but before anything comes out, Silas stares at me while taking the magazine out and gently setting it on the table. I stare at him in shock but he gestures for me to sit back down and when I do, he says "I took this from him when I pulled him out of the car, Hazel. Even if you don't trust me, please trust the fact that he's not going to stop. And maybe this is only going to upset you more, but I don't see what other choice you have besides letting me handle it".

As naive as it is, I hadn't even considered guns. Brandon didn't have guns when I dated him, but I believe what Silas is saying since I've seen first-hand how unhinged Brandon has become. "Do you know how to store and shoot a gun?" he asks me.

After going to the range several times with different men in my family, I know I am okay with a gun so I confidently say "Yes".

He raises an eyebrow, clearly not remembering that ever being a conversation in the past. He slides the gun and magazine to my side of the table and says "I'm sure you want to use it on me- and once Brandon is out of the picture, go ahead. But please for now, please just let me protect you".

He looks so unnerved that I just say "okay" and without knowing what else to say, I just stare at him until he takes a breath and continues: "Like I said, saying sorry doesn't even begin to cover it. But if nothing else, please remember how much I loved you then and trust that everything I've done was for your safety'.

'Even though my feelings haven't changed since then, I completely understand why yours have, and I won't try to convince you otherwise. But you will not stop me from doing everything I can to keep you safe- I don't care if it annoys you or makes you mad. All I've ever cared about was keeping you safe, and that is something that will never change".

His words become more and more passionate as he speaks and towards the end, he looks emotional. But rather than focusing on that, I realize something else "How do you know Brandon's name?".

At his confusion, I clarify "you just said it". He looks annoyed at the question but answers "I looked at his wallet when he was knocked out in your front yard".

I'm amazed how quickly he was able to get to his wallet, but I don't want to get too distracted from our conversation with more details about that night, so I go back to what he was talking about just a moment ago. I stand and ask "Well, will you ever be able to tell me why you left in the first place? I deserve to know. I thought you died".

He doesn't say anything, but he gets up and walks around the table until he's in front of me, and he swears in barely above a whisper "I will, I promise". And oddly enough, I believe him. After the past few months, years, and all of the lies- when he takes another step towards me and wraps me in a huge warm hug, I hug him back.

This is the first time since Abby left that I truly feel safe and I don't pull away very quickly, instead I savor it. I quietly inhale to savor his scent that is just the best mix of musk and soap that I remember instantly.

I'm snapped out of cloud 9 when Silas begins to gently rock me side to side while holding me, and then says over my head "I'm sorry for scaring you by coming in here. I'm going to go back to my place but let me know if you need anything". I nod and pull away, about to put distance in between us when he steps forward again, leaning down so we are face to face.

He holds my face in his hands and smiles, with a slight show of his dimples in a bittersweet expression and whispers "It's going to be okay. I promise". I say nothing as he turns and leaves, shutting the door behind him.

CHAPTER 21

I stand there in silence for a few moments, spacing out and trying to organize everything that's happened in the last few hours. The teddy bear from Brandon feels like yesterday and I try to focus my thoughts on that since it should be the priority.

But my mind keeps going to Silas comforting me and protecting me, after all these years. What could his reason be? He was so genuine, unless he became a really good liar in the last few years, I think he's somehow telling the truth but I just can't understand how.

When I look and see the gun in two parts on the table, I pick both up and gingerly take them upstairs to lay on the floor behind my bed. I debate on telling the cops about the bear and about the gun but I honestly don't believe that they can do anything about Brandon right now, so I just take pictures of both and keep track of any messages from him so I can file a restraining order.

Walking around the top floor, I make sure windows are locked and then look out towards the front street. I move the sensor on my motion camera to cover the sidewalk as well and all of Silas's property so I can see as much as possible.

After awhile, I call my parents to let them

know about everything besides Silas (that's just way too much right now) and warn them to keep an eye out because who knows what Brandon is capable of at this point. I should have known it wasn't going to be a quick conversation as I spend the next hour convincing my dad to not come to my house and stay for as long as he can.

My dad takes a deep breath and calmly says "We should have done more Hazey, I'm sorry. If I see him- I'm putting a bullet in his head".

I scoff out "Jesus, Dad!".

"I'm serious".

"I know you are but… it's going to be fine. If we are just mad, we aren't going to think as clearly. I have cameras facing every direction, motion sensor lights all around the property, and I can check my doorbell camera even when I'm away from home. It's going to be fine, we just have to wait him out a bit".

"Well, I would say go get a gun but it sounds like you've already got that covered. Go to a gun range and get some target practice so you don't just injure him". It sounds like he's still considering coming when we hang up, but I think I held them at bay with promises of keeping them updated and coming home immediately if anything happens.

A few nights later, I've calmed down a bit and am back in the motions of my routine. I get into my car, planning to meet Carly at a diner so we can plan a shopping list for the barbecue. When I go to turn the ignition on, it doesn't start. I try several times, each time it sputters and sputters, but I give up when nothing happens. My first impulsive thought is to start punching my steering wheel but I just pinch my nose and take a few breaths.

Luckily, I was planning on getting there earlier than her anyways so by the time AAA comes and helps I should get to the diner around the same time as her. I pull out my phone to text her and call AAA, but just as I turn the screen on, I hear a loud knock on my window and scream.

When I look out my window, I see Silas- standing there in what looks like lounge clothes, rumpled hair, and a tired expression. Why can't I ever have privacy when my life is being a shit show? He tries to open my door but it's locked so he just stares at me with an impatient head tilt until I open it. When I do, he just quickly says "hi" as he bends down and pulls the lever to release the hood, quickly disappearing in front of my car.

He looks like he was in bed and ran out when he heard my car sputtering. With a quiet sigh, I get out to look at my battery as well. Before I can say anything, Silas beats me to it with "No one did anything to it, it's just dead. I can go take you to the store right now and get a new one".

"Thanks, but I'm meeting a friend in a few minutes so I don't have time to go to the store. I'll be fine".

I pull out my phone to start calling Carly but before I do, Silas interrupts my thoughts with "I can take you".

At my surprised face, he asks "Is it close?".

When I tell him the name of the diner, he closes my hood and pulls out his keys. "That's two miles away. I can just drop you off, get you a new battery, install it and drop your car off at the diner". He's making it sound so easy but it's definitely an annoying last-minute task.

"But how will you get back?" I ask and he gestures for me to walk with him over to his jeep and when I do, he chuckles.

"It's two miles, Haze. I can handle it, don't worry". I decide to ignore his use of my nickname while I make my way to the passenger door. I know he can walk back- but it still feels like a lot. But then I remember it's Silas and he owes me... a lot.

So, I shrug "Okay" and get in his car while I wait for him to get in and turn the car on. His car is spotless and organized and I think he really must have changed, since his car in college looked like someone lived in it. The car ride is short, but it seems like he's trying to make the most of it "So the friend you're meeting up with, is it the woman that thinks I'm hot?".

I scoff, not even making a point about how he was able to hear us. It's been long enough that I begin to doubt how loud we were or if there was a window open. He's entirely too satisfied so I lie "You haven't met him" and when I sneak a peek over at him, he's just making small nods with a serious face. I'm annoyed at how fast we went from me hating him for ruining three years of my life, to making small talk in his car. He broke my heart and I only got to slap him twice...

Pulling in front of the diner, I quickly step out and close the door behind me without saying anything to him- hoping that Carly doesn't see my ride. I quickly walk inside and see Carly who looks like she also just got here so I join her at the booth and sit down across from her with my back to the door. "Oh, good timing, it's happy hour!" Carly exclaims as we look at our menus excitedly.

The diner's happy hour has all of their appetizers half off so we strategize how we will order a few plates and share them. We also get a few dollars off of cocktails so at least this night will be cheaper than expected. "Do you want to share some onion ri-" when I look up mid-sentence, Carly's looking kind of confused at the door behind me so I turn and see Silas. And right now, the adrenaline of getting caught in an embarrassing lie, I might as well have seen Brandon.

Luckily, he's calmly walking towards the register, not even acknowledging me so I feel relief that we are just going to ignore each other. I see him order food and wait for it by staring at his phone at the side of the counter. I realize that Carly is staring at me now with a look like she's trying to piece things together but I just try my best to power through. "Should we share some onion rings?" I ask and she's still in her thoughts when she just shrugs and says "Sure, those sound good".

I see Silas get a bag of food, and two large cups that I try to not notice him filling both up and focus on whatever Carly is saying about him looking familiar when he walks past. I inwardly cringe as he stops at our booth and leans in a little to set one of the full cups in front of me.

He smiles and says "I'll have your car here in an hour" and then turns to Carly, smiling and saying hi. I feel myself stiffen as he turns back to me, winks and strolls out like the cat that ate the canary. I look down at the full cup and take a sip- to Carly's dramatic surprise and caution- it's half lemonade and half strawberry soda. That was my favorite combo in college and that was all I would drink when we would go to "our diner".

I look back to see him but he's already gone into the night. We place our orders quickly and Carly doesn't miss a beat. "I thought he looked familiar… is that your neighbor? Why does he have your car?" I close my eyes for a few seconds and resign myself to the next couple of minutes of summing up my day- without the backstory and any drama to keep it as simple as possible.

"Oh my god, Hazel. He's either the nicest man ever or he's definitely into you- nobody would just do that for a neighbor they don't know" she looks so excited and I can tell that my lack of emotion is ruining her joy, so I put the spotlight on her instead.

"Maybe he's from a small town? I can introduce you guys and maybe you'll hit it off?" I don't know if I would mind. Should I? I don't want to care, but I guess it would be very unsettling to see them together.

She obnoxiously scoffs and says "Yeah, right! He only had eyes for you, girl! That was intense- I almost started sweating. How are you so calm!".

"It's just been the longest day! I'm sure I'll wake up tomorrow and be like you". We get our food and I hope to God this is a good enough change of subject but to really make sure we are moving on, I exclaim "This looks so good, good choice! Should we make wings for the barbecue? Let me pull my list out so we can go over it".

And thank God that's where the Silas conversation ends for the night. When I get a chance to go to the bathroom later, I spend an extra minute washing my hands, wondering why his personality was so different tonight. I've seen him be angry, quiet, insistent to help me, but he was definitely flirting with me earlier. Why didn't I push back? I resolve myself to be cold to him- no matter what.

He broke my heart, I'd be an idiot to even be friendly with him after everything- especially with the lack of answers he's given me about anything.

CHAPTER 22

Silas was a man of his word. My car was in the parking lot with a new battery and it had also clearly been washed and vacuumed. When I get home, I hope I can just disappear into my house without seeing him, but my unlucky streak continues when I make eye contact him as I get out of my car.

He has an armful of boxes and he's already smiling like a Cheshire cat so I flip him off while rolling my eyes when I turn and walk inside. I hear his laughter and I say "We aren't friends, Silas" to shut any joy he has down. I think it's successful as silence takes over when I go inside and shut the door.

I go upstairs and get ready for bed and fall asleep after a few minutes of replaying the embarrassing moment. But it's more because of his smug reaction, not because I should feel embarrassed by anything Silas thinks after the last few years. He seems so confident that he left for a good reason that it's hard not to trust... but what could be good enough?

I need to find out as soon as possible, because he's already getting way too comfortable in my life when I don't know if he should be in it at all. I don't see Silas for the next week and before I know it, it's the day of the barbecue. I check my phone and Carly has already texted me a few times, nothing urgent just questions about party logistics.

Since I usually hang out with her group at night, we are planning for it to start at 7pm and go until after midnight. We already decided to move the party inside if it gets too loud- I don't have an HOA, but I still want to be a good neighbor. I get ready, prepare food and clean the house for a few hours.

As soon as 4pm rolls around, Carly comes over with bags and trays of food and other supplies. After the food I made, we have to strategize to fit everything she brought inside my fridge as well. Most of the others are bringing alcohol and more food but I think we should be set even if the party went on for several days.

While Carly starts filling coolers with ice, I go set up the fire-pit with wood and go back inside to start putting plates and bowls out to be filled soon with snacks and appetizers. We still have an hour or so, so she brings in her speakers and we turn on party throwback classics as we finish up making everything look "insta-worthy" as Carly puts it.

Her photographer mind is never off-duty. We pre-batch some strong cocktails (essentially jungle juice) and I pre-game a tad bit more than a host should as I tell myself it will set the mood. I'm a good drunk so I don't really worry about doing anything too shameful in front of everyone.

Soon, some guests arrive a little early but we don't mind since everything is ready and we were starting to re-adjust bowls and plates several times just for something to do. Within the first hour, there are 15 people here and more people are slowly trickling in. Even with several men standing around the grill at all times, we still can't keep up with the burgers and hot dogs that everyone is eating.

Mostly everyone is in my backyard, but I left the back door open so people can go in and out for drinks, the bathroom or extra snacks. I recognize most people from previous nights out; the others are friends of friends or significant others that everyone else knows. This is the safest I've felt since I've moved- like nothing can happen with so many people here- so I take a few more sips of my drink as I unwind for the night. The speakers are outside but we turned them down a tad so people don't have to yell to one another.

Another hour goes by and people are mostly done eating but the alcohol has helped people mingle and I spend my time chatting with everyone and trying to get to know more about people I met briefly. I don't want to rely on Carly for her friends but I also would like to know as many people as possible since Carly is my only friend here. Silas pops into my head but I forget about him since I don't even know what he is. A memory, I guess.

As I go around handing out jello shots and just plain shots, I can tell the alcohol is helping people get into a dancing mood and I start to see people who didn't arrive together, dance like they may be leaving together. I bring around waters as well just so nobody gets too drunk, and as I walk around passing them out, I notice a couple that came in together start to get more distant and cold with each other the more the night goes on. I think they got in a fight and are trying to cool down but I can't tell without staring too much and I have enough going on just trying to keep more than 25 people happy. While I talk to Zach- one of Carly's friends- I occasionally look at the couple again.

Now, I can tell the boyfriend is definitely ignoring her to talk to his friends and as they get more boisterous, she begins to get bored and wander off. Good for her, he seems like an asshole. Maybe she did something to make him mad but he doesn't seem to handle it maturely.

I haven't met them and I'm not sure who invited the couple, but it might be a good thing that they are getting space. I hate when couples fight- well I like when they argue and I get to eavesdrop, but I don't like serious fights. They make me feel like I'm waiting for something bad to happen.

I've met Zach a few times and he's really cool, I can also tell that he's into Carly and has been for awhile. She never mentions it so I don't know if she knows, but whenever she's in the vicinity, he keeps his eyes on her. One of Zach's friends introduces himself to the girlfriend being ignored and she immediately starts smiling and it doesn't take long for them to start dancing. It's innocent and playful at first and I see her boyfriend notice and try to ignore them.

Once the playlist switches to a more slow and sexual song, they start to change how they are moving to match the song- and its undeniably intimate. It only takes a few seconds of that before the boyfriend notices and hauls over to them to pull them apart Even though he wanted to fight over her, she's again forgotten to the side as the two guys begin to argue.

Zach and I at this point have stopped talking and are just watching this happen. He looks at me and then at them "do you want me to break it up?" and when I look back at them, they are full on fighting now. I don't know who hit who first, but now they are on the ground wrestling and everyone has stopped what they were doing to watch as well. I look back at Zack to tell him "Yes" but someone in my periphery has already moved.

Somehow, Silas is here. In my backyard.

He's holding them both back by the shirt collars, and crouching down so he's at eye-level with them, saying something menacingly. Zach looks at me with a confused expression and I just shrug, not wanting to explain my neighbor right now. Everyone else looks just as confused about a stranger being in my yard, breaking up a fight.

They look like little boys in comparison to him, and they look too scared to try to get out of his hold. Instead, they are intensely listening to whatever Silas is saying and at this point I've walked up behind him. The music is still playing but everyone is silent so I hear Silas grit out "get the fuck off of her property" and then releases them aggressively so they both fall back.

Oddly enough- when the guys get up, they calmly walk out together- the girlfriend following them out. Silas is also watching to make sure they leave, and everyone else is staring at him with an open mouth and then staring at me. I just smile and shrug like "crazy, right?".

That's all the crowd needs to go back to their conversations, which is obviously now about the scene that just unfolded in front of them. I look over at Carly and she's the only one still paying me attention, her head is tilted in confusion but she has laughter in her eyes like she is delighted at the last 5 minutes. I roll my eyes at her and then turn around to face Silas, who is standing there like he is about to confidently take a scolding.

Instead, I quietly ask "Come inside with me for a sec?" before turning and walking inside, not waiting for an answer. I can hear his footsteps behind me and the door close behind me so I know he followed me in. He follows me inside until we are in the hallway to my garage which is out of view to anyone who may be in the house even though I don't see anyone in here.

With the back door shut, the house seems so quiet in comparison. I quickly turn to look at him with my arms crossed and ask "What the fuck are you doing? You weren't even invited!".

"You're not happy that I broke them up?" innocent confusion is all over his face- he's shocked that I'm not happy.

"Why don't you think I could have handled that myself? I could have separated them without causing everyone to watch!".

Now, instead of everyone making fun of the two guys, they are probably talking about me and my crazy neighbor. Silas squints his eyes for a brief second before saying "I know you could have handled it yourself. I didn't want you to. One of them could have accidentally hit you". Before any other thought comes to my brain, I ask the main thought in my head since a few minutes ago.

"How did you even get over here so fast? Were you in my yard?" and he finally looks uncomfortable.

He looks around for a second before looking at me and confidently saying "Yeah, I was by the backyard when I heard guys yelling so I ran back there". That excuse doesn't make sense at all, even people right by them were unable to walk fast enough… at least I think so? I keep questioning myself around him because Silas defies logic these days- if someone told me he was a fever dream, I would believe them.

After a few moments of silence and glaring at each other I say "Alright, well... crisis averted, you can go home now so I can get back to my party". I finish with crossing my arm and putting weight on one hip, aiming more for aggressive than pubescent. His eyes get a gleam in them as he looks at my crossed arms and my uneven hips and back up at my scowling face, causing me to glare even harder.

I tiredly sigh "If you aren't going to really answer my questions, and you aren't going to take me seriously- then please mind your business, and please go home".

He just arches an eyebrow so I add "I really can handle everything on my own" I realize he's slowly backing me into the wall. I see the muscles in his jaw clench as he wrestles himself before calmly saying "I don't think you can", and that's when I snap.

My arm moves faster than my brain and I

land a square punch in the center of his face. Even though it hits his nose, he barely flinches and seems more concerned for my hand. He wastes no time grabbing my fist to inspect it. I use all my energy to pretend it didn't hurt, just like he's doing right now- even though I don't even see blood or slight redness on his face.

I try to pull my arm away from him but he holds it until I stop moving and look back at him. He softly says "I deserved that". Looking back at my hand to softly stroke exactly where it hurts and now I let him since I'm worried I broke it.

He nods towards the kitchen "Let's get some ice on that".

I almost follow him before I stop and growl "Stop trying to help me" he turns around, leans in and tucks my hair behind my ear.

We are completely silent before he leans in, kisses my cheek and whispers in my ear "God, I've missed you". I can't tell if he's mocking me or not, so I use his distraction to kick his most sensitive area. He blocks my attempt too quickly and is now unfortunately holding my ankle, daring me to try anything else with just his facial expression.

With one foot stuck in the air, I ask "What drugs are you on? Every time I see you, you act differently towards me".

He scoffs and says "I wish I had drugs, Haze. It would probably help make this easier".

He looks so sad for a moment but I ask "You thought what would be easier? Me?" and he's back in his laughing mood because he chuckles and says "No, I know you never are" before slowly releasing my ankle.

I close my eyes in frustration, trying to figure out how to get him out of here when he adds "I thought it would be easier to stay away from you. I was just going to be over there, living next to you until I knew you were safe… but I've changed my mind". When I look up at him, he looks like he's not breathing, eager to hear my reply with half-closed eyes.

"Maybe that's not up to you" I say, attempting to reign in my emotions and looking back down because I can't think straight when he's looking at me like that.

He's brushing some of my hair back over my shoulder when I hear him say "It's always up to you, but I think I can help change your mind" and when I look at him, he's got a little hopeful smile on his face.

I put my hand on his chest to keep him at a distance "My mind is never going to change if you don't start telling me some things. No, not 'some things'" I correct myself "everything, Silas. You need to tell me everything if you even want to talk to me again. You owe me". My eyes start watering when I hear my desperation so I look away again. So he doesn't see my emotions all over my face, my pathetic and embarrassing emotions showing how weak I really am.

"Hey" he says, in a gentle voice like he's scared of tipping me over the edge. And then his hand is on the side of my neck in a gentle hold as he uses it to guide my face up to look at him. He's leaned in and only a few inches away when his eyes flick in between my own, and with the truest sincerity I've seen in a person, he says "I will, I swear on everything".

And then he kisses me.

I don't pull away but I don't go any farther than our lips touching, and neither does he. As soon as his lips open the tiniest bit, I hear Carly's voice calling for me by the back door. I look to confirm no one saw us, and when I look at Silas, I can tell his mind is in another place, maybe he was hoping it was just the beginning of something. "One second!" and then I stomp on his boots and whisper yell "Do NOT do that again!" and walk out of the hallway into the kitchen.

When I see Carly, she looks concerned, confused, and then she looks behind me, looking a little smug. I ask "Is everything okay?" ignoring Silas. Hoping that I am coming across as calm and normal like the last 5 minutes didn't happen. She has contained excitement all over her face as she's also trying to ignore Silas, who's rooting around in my freezer for something.

"Yeah, I just wanted to check on you since you disappeared-" She's cut off by Silas standing by both of us, as if he's a part of the conversation as well. Without saying anything he puts an ice pack against my knuckles. When Carly looks at the source of our attention her eyes go huge as she looks back at me "Holy shit you split your knuckle! What happened? Did those guys not really leave?".

Before I can say anything, Silas says "They are definitely never allowed back here, but this is because my face accidentally walked into Hazel's fist… hard. But I think she's fine". He's looking at my fist and then at me, smiling at our little inside joke- I don't think I've seen anyone that takes a hit as well as him. Or that kisses as well as him.

Carly just looks confused and backs up a step saying "oookay… well the party is still alive and well if you guys want to join" and then she wanders back into the yard. Once she's out, I see Silas looking at the time on my stove- so I look too and see it's midnight. I usually go to bed pretty early, so this feels like it's the middle of the night. Since my hand hurts anyways, I make a drink and tell Silas I'm going to go around to talk to everyone. He nods and stays inside and while I'm out talking to everyone, I see him cleaning up and putting things away slowly.

A lot of the people I talk to are mostly sober so they are figuring out ways home and the rest are either sober and driving themselves or drunk enough to have someone else figuring it out for them. Within the hour, most of the party goers have safely gone home and based on what they told me, I feel pretty confident that it was a great party. Now with about 10 people left, Carly and I are finally alone enough to talk, and she immediately exclaims "I am so sorry about those guys, Haze! I should have told Zach not to invite his friend, Jesse- he can get pretty rowdy".

I hug her and reply "It's totally fine, things happen! Who doesn't like watching a little drama every now and then" and she laughs at my half-assed wink. I'm not sure where Silas has gone but I figure he went home. I already know that I'm going to be lying awake in bed tonight for awhile thinking over everything. He disappears, years later we are somehow neighbors, and now he kisses me? If he really does give his story, I can't imagine what he would have to say for it to make sense.

A few more people have gotten rides home so Carly and I yawn and debate on just letting the four drunk people sleep. I have a couch and guest room but as we talk about it, I see Silas calmly walk in through the backyard again. I watch to see what he's doing, and he's going up to the three drunk men and one woman, coordinating their rides home. The woman, Sarah, thinks he's asking to take her home and I actually feel bad when he gently clarifies that he's ordering her a ride alone.

The app he uses has a confirmation that the rides he ordered for others got to their destination safely which makes it take very little time as he circulates getting everyone out and home safely. As he does that in that backyard, Carly and I are inside and I'm helping her pack up her dishes and trays that she brought and loading them into her car. I notice her eyeing him suspiciously, which I completely understand because if he was just a neighbor, he would be acting very odd. Since the others left, he's been cleaning my backyard up and I think Carly feels nervous to leave me alone with an overly comfortable and aggressive neighbor, no matter how good looking he is.

I see her eyeing him as we are saying goodbye and when I hug her, I tell her "It's fine, don't worry. But text me when you get home even though you're close". She agrees and walks out to her car, waving to me as she drives off.

CHAPTER 23

I go to the backyard where Silas is still putting empty cans and water bottles into a recycling bag "You can go home now. I'll get the rest tomorrow".

He keeps cleaning like he didn't hear me so I walk over to him and cross my arms "I can handle it, go home".

He looks at me and keeps cleaning, so I know he's ignoring me now. I change tactics- "Why did you kiss me?" he immediately stops and looks at me.

"Because I wanted to… I've wanted to since you moved next to me…. and for the last three years. And because I could tell you wanted me to". The scoff bursts out of my mouth before I can say anything but finally, when I see him looking at me like he thinks I'm playing dumb, I add "What?".

He walks a few steps towards me and puts his hands in his front pockets "When you first recognized me, you were obviously shocked and very upset. But the very first look in your eyes when you realized it might be me? It was excitement… and love".

I feel my eyes rolling before my mouth even opens but I manage "Yeah, I was happy you weren't dead. That doesn't mean I want to make out with you".

"Maybe… but that kind of love doesn't just disappear in a few years, at least not for me". He's analyzing me, trying to see if my facial expressions tell him anything.

I don't really care about his feelings so I explain "I think it does when you think someone either died or ghosted you. Also, you're so different- you're kind of a grumpy asshole now". I have to fight my face to keep from smiling but I give up when Silas tilts back his head and laughs.

He matches my crossed arm pose and replies "I'm just focusing on keeping you safe, I'm still the same Silas just with a few years added on". He looks me up and down before adding "And I think you're still the same Hazel that I've thought about every day and night for the last three years. Just with a few extra layers of sass… but I'm realizing that I think I really, really like that".

His wicked smile fades a little when I say "I'm not yours and you're not mine, anyways- go home. I'm going to sleep".

Then, I turn and walk inside. He's still cleaning things up as I get ready for bed. When I peek out the window, he's gone and the yard looks like I just moved in. That night, I definitely dream about Silas. What was before just a montage of feelings, is replaced with the real, tangible present-day man that I've come to know. And somehow, it's just as comforting. I wake up feeling safe, and well-rested, resisting waking up the next morning.

The next week goes by too quickly and I hardly see Silas at all. When we do see each other in passing, it's usually a head nod or a wave. I need more time before I talk to him again. I get confused every time I see him- how can he be so confident about us being together when I've spent the last three years thinking he was going to be gone forever? Focusing on work for the week, I ignore the frequent calls from unknown numbers that I know are Brandon. Silas shouldn't be my main concern right now, but he is definitely my greatest distraction.

Earlier today, I delivered a large order from a new and local company. To celebrate, I bought a nice bottle of wine and head to the back patio and lay down in my lounge chair. The weather is perfectly sunny with a slight breeze so I bring a new book I've been wanting to read along with some chips that I set in a bowl on the little table next to me.

The sun is right at the point before it begins to set and that last two hours has flown by as the book I'm reading is better than I could have expected. I drank several glasses of the wine and I feel a little sleepy as I close my eyes to listen to birds' chirp and the grass sway... I wake up what feels like minutes later (but has to be longer than that because the sun is fully down) and I realize I'm being lifted into the air. It has to be Brandon. I flail and swing my arms to hit him and to get out- but all that happens is the grip gets more secure.

I hear Silas's deep grunt "For fucks' sake. Can you stop hitting me?". I stop moving and squint up at him to make sure it's not anyone else.

"What the fuck are you doing? I thought

you were Brandon".

He is carrying me inside "Well flapping around like a crazy person isn't going to help you. I just wanted to set you inside so you don't have a sore neck tomorrow".

He sets me on the couch and steps back so I sit up, fully alert now, "How did you even know I was out there?".

He stares at me for a few seconds before nonchalantly saying "I have excellent senses", grabbing a throw blanket to put over me. I don't say anything else because he seems focused as he goes back outside to grab everything and sets them on the coffee table in front of me. Once he locks the door, he sits on the other couch and just stares at me, looking comfortable on my new furniture.

I push the blanket off of me "Thanks for… that. I'm going to go up to bed". I stand up and look at the door and hope that's an obvious enough signal for him. He nods and then stands as well as I open the door to coax him out of my house.

On his way out, he kisses the top of my head and says "Goodnight, don't forget to lock the deadbolt" and I close the door, doing just that before heading upstairs and getting ready for bed. The next morning, there is a new and very nice bottle of wine on my porch with a bow on it. This time, I don't worry about strange gifts on my door because I know exactly who this is from.

Carly wanted to meet up to talk about the party's other little dramas between friends at Cafe Marigold, a cute little coffee shop by her place. We decided to have coffee while we catch up and then we promised to work on our separate businesses together. She doesn't ask about Silas and I think it's because she's waiting and hoping I bring it up, but I take the opportunity to not bring him up at all since I wouldn't even know what to say about him… or us.

Instead, we talk about the typical petty drama that also happened at the barbecue and most of it is so lighthearted that it's actually fun to talk about. I thought about that kiss constantly, our lips touching was one thing, the way he held me was one thing as well, but the way he looked at me so tenderly the moment before and after just made me feel so safe, even despite our past. It made me nervous to be around him; while I do think feelings can fade with time, I am scared that love can't.

Since she's editing photos for her photography business, we are able to work in companionable silence for a few hours with random interruptions of conversation. Once we both close our laptops with wide eyes and a deep breath each, I say "Okay, I think we deserve a little treat" and her smirk looks sinful as she nods and I get up to buy the last berry tart.

When I sit back down and we grab our forks she says "So, Nikkie was telling us last night that some of the group is going to check out a new club called 'Siren' this weekend, do you want to go?". I look it up on my phone and even though it is new, it already has a good amount of reviews and pictures of a very, very fun looking bar.

We look over the photos together and I say "I'm so happy that it's themed like mythological sirens and not the loud noisy things" she laughs and confirms with Nikkie that we will both be coming too.

When I walk home, I check the mail like usual and besides the typical ads in the mail, I see a letter with no return address. It's a thin plain envelope which didn't tell me much and it was thin enough to only have maybe one or two pieces of paper inside it. I quickly open it, too weirded out to delay- there is one piece of paper in it and nothing else, but it is filled with words.

I unfold it and read it immediately, standing there as I quickly scan the page. I instantly know it's from Brandon. It's a long-winded letter about how he will do anything to get me back: counseling, pills- whatever. And how sorry he is about everything. It's surprisingly pitiful and submissive and I get instant hope that he's starting to cool down and reflect but I also feel unnerved by him ending the letter with "I'll do whatever it takes".

I keep staring at the letter, looking it over for any other things I may have missed but don't find anything. "Is that from Brandon?" I make a loud yelp and swivel to the voice behind me but it's just Silas with his hands up looking innocent.

I gasp out "Jesus! You scared me!".

He walks over to me while muttering "I can tell" and looks at the letter in my hands before asking "Can I see?".

When I hand it over, he's lost in concentration and I see him read over the letter and the envelope several times just like I did. "Haze, there's no stamp on this. It had to be dropped off-

When was the last time you checked the mail?".

I answer quickly "last night". He puts his arm on my shoulder to walk me inside.

"He might still be around so be cautious, okay? I'm going to look this over a bit more and check the cameras- then I'll bring this back". There's a lot of thoughts swimming around in my head at once so I just nod at him and go inside, he gives me a smile and an encouraging nod before going back to his place.

I nervous clean for the next hour until I hear knocking on the front door and once I confirm on the camera's app that its Silas, I open the door and let him in, noticing the envelope in his hand. "He dropped it off at 1am last night before driving off. Find the recording on your app and screenshot it so you can show the police and they can keep building a record on him".

He stands by the door like he's not planning on being here for very long. This makes me happy since I don't want him to be comfortable in my house, but also a secret part of me wishes he would stay, just so I don't have to be scared of being alone right now. "The letter didn't seem very threatening, do you really think I need to do that?" I ask with anxiety spilling out.

With slight pity in his eyes, he answers "Yeah, I think that was all B.S., I'm assuming he was just making a point that he's in the area and that he can be here without you knowing".

I think it over and lean against my counter "I'm going to keep doing exactly what I have been, I'm not going to live in fear of him" I say, with a surprising amount of confidence. Something in my voice tells Silas not to argue, but he does add "I can't be here all the time… especially on some weekend nights. Please be careful".

I walk over to him and cross my arms "Oh yeah… what is up with that?" he tilts his head in confusion so I add "Are you like a delivery driver or something?".

He gives a confused chuckle and answers "No, I've been helping a friend out" but even in the way he says it, it just adds more confusion.

I start losing my patience so I say exactly that to him "I'm starting to lose my patience. When are you going to start telling me about who you are now and what happened to you?".

He leans against the wall with his arms crossed "If I could have told you everything when I first saw you, I would have. I'm not trying to keep anything from you but I also don't think right now is a good time to open up that can of worms, you're already dealing with so much".

Can of worms? "Don't you think that's my decision to make, how much I can handle?".

I try to stay as unemotional as possible but Silas sees right through me, so he walks over to me and puts his hand on my shoulder "You're right. Let's find a day where we can talk about everything because it's going to take a while and the focus right now should be reporting that letter and keeping you safe, okay?". I open my mouth to argue but he cuts me off with a look "It's not a 5 minute conversation, Haze. I don't want to give you a half-assed answer, you deserve a real conversation. I'm not trying to get out of this, I promise".

I solemnly nod and say "It must be one hell of an explanation then".

At that, he sparks back to life with a passionate "Of course it is. We were perfect together- I wouldn't have given any piece of us up unless I had to. Did I ever seem hesitant when it came to you? Disloyal? Apathetic?".

His insistence stuns me so I just think it over and say in agreement "No… You didn't, I just couldn't think of a reason good enough to not even give me an explanation".

He sighs "I can only imagine how frustrating it is to be on your side of this, but honestly my main priority is keeping you safe. Transparency is the second priority but I can't do that when we are worrying about stalkers outside your house in the middle of the night".

I know he's right but I'm still frustrated "Okay, okay. Let's figure out a time to talk but then you have to tell me every single thing". He agrees, we say goodbye, and then I go back to normal life and work the rest of the day in my garage.

CHAPTER 24

A few days later, Carly is texting me the logistics for tonight and what time she's picking me up along with who's all going. It's going to be Carly and I in her car, along with a couple who I haven't met yet. We are meeting four others at a restaurant before going across the street to Siren. I asked Carly about who all was joining us and so far, it sounds like neither of the guys from the fight are coming.

As fun as the barbecue was, I was busy hosting and checking on others so it wasn't a carefree night. Truthfully, I love dancing and I'm just excited to truly have fun and dance until I have to leave. I've had the morning to make shirts for a local bakery and get a few chores taken care of, so I start to get ready pretty early. More out of eagerness than thinking I really need that much time to get ready. I lay my outfit out and start an "everything" shower, enjoying the ritual of getting really ready for the first time since I moved here.

After exfoliating, shaving, and putting oil on my body, I then dry my hair and straighten it. Once the hard part is over, I spend an hour on my makeup, moving slowly with enjoyment- watching my face change into a contoured, smokey cat-eyed woman. I keep in mind my entire night when getting dressed- A black deep-v bodysuit with clasps at the crotch so I can easily pee (even if I'm drunk), and a mini distressed denim skirt that is comfortable enough to sit down in at the restaurant.

After years of leaving early because of uncomfortable heels, I finally learned to wear cute combat boots with insoles so I can actually dance all night long. I only have to wait a few minutes before Carly is texting me that she's outside.

Quickly running down the stairs and making sure everything is locked, I walk down my front steps. Silas is going back into his house when he looks over at me and stops walking immediately. I was a lot more demure when we were dating so I've never worn anything like this in front of him. He has a lot of emotions filtering through his eyes: confusion, desire, surprise, and finally- anger. Probably for leaving when Brandon is in the area.

He looks like he wants to walk over and drag me inside, but he sees the car with Carly and friends inside it and looks back at me sternly "Be careful" he says in a low warning.

Caught up in a fun mood, I just smile at him and say a carefree "Always!" before walking over to the car and getting inside. I catch the sight of the muscle in his jaw clenching before I open the door to Carly's car.

She's quick to let out a quick whistle "Look at you! By the way, this is Allison and Theo". I say hi to them and sit in the passenger seat. They seem a little younger than us and kind of shy, but nice, so we make easy conversation until we get to the restaurant. Checking my phone one last time for the night, I see that I got a text from an unknown number. I start to get scared, but then I read it *"It's Silas. Now you have my number. If anything happens just call/text me and I'll be there immediately"*.

I just send a "like" reaction and turn my phone on "Do Not Disturb" for the rest of the night. It feels good to have someone looking out for me after being on my own for so long, but it also scares me because lately he is really becoming someone that I would want to call when something happens. So far it seems like he has no problem dropping what he's doing immediately. Even though I don't fully trust him yet, I know deep down that for whatever reason, he still cares about me.

The four friends are already here at the restaurant so we take over the other two tables that have been pushed together. I overheard Connor and his friend Alex discussing how two or three more people are planning on meeting us in Siren and based on their quickly hushed tones and eyebrow waggles, they are some cute girls. There's also another couple at our table who I met at my barbecue… but I can't remember their names.

Tuning back into Carly's conversation with Allison, I spend the next two hours drifting from different conversations around the room. I'm so grateful to Carly and her group of friends for including me, I probably would be at home in old sweatpants watching reruns. Which also sounds amazing right now, but I already do that often enough.

Once in awhile, one of the guys looks at me like he's considering my looks but I try to keep it light with everyone, not wanting to risk changing the group's dynamic. The restaurant and Siren share a large parking lot so we only need to take a quick walk over to get in line for the club. Since Carly is the driver, she's sticking to non-alcoholic drinks. She does seem to consider my offer to get an Uber for the both of us if she wants to crash at my place.

The eight of us wait in a pretty long line and there are two flasks floating around that we take turns air sipping out of when another friend walks up. Bryce, one of Alex's friends who I've met in passing before ends up standing by us and talking to our little subgroup for awhile. He's flirtatious but nothing uncomfortable, so I just laugh his little quips off and keep a casual attitude. It's easy to do when I see him looking around at other girls so many times.

We finally get inside and immediately disperse- some going to find space for the group to stand and dance, while a few people go to the bar to get drinks and shots for the group. I follow along with Allison and Theo as we follow a few others to a corner in between the exit and the stage as Carly with Bryce go to the bar. The decor in here is amazing, the dimly lit lights are shades of blue and green, the decor is shimmery and inspired by sea elements, and the bartenders all have cute mermaid-style tops on with scale-like shorts.

Compared to the ones back home, it's pretty big with lots of room to dance despite so many people being in here. Most importantly, the music is actual dancing music that's recognizable rather than just the same repetitive beat over and over like other clubs I've been to. One of the women in the group,

Melissa, brings over her armful of drinks along with Alex, and the rest of us promise to get the next round before trying the sea-themed shot.

By our second round, the main DJ comes on stage and based on everyone's reactions, they are a local legend. I stop dancing for a moment to look as well- joining the rest of the crowd staring at the stage. The lights get dark for a second and everyone starts to stare and then we see what looks like a man with a mask hop up and start playing a familiar song that makes everyone cheer and go crazy.

I'm surprised when I see people taking pictures of the masked man and taking selfies with him in the background. The song is a remix to one of my favorite songs in college that Silas would always tease me for because it never got old when I felt like dancing. It's given a deeper bass and made to sound a little sultrier which makes it easier to dance to since it was a little too upbeat before.

Everyone is going back to their groups and dancing but I'm stuck trying to figure the DJ's mask out. It's small red neon lights making the outline of a devil's mask and even though I've never seen it before, it looks familiar. I keep staring when I think that the masked DJ looks up and turns his head to me, tilting slightly in what looks like a confused gesture before looking away again. I quickly dismiss the thought since I usually think performers on a stage look at me, when really, it's the general area and everyone else around me. I give it another minute of staring before going back to dancing my heart out.

The next portion of the group takes their

turn buying the third round and we also go to get some water as well. This shot has little swirls of micro-glitter in it and is a darker teal color- tasting like a mix of alcohol and candy. The drinks are strong but since I've been dancing this entire time and don't feel clumsy, I don't worry about needing to slow down yet. I decide that I can have maybe two more rounds before I'll need to stick to water.

By the fourth round, I start to get curious about the room and what the other people here are like. I say I'm getting some more water and, I do, but then I take a walk around the room. I'm passed the point of caring if I look odd, so I look maybe a little longer at people than is normal for a sober person. Part of me is curious what people here are like, what they dress like- and the little drunk part of me is curious if there's any cute guys. I make a full lap around the room. Not seeing anyone interesting enough to stop for, I go to the bathroom.

After waiting in line for a few minutes, and then waiting a few minutes in the line to wash my hands, I'm back to my group. Carly shouts in my ear "I thought you left us!" while keeping her dance going.

I match her tempo and yell back "The lines here are insane" because I know if I tried to explain in a full sentence, she wouldn't be able to hear me anyways. It's after midnight, and even though I don't feel tired yet, it looks like a few people are losing steam. Some of the couples like Allison and Theo break off to dance and makeout in their own little world. I try not to stare in envy but I have a wave of remembering that feeling.

Even though I do love being single, when I'm drunk, I always feel a little lonely. Luckily, dancing always distracts me from that, so I just turn back and dance with Carly as low as we can before we get back up and laugh about our knees cracking. An hour later, and half of the group is gone. Allison and Theo seemed in a rush to leave after dancing for a few songs, and two of the others left after meeting people and dancing with them for awhile.

Carly and I have been trying to sober up with water and dancing, and Melissa is over at the bar making out with someone. I don't know where Alex is, but he's been gone for a long time now while Bryce is dancing with a woman who is looking at him like he's the sexiest man on earth. Throughout the night, Carly and I have danced with strangers, but none of them were very good or interesting enough to stick around for.

Carly's excitement comes back in tenfold when Zach walks in, joining us from closing his bar down the street. I begin to distance myself from them- it's obvious to me that Carly likes Zach just as much, so I try to give them a little space to let something happen. I go back to what's left of the group- two girls who I met earlier that seemed nice enough. Unfortunately, I could barely hear their introductions and now I have no idea what their names are. We bump into another small group with a few guys and innocently dance with them.

Even though I have been drinking, I am sober enough to realize that Siren is probably closing soon so I check my phone and see that it's almost 2 a.m. Carly and I have already texted that

I'm finding an Uber home and she's going to let Zach take her car back to her place. She's sweet to make sure I promise to tell her when I get home- but I'm so excited that something finally happened with them that I quickly agree and tell her goodnight. I get a water and keep dancing with the newly-formed group and then I open up the Uber app to see how long one would take.

A finger comes into view over my phone, pointing at the app and when I look up, it's a guy I was dancing with a moment ago. I couldn't hear what he said so I move my head, bringing my ear closer to his mouth.

He drunkenly shouts "I can take you home!" and his overconfidence is what immediately tells me that it's a bad idea.

Having already made my mind up I say "No you can't! You're more drunk than me!" trying to say it in a lighthearted but firm way.

He pulls his head back to look offended with very glazed over eyes which he then dramatically rolls to show how crazy it is for me to say that. He stumbles a little as he leans in again to say with a hot and wet shout in my ear "I'm good! What're your cross streets?". I mentally applaud his confidence but when I open my mouth to politely turn him down again, I notice that he's no longer focused on me. He, and the others in the group, are now looking at a specific spot right behind me, right as I feel a gentle hand on my shoulder.

Quickly and with fear, I turn around- hoping it's not Brandon based on the shock on their faces. I have to look up a bit, up the strong chest,

the defined neck and then the smirking mouth as it says "Hey, neighbor".
    Silas.

CHAPTER 25

"What're you doing here?".

That came out a little aggressive. I'm squinting my eyes and realizing that I may be a little more drunk than I thought. I know he hears my question and chooses to ignore it as he leans down to say in my ear "Do you need a ride?".

I can tell he's sober but just to make sure, I still ask "Are you sober?". Even getting into a car with Silas would be better than getting into an Uber this late. The devil you know, and all that.

Forgetting the group behind me, I wait for him to bend down again to say "Yes, I was working tonight so I only had water". I want to ask what he meant about the working detail but since it's so loud I don't feel like having more conversations than necessary in here. And, admittedly, I'm a little too drunk to seriously digest any real conversation.

I see Carly finally walking out with Zach. She does a quick double look in my direction before I wave her off with a smile and look back at Silas who's patiently standing there. "Everything okay?" Silas asks with a stoic expression that morphs into a hopeful one as I nod at him and wave goodbye to my group. Most of them wave back with surprised or confused expressions as we start to walk away.

I'm sure to them it looks like a random man

walked up to me and a minute later we are leaving together, but since I don't really know them, I don't really care to clarify. Since it's more packed, Silas holds his hand out in a gentlemanly pose and as I barely hold his hand, I mutter "Don't make me regret this". I'm officially able to confirm his hearing is beyond normal because somehow, in this loud club a few feet away, he heard me clearly.

He turns around to stand close to me so I can hear "I won't. Because I'll buy you food on the way" and then my drunk brain is appeased and easily led towards the exit. As we are walking out, the bartenders wave Silas off and look at me with a surprised look. We also get stopped a few times with people excited to tell him "Good job tonight".

I obviously notice the way that some of the girls look at him but he just gives a polite one-sided smile and focuses on the door, holding it open and helping me outside. He's not letting go of my hand on the way towards his car and I don't fight it since I have no idea where we are going. As we are walking to the opposite site of the building, Silas asks "What do you want to eat?".

I know my options are limited this time of night, but I still ask "What's open and on the way?".

He doesn't sound excited when he questioningly says "Dollar menu burgers?".

I don't want to admit how amazing that sounds, so I hold in my groan and mutter "Sounds good" as we make it to a different car than the Jeep I've seen.

I look back at Silas "This isn't your car". I say it confidently, so he makes a point to open it with the key like I said something silly and nudges me inside the passenger seat. I don't know cars at all but I can tell it's a vintage black sports car in excellent condition.

Since I don't know what his job is, I'm not entirely sure how he's able to afford something like this. Maybe he's borrowing it? When I acquiesce and sit down, he gently shuts the door and gets into the driver seat before looking at me "It's been in my garage" and turns on the beautifully loud engine.

He looks at my purse before putting the car in reverse and suspiciously asks "Are you sure you have everything? Phone, keys, wallet?".

I double check and confirm "yep, all there" and then he pulls out of the parking lot. After standing the entire night, sitting down makes me realize how exhausted I am, and also how I'm perfectly buzzed for a great night's sleep.

I lean my chair back a bit and close my eyes as an oddly comfortable silence takes over the whole way there. We make our order and he pays without complaint despite my order being double his. I don't even know if I can eat that much but everything sounded so good. He easily sets the bags down in the back seat and I hide my disappointment at not being able to eat it immediately.

It doesn't take us much longer than that before he's pulling into his garage, leaving the garage door open and turning the car off. "Thank you for the ride" I say, looking over to him and meeting his eyes "What were you really doing there?". He looks offended at my suspicion on why he was in the same place as me but answers "I told you… I was working tonight".

I just furrow my eyebrows at his vagueness before he sighs and explains further, "My friend Nate owns that club and they are still trying to find more people to fill in sets permanently. So, I've been helping in the meantime on weekends since I have equipment and experience". When I look even more confused, he reaches in the back and that's when I notice familiar looking boxes of sound and DJ equipment.

Then, he grabs something, bringing it to the front to show me.

It's the red, neon devil mask.

CHAPTER 26

"You were that DJ?" I ask, probably in a louder voice than necessary but I am absolutely confused and surprised. That's not a hobby he was ever interested in, always sticking to alternative and hard rock music. He sets the mask back in the backseat.

"Yeah, it's a long story for another time but basically, he was opening the club up and didn't have anyone to depend on weekends to DJ. I had a full set up with speakers for some other projects so it wasn't hard to just play around with popular music and show up. Plus, the energy is amazing" he has a small, confusing smile about that last part.

"Woah, I never saw you becoming a DJ... I guess that's impressive that you were able to afford a house and cars doing that". Uncomfortable about how impressed I am, I add "that explains why you are always loading and unloading your Jeep". I'm not sure why he drove this car tonight but I'm having so much fun in it that I don't really care.

"What about drums?" I ask with sudden curiosity to which he just casually shrugs "I still have a drum set but I'm not in a band- it's just there for fun". I rotate more to face him and he gets distracted by the movement, focusing on what he sees as he looks me up and down.

His appraisal makes me nervous so I look

down to make sure everything important is covered. He attempts to distract me catching him "I didn't know you were going to be there tonight- I finished loading my car and went back in to say bye when I noticed that you were there so I hung around for a second to make sure you were okay". I'm briefly distracted by the muscle in his jaw ticking.

"Then, I heard that guy trying to convince you to let him drive you home drunk and I decided to come over before he pushed it too far". I start to understand why he's so vague, every time he tells me something, the details don't make sense.

"How could you hear him convincing me? I could barely hear him". He looks past me like he's trying to think about it and I lose my patience. "What happened to you? I feel like I'm going crazy- you somehow can hear every little noise, you are acting different, and you look like an entirely different person. The weirdest part is you expect me to trust you when you might as well be a stranger".

Silas turns to me and says "It's been three years". He pointedly looks me up and down "You don't look the same either. Or act the same" he gets a little smirk on his face quietly adding "I'm not complaining about any of your differences".

Irritation, anger and resentment take up all of my brain. I hiss with disgust "Don't flirt with me like you didn't fuck me over and make me grieve you for three years without any answer".

He puts his hands up and calmly says "You're right, I'm sorry. I know I'll never be able to make that up to you". He does truly look sorry but it doesn't soften my anger. I stare lasers at him until my mouth moves on its own with questions that I haven't even thought about "You're a part-time DJ? How do you own a house at 25 years old?".

He chuckles at my change of topic but thinks for a moment as if he's considering how much to share. "I'm a part owner with my dad and work remotely for the financial aspect of the business- that covers the money part since all I really do is work. The DJing isn't a dream or a career but it's fun and helps my friend out". He ends it with a shrug, keeping it casual but I know there's more to it.

I have so many question- Silas works for his dad and he's who helped me get this house- it's hard for me to even know where to begin. "Did you leave me for someone else?" the question surprises both of us but I don't regret asking it. This time, he doesn't laugh at the question but he does look surprised- and a little offended. "What? God no".

It's said with such vigor that I don't even consider he's lying, but I still need to know what happened. "So, what could have been so important to make you just disappear?" my voice sounds so weak, I hate how fragile I sound. He breaks our intense eye contact after several seconds to rub his face with his tattoo-covered hand. I stay silent, barely breathing while I wait to finally get the answer I've waited this entire time for.

With a deep breath, Silas looks back at me and says "Some... dangerous things happened the night before I disappeared. I thought the situation was going to involve- and hurt- you too".

His eyebrow arches when I open my mouth

but he continues "We both know that if I told you that, it wouldn't have been enough. Time was crucial so my dumb 22-year-old brain panicked and I left everyone and everything I knew". He starts to sound more like he's talking out loud than trying to explain.

With a soft voice, he continues "And then how can I come back after that? You think you were mad when you saw me here- Imagine if I just strolled back into your life. I wouldn't have been able to give you as many answers as you would need and you wouldn't be able to let that go. I can't even imagine what your parents would think". As wrong as he was for leaving, he's right- The relationship would have never been the same, and my parents would be even less tolerant than me.

I'm lost in my thoughts when I hear his voice continue "For the last three years, I've watched you. From afar, wishing I was there with you. All I've wanted to do was come back but I just couldn't think of a good enough reason that I would deserve that. I figured you were happier than you could have been with me so I just accepted my self-inflicted punishment.". With more of a mumble, he adds "...little did I know you attract such assholes".

I'm looking away, trying to get my thoughts- any thoughts, actually- in order. The amount of information I'm finally getting is happening so fast and I only have more questions. I silently wish I had a notebook to organize my thoughts. His abrupt voice interrupts my scattered thoughts "So, now you're stuck with me as your neighbor as I try to protect you from the other piece of shit in your life. And I can't really give you more of an explanation- and for that, I'm sorry".

I notice that my whole body is leaned in, facing him, so I rotate back to face forward and stare out front. My drunkenness has worn off and I am finally getting a few answers from the source of the pain that has stuck with me for years. I feel his hand sweep away the hair off of my left shoulder to get a better look as he leans in. "I don't know how to prove it to you, but I haven't been just living the fun bachelor life for the last three years'.

'I did have a time of trying to distract myself with anything I could, refusing the possibility of ever seeing you again. But I always hoped that if I did, I'd have something to show for it. The majority of the last couple of years was just me focusing and working hard to be the man who could have deserved you in another life". I turn my head to look at him and realize he's much closer than I realized. I try to stay firm in my resolve to hate him so even though my words are firm, I can't help but sound sad.

"Don't expect to finish where we left off, Silas. I want to believe you, and I think I do- but there's a lot of missing information'.

'Honestly, I don't see how I could ever really trust you until I know absolutely everything". Gently, he grabs my chin in between his fingers to look at him- his deep, green eyes looking into mine.

Barely above a whisper, he says "Understood. But in the meantime, please let me be your neighbor and do what I can to keep you safe, okay? If you need anything, I'm here".

His eyes flash in between mine as he waits for confirmation. I promise him "Okay". Then, he leans in a little farther, like he can't stop the pull. I close the distance... kissing him on the lips.

CHAPTER 27

At first, its semi-drunken curiosity. Wondering if kissing him would feel the same. I'm too selfish to worry about the repercussions as I compare his lips to every other one I've known- including his from three years ago. When I go to move away, he cups the back of my head with his hands- holding my lips to his. Opening my eyes in surprise, he's looking at me with a heated vulnerability- silently begging me not to stop what happens next. I don't. He slowly moves in to give me a deeper kiss, lips interlocked and his fingers in my hair.

I hear a contented groan come from Silas as I open my mouth to feel his lips with my tongue. I feel his other hand move to cup my thigh and I shiver at the touch, realizing I haven't felt true intimacy since the last time I was with him. I bite his lip until I'm met with another groan. My hands start to run over his body, feeling the difference from his shoulders to his hips.

I don't understand how someone can be so different within just three years but I savor his new warmth and strength that I can feel just from us embracing. His hands also roam my body and as soon as I feel his palm near my chest, I unbuckle the seatbelt and nudge him to his seat- which he does not fight. He too willingly moves backward into his seat while he ensures his lips never leave mine. When I straddle him, he pulls back to look at me. For the first time since I first saw him in the driveway, he looks completely out of control.

Gone are the bored, closed-off eyes as I take in his intense, dilated ones looking at me now. His lips, moist and plump from kissing, are slightly parted- showing the pointed tips of his canine teeth. Both of his hands go to my outer thighs in a hold. My hands go under his shirt, feeling his defined abs that were once so lean, but are now thick with earned muscle. With the tip of his tongue, he is tracing my neck from my collar bone to my ear.

Suddenly all I hear are my own pants and his little grunts of satisfaction as he gently starts to bite me all over. I feel one of his hands leave me to pull the seat back, and now we are falling a few inches back until we are flat in his seat, our bodies aligned perfectly. I can't help myself as my body starts to do a little rocking motion, desperate for friction as my denim skirt rides up to expose my legs fully.

He grabs my jaw to align our mouths again but before he closes the distance, I see him look down and I realize he can see in between my leg to my bodysuit. "Fuck." he whispers in desperation. Our faces meet and our teeth, tongues and lips clash- taking turns being dominant with one another. His hands move from my outer thighs, to the tops of them. He slides them up, up, up until they are tracing the hemline of my bodysuit, along the line of where my hips meet my thighs.

The noise that comes out of me sounds feral

and unfamiliar. My desperation becoming more obvious as I move against him even more, gently sucking on his throat, feeling the vibrations from his moans. Craving more, I pull the bottom of his black threadbare tee before he quickly snatches it and takes it off himself. He throws it in the passenger seat so he can go back to scraping his teeth along my shoulder. He keeps whispering how good I smell and taste and I wonder if his hearing isn't the only sense that improved, since he seems so focused on inhaling and licking with heavy-lidded eyes.

When we go back to kissing, he whispers "Please don't make me stop". He slowly and gently traces my lips with his own as his hand grazes the clasps of my bodysuit, causing me to shiver. I hear his quiet, tortured noise as if debating on opening the clasps.

Once the shock of feeling his hand there subsides and the sensation of his hand gently rubbing back and forth makes me moan, I sober up a little. Not from alcohol- because I'm not that drunk- but mentally, my trance is broken. I don't want to go any further when I don't even know who he truly is. I know I'll regret going further if I don't get more answers out of him first. As much as I want to continue, to feel him inside me again with his huge strong body against mine, I stop my wandering hands and give him a quick peck on the lips to snap him out of it as well.

When his eyes snap open in confusion, I grab my bag of fast food from the backseat with my left hand- and grab the door handle with my right. As I open the door and get out, he weakly says "I said please". Even with his pained and tired looking eyes, he still stares at me with a lust that I've never seen one anyone, not even him in the past.

My lust dissolves into satisfaction when he moves his head to blankly stare forward until he takes a deep breath, while I readjust my clothes and look at the tattoos almost completely covering his torso. I figured he had a lot since his arms and hands are covered, but seeing how much he's covered in three years is surprising. It's dark, so I struggle to see what the actual designs are but before I have a chance to lean in and look further, Silas hops out of his seat, grabbing his shirt on the way along with his bag of food.

When he closes the door and places the bag of food on top of his car to put his shirt on, I look at his back designs which are also taking over most of the space.

So far, most of his tattoos are in black and white but there's a few that pop with vivid color- And that's when I notice several red dahlias on his right shoulder.

CHAPTER 28

Most of his tattoos are in black in white so the bright red flowers pop out to me immediately- that, and because he knows they're my favorite flower. Without thinking, I slowly reach my hand out to touch the tattoo, whispering "dahlias…" in wonder.

He stops moving and stays still, quietly asking "Are they still your favorite flower?".

I just hum "mhm" before looking over more of his tattoos.

He slowly turns around- he's trying to figure out what I think of them, and I can see he's a little nervous. I hardly notice him as I keep perusing his tattoos, looking at what else he has and seeing if I will recognize any with significance. His garage is dark, but since the door is open, I can make out the tattoos from the semi-distant streetlights.

Shocked, I start to notice several more tattoos in color- all relevant symbols from our relationship. A monarch butterfly (he bought me a small, gold butterfly necklace for my birthday that I never took off) and Persephone and Hades embracing (we went as the pair for Halloween one year). Those are some of the first color tattoos that I notice, but I keep scanning for more. The different styles, sizes and themes are different, but somehow, they all flow together and the placements turn his body into artwork. I keep scanning, paying more attention to the ones in color as I remember the backstory of each one (ignoring his nervous stare), and then I see it. My eye.

Detailed and right on his chest "is that my eye?".

Gauging my reaction for a second, he unemotionally says "yes." and I start to see that he really has been suffering the last three years. What would have happened if we never saw each other again? Would he just be a walking canvas of our short two years together?

He sees me looking at a little red heart with an H in the middle on his wrist and says "I have a few more I can show you another time" with no implication in his voice- so I match his tone "I'd like that".

We aren't far, so I only have to lean in a bit on my tip toes to kiss his cheek "Goodnight, Silas".

He smiles down at me "night" is all he says, so I turn to walk to my house until I hear "Hazel?".

I turn to face him "Yeah?".

His smile returns "Do you still have our tattoo on your ass?". Not wanting to answer I just squint at him suspiciously until he adds "because I do" with the smuggest smile I've ever seen. We smile at each other for a few minutes but I just roll my eyes and say "thanks for the ride". As I turn around and walk away, I can still hear his chuckle as I close the door.

At this point, my food is cold but I sit on my couch and start to numbly eat, knowing I won't be able to fall asleep. Being at Siren feels like years ago, so much has changed and shifted even though I still haven't really gotten many other truth's out of Silas.

I think over the entire night and our whole conversation to make sure I didn't miss anything and then I realize how late it is. I text Carly *"Thank you for tonight! I'm home, let me know when you get home safely"* I have to text extra fast before my phone dies from low battery. Once I'm done eating, I go upstairs and brush my teeth, plug my phone in the charger and then pass out.

I wake up at 11 a.m. which is late for me, but I know it still wasn't a full night's sleep. I'm already planning my nap that I will definitely need in a few hours. Turning my phone on, I use the bathroom and get ready for the day while it powers up. I only care to make sure I got a text from Carly, confirming she's fine. When I check my phone, I see that I got a text, so I quickly open it to see what she says.

"Cute. I can see why you left me for him".

I'm confused until I see the text isn't from Carly, but an unknown number and then I realize it has to be Brandon. And that Brandon was watching us last night. I screenshot it and send it to Silas, not really knowing what else to do.

When I go downstairs, I reassure myself that Silas's windows are heavily tinted so it's not likely he saw us making out, but he definitely saw us outside of the car looking way too comfortable to just be polite neighbors.

CHAPTER 29

An hour later, Silas is at my door with a quick knock. Letting him in, I do a quick scan outside, then shut and lock the door. I try not to comment on it taking him so long to walk over here. Before I can say anything, he's opening his phone and holding it open for me to see the screen, which is on his photo album. "It's the vacant house across the street" I say in confusion as I wonder where this is going but he keeps sliding, and then it makes sense.

The photos get closer and closer on the house until there is a camera on the porch, facing our houses. "That's how he saw us last night, he wasn't here in person watching" he explains but it hardly makes me feel better.

Silas continues "When I checked the camera for footage from last night and didn't see anyone. I looked around for any other way for him to see us and then I noticed it".

The last photo he shows me is the same camera in a dumpster and then I finally do feel a little relief. "When do you think he installed it?" I ask, because if it was recent, he might still be in the area.

"I can't tell, I tried to check the video recordings but I can only confirm it wasn't in the last few days. Either way, I'll send these photos to you so you can add it into your police record for him".

He looks back at his phone and I can see that he's sending the photos to me so I ask "Do you want some coffee? Or tea?". Distracted on his phone, he sits down on my couch without looking up, but answers "No, thank you".

He puts his phone down and looks around the house like it's his first time ever really looking at it "You've always had the best taste, it looks amazing in here". He takes his shoes off so I assume he's planning on staying for awhile, so I go to the love seat perpendicular to him and sit down. He looks at me in confusion and then looks at the seat beside him.

Before he can say anything, I beat him to it "Don't get cocky, I'm happy over here. Thank you". The proud smile on my face falters when he just stares at me with a cocky smile, and as his eyes are sparkling, I ask "What?".

After a shrug, he answers "Nothing… it's just nice to be here. With you".

"Now what?" I ask him since he's in my house like we made plans to hang out and I'm not really sure what to do with him. He acts like he doesn't have a care in the world when he says "Tell me what I've missed. Tell me everything".

After how much information he's avoided telling me, it's hard to keep the anger out of my voice when I say "I'm pretty sure we agreed that you were going to tell me everything- Do you not remember?".

He moves to the seat that he was trying to

get me to sit in earlier, so he is closer to me. "Tell me about the last three years. I'll tell you everything after".

I look at him skeptically "Right after? As in, today?". He nods once in promise.

So, I do. Quickly. "Let's see… three years ago I thought you were dead so I spent months looking for you. Then, when I never found you I grieved while still hoping, since I didn't have any closure. After about a year I was pretty shut down mentally so some family and friends intervened and I had to start therapy-" a text notification from my phone interrupts me. Nervous that Brandon somehow knows that Silas is in my house, I stop talking to immediately check. I dramatically sigh with relief when I see that it's Carly.

"I can't wait to hear about last night! And to tell you about mine ;). I'm in the area of I can stop by soon?".

I'm not sure what all I feel like confessing to from last night. But I want to hear about her night bad enough that I reply:

"Yes, stop by whenever! My neighbor might be here but just disregard him if so".

Pressing send, I say to Silas "Carly might stop by to chat".

"Do you want me to leave so you two can have girl time?" I don't miss the disappointment in his eyes. I smile at his consideration but shake my head "Sounds like she's running errands and just plans on stopping by for a few minutes".

"Well, I'll make you both drinks when she gets here. In the meantime, please continue your update"- so I continue my summary for a few minutes about trying to move on, Brandon, and how I ended up moving here.

The mood has gone from a casual chit chat to a very quiet and stiff atmosphere, but I don't feel bad. I become resolved when I talk about it but Silas is clenching and un-clenching his jaw over and over, mulling over everything I said. After a moment of tense eye contact, he mutters "I should have just taken you with me". Louder, he says "I didn't want to drag you into my misery and take you away from your loved ones. But, if I knew that this was how it was going to go, I would have just brought you with… starting fresh together".

Surprise hits me first, but then reality is soon to follow "We were college sweethearts, Silas. You did me a favor. We were about to move in together and we would have ended up breaking up a long time ago anyways". I can't put on a fake smile, so I give a half-hearted shrug instead.

He's quick to reply "No- We wouldn't have." in absolute confidence, so I push back.

"Of course we would have! How often do relationships at that age last? Eventually, you would get bored and want to experience more girls and life- or maybe I would have had to take a job in another state. Things happen".

All levity in his face that was there a few moments ago is now gone. He's staring at me with seriousness and slightly scrunched eyebrows "Is that why you think I left? To 'sew my wild oats'?".

I shrug to keep it light despite his intense stare "It's the best one I can think of. Unless you owed loan sharks money…" I try to gauge his reaction to see if I got it right, but he only scoffs.

I add "Because if you really gave a shit, you could have at least written me a letter, right? Sounds like your parents were in on it this entire time too".

In hindsight, that does make sense, why they seemed to accept his disappearance so well. He looks away for a moment in contemplation before looking back at me, saying carefully "I… do you remember how the night before I left, the band had a show?' I just nod once.

"Well, a band that I wasn't familiar with opened for us, and the guy playing bass… wasn't- something was off and I couldn't figure out what". Not wanting to slow him down, I just keep looking at him so he can continue.

"So, we play the show, everything goes fine. But then we are all hanging out after and making small talk. Anyways… something happened. Something changed… I was changed. And I just knew that I had to get far away as soon as possible".

After waiting this long, I just feel impatient. I have even more questions now. "Silas, I don't even understand what you're talking about. Can you be less vague? 'changed' could mean anything". He gives me a desperate look like he's hoping I can just guess, so I say with even more impatience "Look. You either trust me or you don't".

He gestures to his body "You said it yourself- don't I look different?".

"Yes, you look different. And just like you said last night, it's been three years. Change isn't a crazy thing to happen" I say, clearly still confused.

He leans in "These changes happened

within a week, Hazel. I grew 4 inches in a week. I don't look that much different than I did the week after I last saw you".

Staring at him with an open mouth, I wait because I can tell he's not done, so he continues "How could I have explained that to anyone? Even HGH doesn't do that to people".

Nervously, I ask "So, what does that to people then?". He makes an exasperated sigh and looks towards my front window like he's lost for words.

I practically beg "Just tell me. I won't tell anyone if that's what you're worried about".

He snaps "I'm not worried about that!". Then, he takes a breath to calm himself down before saying "I just don't know how to make you think that I'm not crazy".

Annoyed, I say "Well, I'm about to go crazy if you don't tell me".

I have lost all patience in this conversation. He puts his arms up in innocence "Okay… Well, me and that guy were outside with both our bands and after awhile, people started trickling to their cars to go home. Then, it was just me and this guy. He was huge! Bigger than me now and he was around the same age as me then'.

'Once we were alone, he got quieter but started acting more aggressive and it started creeping me out so I was planning on getting the hell out of there. Out of nowhere, he asked if I had any drugs. He didn't even specify- He just said 'drugs' so I said no. I was just trying to get home so I said how I should probably start heading out and before I know it, he slams my head into the brick wall- I blacked out immediately".

I hear myself gasp and leaned in a little but he keeps going "I woke up a few hours later. Alone, with an aching head and a pain in my shoulder like a scorpion bite".

"Scorpion bite?" now, he lost me.

His hand makes a "one moment" gesture so I press my lips together to resist asking more questions until he's done. "So, I get home in the middle of the night and sleep for a few hours.'

'The next morning, I told my parents about it- Before I even said anything they freaked out about how different I looked so I just gave up and immediately told them everything. I couldn't hide the fact that I was already larger, and I was panicking about the wound on my shoulder. It looked like a huge black and purple bruise but the veins around it were also dark- the pain felt like the worst bruise and stab wound all at the same time".

He looks at me, debating on telling me the next part so I nod to urge him to continue and he quietly says "And when they looked closer, there was a bite mark". "He bit you?" I couldn't help but yell that, why would he bite Silas? "Well, at first, I thought it was some weird way to get back at me, or just a drug addict being aggressive. But now I know. When people do drugs, their blood tastes different while it's in their systems… and he could smell that I was clean. I guess he was desperate".

Not knowing where the hell this is going, I just ask "Desperate for what?" after a moment he just answers blankly "Blood".

I don't sound like I believe him when I ask "You're saying he, what? Drank your blood?".

Devoid of emotion, he answers "Enough to change me. Not enough to kill me" and I pick up on his disappointment in the latter.

"Changed you into what?" I ask, going along with this weird skit for no reason but my own torture.

"With the lack of another word for it…. a vampire".

A loud, choked laugh bursts out of me, and I don't give him a chance for another word. "So, you're going to mock me? Really? When all I wanted was to know why you fucking left me!".

He has the nerve to look surprised and hurt at my disbelief "I'm not mocking you, Hazel. Call it whatever you want. I get it, the word 'vampire' is a very commercial term but there's not exactly a lot of other names for this".

He's so serious that I play along, and ask in a sarcastic tone "So, you drink people's blood?".

He actually scoffs at that before replying "Only a piece of shit would do that". And then, in a too factual voice, he adds "Actually, that's more of a high anyways- not sustenance".

"So, you're a food eating vampire?" and I hold in my mocking joke that I also am.

"I mean, I can eat food but I can fully sustain myself with people's energy".

I remain calm, and gently ask "Have you talked to a professional about this?" he looks offended, so not wanting to piss him off, I add "I have a therapist and she's been really awesome, Si.

She can give you a referral for someone in this state to help you". I'm not sure if medication could help him but, maybe, since he seemed mostly normal until this very moment.

"Hazel, trust me I know how crazy this sounds. I've had three years of knowing. Why do you think I didn't just continue my perfect life? You're so damned stubborn. I know you won't believe me until I prove it to you".

He looks determined so I back up in my seat "You don't need to bite me. Let's just stay calm and talk to someone about this. You don't have to suffer alone". He's starting to look amused, at least.

"I'm not going to bite you. Jesus Christ." I sigh, a little relieved, but casually scoot back as much as I can. He rolls his eyes but then says "Although, I'm sure that would be… fascinating". He's looking off in the distance with glazed over eyes, so I move my head into his line of vision and he snaps out of it.

"I can actually prove it to you while staying over here, and with you over there" he gestures to the love seat I'm on.

I consider, debating if there's any way that this is a trick but then say cautiously "Okay. If you promise to stay there…". He focuses his gaze on me but looks normal and calm so I just stare back, not knowing what I should be feeling for.

My eyes droop a little as I feel a little lethargic, suddenly craving a nap, but I mentally fight to remember that I didn't get a lot of sleep. He smiles a little at my change but doesn't change his focus. I'm fighting to stay awake but slurring, I try to say "so far so good" and my head quickly falls for a second before I catch myself, using all my energy to keep my eyes open.

Why do I feel so heavy… His brow quirks "oh, really?". I just mumble out "mhm" and lay down on my side hoping that it will help a little.

He stands up and walks a few steps over to stand over me with his hands on his hips and I realize I've been compromised but also feel too tired to fight it so I just stare back up at him. Suddenly, the pressure getting heavier stops but I am still fighting to stay conscious, to make out Silas's next words.

"That was me barely trying, and I was concentrating on doing it gradually". His head tilts to the side as he analyzes me.

Still too proud to admit anything, I grit out "What're you talking about… I just need some coffee?".

He barks out a laugh and after a shake of his head, says with a grin "How are you even more stubborn now? Hold on".

Somehow, this experience is getting even weirder. He sits on the edge of my loveseat and links his fingers through mine, so we're holding hands and I suddenly feel almost how I did before this whole experiment started. He moves back over to the couch in the seat he was in a moment ago and just watches me, waiting for a reaction. I sit back up and say, with resignation in my voice "So you're what? An energy vampire?".

He looks ashamed and says "Ew… I wish there was a better word for it. I feel like you're imagining Edward".

I laugh but still ask "Does your skin do anything cool in the sun?" and finally he smiles genuinely "Nope. Not at all".

"I was beginning to wonder if that's why I don't see you in the daytime very often". After a moment of silence, Silas replies "That would make sense. But I just got used to a nighttime schedule helping Nate. And then, I started… trying to avoid running into you".

For the first time, he looks genuinely embarrassed. "Why?" I ask.

He answers quickly "I panicked. I wanted to get you away from him and near me. Quickly. But I didn't think about what it was going to be like- seeing each other again". I just raise an eyebrow in question until he adds more.

He sighs "As soon as I saw you and Abby hop out of your car, I realized I had no idea what I would even say to you... so I was hoping to delay it".

"So, you thought being rude to me was better?" I can't help but ask that, I've been wondering ever since.

"Well, I figured you were less likely to look at me and recognize me if I was an asshole" he's right, but I make a note to myself to stop seeking out assholes. A few seconds of silence happen as I think over everything he just told me. As my eyes wander back to Silas, he's looking at me with a cautious gaze, like he's debating on telling me something. So, I wait.

After a moment, Silas looks away and then looks back at me with a careful voice "Hazel, that first night I got bit? I kept having the same horrible dream- over and over but in different ways. I dreamt that you were there with me and without even thinking, I ripped your throat open with my teeth and didn't stop until you were drained completely dry of blood".

He's looking down now, with his elbows on his knees as he adds with a little embarrassment "When I woke up, instead of being horrified- I was scared, but I also couldn't stop fantasizing about it. I didn't understand it- I started fantasizing about draining you of your energy- until you were pale and stiff. It was disgusting".

His lip goes up in self-disgust and I can't take the look of pity off my face- there's no way he could be making this up. But my brain just can't picture how this actually happened. He lets out a sarcastic chuckle as he shakes his head "When I told my parents about that, when I started crying in fear of my own thoughts, they told me how they loved you too. And how because they love you, they didn't want me around you unless I knew I wouldn't do anything to harm you". I can't help the feeling of gratitude that I wasn't around for that, even if not knowing felt worse at the time.

"So, I just left. Without any of my things and just went and hid out in an apartment for a few months on the opposite side of the country- it was like a self-imposed rehab'.

'I was in isolation until I knew for sure I wouldn't hurt you- or anybody. But, by then, it just felt like I was too late. I kept having dreams of calling you and convincing you to come to me, alone, and hurting you in these horrible, disgusting ways so I never wanted to contact you at all". I jump when my phone starts ringing- Carly must be here. Silas and I look at each other for a few seconds, before I stand up and answer.

I can hear her car in my driveway so I just say into the phone "come on in!" and go over to open the door for her. She makes her way to the door quickly and I just greet her with a quick hug and say "My neighbor's still here. Are you sure you don't want me to kick him out? He won't mind".

I look at Silas and he innocently smiles at Carly, waiting for a response. "Silas, right?" she flips a casual point in his direction and he looks at me in surprise. I don't want him to think I've been talking about him, so I mutter out a casual "wow, good memory" so he doesn't get too cocky.

Carly looks at him and replies "Well, your entrances- and exits are hard to forget. Our group of friends are big fans". She says it so innocently but we all chuckle thinking about the dramatic barbecue scuffle, and the quick exit from Siren. Silas quickly gets up and gives her a handshake (she slaps has hand away to go into a hug that he reciprocates with a chuckle) before walking into the kitchen, easily finding and taking out barware like we aren't here.

I decide to ignore him and gesture for Carly to sit down with me at the kitchen island counter. I ask Carly about how her night went as I notice Silas working in the background on pulling out three glasses, ice and a shaker before pulling out the ingredients.

CHAPTER 30

Carly does not care at all that there is a strange man overhearing everything that she's saying. She quickly explains how her and Zach have had secret flings in the past but lately things seem to be more serious between them. She's mentioned a mystery man before but never specified who it was and I don't push- I know what it's like wanting to keep your love life private. She doesn't go into too much detail, but she does talk about how they left together last night with an unmistakable smirk.

"And then what?" I ask with a smile, because I know they went to her place together.

She proudly rolls her eyes and says "Let's just say… that we just left my place". We both obnoxiously laugh- I love how proudly she says it. I can tell Silas is trying really hard to look like he's not paying attention, but I see him barely holding in a smile at the gossip. She holds her hand out for a high-five which I immediately hit and then we both have two drinks in front of us.

Silas easily grabs one of my heavy bar stools over to the opposite side with his drink (I make a note to ask how alcohol affects him), and sits down like the three of us had plans to chat today. Carly is not bothered at all by the addition and talks for a few minutes about her plans with him tonight while

I sip on the drink that is refreshing and not too sweet.

After a few minutes, Carly stops talking and gets a sly look on her face while looking at Silas, and then back at me. "So… Hazel. Our friends were pretty excited that you with a 'very hot guy' that appeared out of nowhere".

I stubbornly stare at her, not wanting to play into this game but I can barely hold in my laugh. I know she saw Silas and remembered him, but she's having fun putting me on the spot. Out of the corner of my eye, I see Silas lean in a little- and Carly definitely catches the movement as her little canary-eating smile gets a tad bigger. I pretend to think "I don't know if 'very hot' is accurate. But, Silas did let me ride back with him. He's a pretty good neighbor". I happily say the last part in hopes that we latch on to the neighbor portion.

Carly looks to Silas in mock-surprise "So you're the 'hot guy' everyone was freaking out about". He just politely stares back waiting for her to go on, which she does "and you gave her a ride home because you are neighbors". Silas and I look at each other wondering where this is going. Carly looks at me and then looks at my neck for a second which makes me nervous.

"Hazel, is that a hickey on your neck?" I immediately tilt my head down, thinking it will somehow conceal it.

Silas is doing everything he can to hold in his laughter but his eyes give everything away.

"It's probably from my curling iron" I say, as I move my hair to cover both sides of my neck, I realize my hair is straight but Carly is already content enough to not point that out. Silas is gone- he's pretending to look at something in the opposite direction- but I notice a slight shake in his shoulders.

"I got a ride home, since you were busy with Zach... and then I slept alone and I slept wonderfully. Anyways... do you want some food? I can make you guys something".

I start to get up but Carly says "It's okay... Zach and I are getting dinner so I think I'm just going to eat light until then, but I should get back so I can rest and give you guys some privacy". I make a loud frustrated noise, but I've never seen Carly look happier so I just end up laughing and walking her to the door.

"I'll pick you up for drinks next week, we can talk more then" I say in a quiet rush to Carly as we walk to my door.

I know Silas can hear me but that fact is easier to ignore when I almost-whisper and am facing away from him. Carly and Silas say 'bye' and that it was nice to officially meet each other as I open the door and she walks past after a quick hug. As she walks out to my front yard, she turns and says "Oh, don't forget we are going back to Siren for that DJ in two weeks! He's so good!".

I remember that Silas wasn't wearing the mask when we walked out so Carly and the rest of the group have no idea it's the same person. "Oh, yeah! Let's plan out the details next week" I assure her before shutting my door. Silas looks annoyingly satisfied when I walk back in.

"Your friends think I'm hot... and that I'm *so* good", he brags, goading me into a response.

I give a casual shrug "Nightclubs are notoriously dark- everyone looks hot. Especially to people as drunk as they were". He's not bothered at all by my attempts to humble him.

"I like her" he says, slowly walking over to me and moving my hair to look at my neck, eyeing a hickey from last night. He says in a gravelly voice close to my ear "Since the cat is out of the bag, why don't we go check out that pizza place down the street?" and walks over to put his shoes on. I don't really have a reason to say no, and I think this would be an excellent way to get more answers. I tell him to give me five minutes while I put on leggings and a tank top with sneakers.

CHAPTER 31

We only have to walk two blocks over which doesn't take us long at all and Silas picks a booth towards the back. He orders a large pizza for us to share, and when we get our food, I (again) wonder about his dietary restrictions. "Wait… so you just eat normal food? Like a normal person?" I try to say it as quietly as possible.

He scrunches his eyebrows for a moment in confusion before realizing what I meant "Oh. I'm pretty sure I can survive without eating… or drinking anything as long as there's some sort of energy around for me to absorb. But I've never tried- I like food too much". I laugh, remembering his college-kid appetite that was always insatiable.

"So, you just have to be around people to source energy? What happens if you're isolated?". I can tell from his face that he doesn't know much more than I do. For a moment, I feel bad imagining navigating a "disease" that I didn't know anything about.

"I'm not totally sure, I've never been truly isolated for long enough to see a difference".

He thinks for another moment, "From what I can tell, as long as I stay in populated areas, I should be fine. Areas or places with more energy are what makes the biggest differences, and one of the reasons I'm happy to DJ for free" he flashes a smile.

"So going to places like clubs is kind of like a power-up for you?" which makes sense, because he definitely never cared about clubbing before.

"Anywhere that you would describe as being 'energetic' would be my main sources of energy- nightclubs, gyms, even shopping malls. Or even activities with others like… sports" he says awkwardly and I know he was thinking about different energetic activities.

Good to know he was sleeping around when I was having the worst time of my life. I blurt out "So, I take it you've been eating a lot of good food and doing a lot of good fucking these past few years?".

Without faltering, he answers matter-of-factly "Not really. I hoped it would be like that though" he darkly chuckles to himself and adds "Like I said, I kept an eye on you over the years. So, when I saw you in pictures after awhile with Abby and partying with men, it seemed like you were moving on'.

'I was in such a shit-place but I was so happy for you- I know now that you weren't happy- but in photos you faked it so well. So, I tried to do the same thing, thinking it would help me.". He looks at me with such an open expression that I keep listening.

He chuckles "It didn't help. I felt worse. I kept trying to tell myself that we were both moving on with life but it just made me miss you more. It didn't take me long to feel like 'is this what my life is now?' knowing that if I never left, we would have been building a life together".

"So, you never dated anyone else?" I don't know why I feel like I have the right to ask that, but instead of looking surprised like I expected, he looks disgusted.

"No. Why would I date anyone if I couldn't have you? What would I find in someone else if you and I weren't going to be together?". I open my mouth, hoping to think of a reply, but I'm just surprised by his honest and disgusted reaction.

Surely, he must have met women that he could have spent more time with. "So, you just casually slept around and never wanted to see anyone? Even casually?".

He's already shaking his head before my question is finished and answers "Nope. I will always crave energy in all forms". He looks at me briefly with embarrassment before continuing "but I don't need anything- or anyone- else.'

'When anyone tried to stick around, I would just resent them for not being you and that's not fair to them". Obviously, it's hard to hear that at some point he slept with another woman for the first time, and then continued doing so, but I also know that I did that too, and it never took anything away from what I felt for Silas.

Silas looks forlorn and ashamed but then says "Anyways… 'poor me', right? I'm sorry that it sounds so stupid- but I also had a life that was uprooted, and as selfish as I was, I just wanted to live again. But we are both here, eating pizza together- and I wouldn't change it for anything".

I try to get this conversation back to a more

casual place "Speaking of pizza…. turns out you can eat garlic". He laughs, accepting my topic change "Forget everything you've read. I know I don't know a lot about this but so far none of the urban legends are true".

His face turns mischievous "In fact, lately I'm beginning to think that my old human urges are even more intense now". I roll my eyes. But then my mind wanders to what and how different being with him, like that would be now. When my thoughts snap back to reality, I look at Silas and he's looking focused and satisfied like he knows exactly what I was just thinking about, imagining. My mind still in the gutter, I attempt to casually observe his features: soft and tousled hair, forest-green eyes, perfect mouth that I know for a fact kisses so decadently. … And now his perfect dimples are coming out in a smile.

I attempt a breezy tone "I bet those urges are easy for you to satisfy. I can't imagine a lot of people turning you down these days- getting energy can't be much of a problem". He looks simultaneously offended and complimented, like he can't decide which part of that to focus on.

"These days, I wouldn't have the slightest idea. I rely on going to energetic places- but if you're offering, I wouldn't say no". I think for a second "In the past, I would have been the first in line- I don't feel very energetic lately".

My attempt at a joke and keeping the moment light falters but Silas can read what I was going for and indulges me. "Don't worry, you will be again. And Hazel… I'll always be the first one in

your line". My mouth slightly opens in surprise.
He just smiles and asks "Ready?".

CHAPTER 32

The two weeks before Carly and I return to Siren go by way too quickly. Focused on my business after so many distractions, I spend most of my time in my garage working. The breaks I give myself are my daily runs at the park and getting coffee with Carly mid-week. Silas went back over to the vacant house a few times and it looks like we are still free from any cameras or other insidious things.

Other than that, I don't see Silas often. I told him I needed to let the information he told me "marinate"- I needed to go back through my memories from three years ago and think about his side of events. Mostly, I need to decide if I'm really going to believe and trust him- because there's no gray area in this situation.

Maybe he handled the situation like a dumb 22-year-old guy, but that doesn't mean he's an awful person. I knew that if I saw him all the time it would be harder for me to see things clearly so we left that I'll take some time to process, and that he's there if I need anything. As weird as his confession to me was, he hasn't wavered from that, so I am resigned to just going with his theory until proven otherwise.

His hearing is definitely abnormal, and so is his strength and speed- and just overall changes. But I'm hoping there's a more normal reason- especially since it seems that he doesn't even know that much about the "disease" he carries or where to find out more information. In movies, they always have a lot of lore and information about the supernatural- but what if it was just someone trying to figure out their new life on their own? I can't imagine how lonely it would be to go through something away from everyone I know, and not know if I'm even really okay. Or if I'm going crazy.

Most of my questions for him get met with shrugs or equal confusion- and I definitely don't understand the concept of taking and giving energy as sustenance. Despite my confusion through all of this, I trust Silas. I don't think it's just from our past together, but also because he's been genuinely steadfast in my well-being so far.

The day before my night out with Carly, he asks me out for coffee and I say yes quickly, secretly eager to see him after two weeks. Its early evening when Silas and I hop into his car and go to another cafe. Silas mentioned that he wants to show me all the best ones in town while I still learn this beautiful city. This one is simple and small, so we easily find a table and don't have to yell over loud music to communicate. Which is preferred after the last loud brunch cafe that Carly and I went to.

"So…" Silas interrupts my perusal of the cafe with a smile "I actually have different motives for this little coffee date".

I raise an eyebrow "Coffee date?" he just nods and continues "I have a business proposition".

I laugh at his seriousness but then give into his mood "Alright… what's your proposal?".

He wastes no time "The customer-facing

employees in our company could use new re-branded company t-shirts. And some other things like stickers, and a few other merchandising items. So, I'd like to work with you on a design and once that's agreed on, I'd like to place a fairly large order".

I feel my eyes grow big "How large?" when he tells me the amount, I try to keep a calm face but it's definitely the largest order I've ever had. I know I can do it, but it would be a lot and I wouldn't be able to work on anyone else's orders for awhile. We spend the rest of our "coffee date" going over timeline, prices and quality. He and his father agreed on ordering them in a few months, so I have plenty of time to prepare. Which makes me feel better since I can do a little at a time.

We sign an e-contract to give both sides security and agree on a timeline of when to start meeting for design ideas. I try to be cool about the order- but it's enough money to pay my mortgage for the year. He might be paying more than he needs to but who am I to argue? I put my hand out for a handshake which he quickly takes and shakes.

Then, instead of pulling away, he gently pulls it down to lay on the table to take soft swipes with his thumb, swiping my knuckles. "I hope you're more professional than this in our other meetings. Or we are going to need to circle back regarding conduct and behavior" I joke, trying to keep the mood light.

His adoring eyes aren't affected "I'm so proud of you and your business".

I briefly squeeze his fingers before slowly

pulling away, his eyes focused on my hand. "Thank you, Si. You too. Who knew that you'd be a real estate mogul". He just responds with a self-deprecating face. When he parks in his driveway, he insists on walking me to my door and I think he's just using it as an excuse for a kiss goodbye. But as we walk over to my door, I'm reminded that he has other motives for keeping an eye on me for as long as possible.

When I look up at him, he looks a little confused and concerned… and a little angry, but I have no idea why… until I follow his gaze to my doorstep. My doorbell camera is gone.

There are small fragmented pieces of it all over my porch- clearly smashed to bits. I'm frozen a few feet back as Silas stalks over to it, swearing and looking around for any more evidence. He quickly takes a picture and walks quickly back over to me "I'm going to walk you over to my house, I want you to stay in there for a few minutes while I look around your place".

In shock, I just nod my head and take his hand as he walks me to his front door until he unlocks it. I remember the gun in my house and worry that Brandon is still in there "There's a gun in my house, be careful!".

He quickly turns back to me and says quickly "Remind me to tell you later how hard it is to kill me" and turns back around like he is planning on doing the killing. I shut the door and lock it, then I look through my security app to see if the camera caught anything before its demise. It's just a blank screen and the recording ended about 30 minutes ago with no sign or reason why.

A few minutes go by and even though this is my first time in Silas's house, I don't stray far from the door. I feel too nervous and on edge so I just stand in the same spot and take a look around his place. It's cozy yet minimalist- most of the furniture is cold-looking. But his couch… it's huge and has thick cushions in a taupe color.

It looks like a huge teddy bear got turned into a couch- and I decide that the next time I'm over here, I'm going to lay on it the first chance I get. There's also a ridiculously large TV hung on the wall and the overall vibe of Silas's decor is that he doesn't need much- but whatever it is, it's going to be very nice, very comfortable, and probably very expensive.

When Silas returns, I tell him that my camera app didn't record the break-in and the only conclusion either of us can come up with is that the doorbell might have been smashed in from the side before it got a chance to notify me. He hands me the same gun that Brandon had before "Just keep this on you from now on, he's definitely not there or in the area anymore… but he was inside for a few minutes".

Panic surges inside me "How do you know?". My thoughts go to smashed glass, torn couches, anything destructive.

"Nothing is wrong in there, but I could smell him in almost every room" he looks as disgusted as I feel. I take the gun from him and with an uneasy look out his front window, I head to his front door, but stop when I hear Silas say "one second".

He's off- bounding up his stairs two at a time before I could get a chance to reply so I do just what he says, I wait. After another minute, he's back with a small bag, walking over to me so I just keep staring at him to try to figure out what he's doing. He opens the door, gesturing for me to walk out and then he follows too before locking his door behind him.

"What are you doing?" I ask after giving up on waiting for him to explain what he's up to. He looks at me in surprise "I'm spending the night at your place" after a moment he adds "on the couch, obviously".

And after another moment, he clarifies "until you get a new doorbell". I try to think of an alternative but honestly it sounds like a good idea.

"Thank you" I say and he just gives me a polite nod as we enter my home.

"What do vampires need for overnights?" I ask before I can talk myself out of it. He looks at me like I'm speaking gibberish, but answers "Toothbrush… since we still have teeth. A charger for my phone…".

Okay maybe that was a stupid question- I don't know what I was expecting to hear.

From a quick look, I can see a few differences from Brandon being in here but nothing too threatening. A picture frame of myself and my childhood dog is missing, random decorations are knocked on their side but so far nothing is broken. I go upstairs and Silas silently trails behind me, and I go to my bedroom where Brandon clearly did a quick look-through in the drawers, through my bed sheets and my bathroom cabinets.

My only proof that it was Brandon and not anyone else is the note on my bathroom counter. It says "good luck" along with a ripped-up photo of us, taken at a friend's Christmas party. What a diva. Silas takes pictures of everything and sends them to me so I can save them for more evidence to give the police. I don't call 911 because other than the evidence I sent, I'm not sure what else they could really do for me besides knowing he was here.

Silas helps me tidy up, but it doesn't take long since Brandon was only in here for a few minutes. Even though I could handle it on my own, it's nice having someone here with me. I go upstairs to use the bathroom, and when I come back downstairs, I notice that Silas changed into some loungewear he brought from his house.

Despite everything going on, I take in his thin white shirt that shows off his arms and toned chest, and his black jogger sweats that looks so soft I want to touch them. Silas focuses on me and it's obvious that he can tell I was checking him out so I try to distract him.

"I guess I don't need to tell you to make yourself at home" he chuckles and walks over to my couch and sits on it, unbothered, while propping his socked feet up on the ottoman. He looks happy like a little kid so I decide to indulge him since he is being my guard dog for the night. I begin to preheat the oven and pull out some frozen pizzas. I hear him behind me, close "I like where this is going… I'll make us some drinks" he says it in such a risqué tone that I laugh but say "I'll take tea, thank you".

I don't want to risk drinking alone with Silas after every other time I've drank around him has led to my lips on his. Not missing a beat, he says "Tell me where the kettle and tea is and I'll get some going". Appreciating the quick recovery, I tell him where it is. After twenty minutes, I'm wearing my softest sleep shorts and tank top, taking pizza out of the oven and carrying a hot cup of herbal tea to the couch.

Silas is a few feet from me on the couch with twice the amount of pizza and a hot tea as well. I say "We might as well start a show, right?" and he has the happy, kid smile again so I take that as a 'yes'. I pick a new one that I've heard a lot about, but haven't had a chance to watch and Silas confirms he also hasn't seen it so we start it and eat in silence. After two episodes, we take an "intermission" to wash the pizza dishes, brush our teeth and go to the bathroom. Once we are seated back at the couch, I notice that Silas has sat a few inches closer to me on the couch, but nothing too obvious.

He has his arm on the back of the couch, a few inches behind my head- and our feet on the ottoman are almost touching. So weird to be here with him, like this- and the combination of new and familiar. It feels like a first date while also feeling like best friend is right next to me.

Thirty minutes go by, and I begin to nod off. I try to fight it but my eyes keep shutting for just a little too long. I feel Silas's hand on the side of my head, gently pushing my head to the side until it's resting on his shoulder. "It's fine, Haze. I won't make it weird" so I give in and enjoy the strong but comforting muscle below my head.

He readily adjusts to make it more comfortable for the both of us and I whisper "Just until the end of this episode" because I know I need to get into my bed- alone. And then I fall asleep.

I wake up hours later, my head is on his chest but we are fully lying down- snuggled close on the couch with a throw blanket over us. The TV is asking if we are still watching and it looks like dawn is coming up soon, so I realize we must have both fallen asleep. He's still, and breathing in quiet, short breaths- so I'm positive he's asleep and I don't want to wake him when I get up. I slowly start trying to get up and I hear him ask "Where are you going?" in a long-forgotten sleepy voice that makes my heart race. "Going to my bed... goodnight" and I quickly hop over him and walk upstairs.

I grab a blanket and pillow and head back down which he gratefully accepts with a "Thank you, Hazey." and then I head back up. This time it's a little harder to fall asleep, but I eventually do, wondering if Silas drains energy without even trying. I add the question to my note's app in my phone among all of the other questions I have been asking him lately. I wake up early in the morning and immediately head downstairs, and find Silas in a fresh change of clothes quietly working on his laptop on my kitchen counter. He looks up when I enter the kitchen and has a slow but pleased smile.

He waits for me to say "Good morning" before he says it back. "How did you sleep?" I ask, genuinely curious how my couch held up to his huge comfy-looking one.

He shuts his laptop and answers "I slept…alright. How about you?". I can tell he is trying to be polite but it obviously is nowhere near his standards.

"I slept pretty good considering the situation. Actually, I never woke up throughout the night… did you do something to me? Like, your little energy trick?".

His confusion changes into offense before finally settling on earnest "Hazel, I would never do that without you knowing, that would be no different than drugging you.". My response to him is a hug- which he returns tightly- before I walk over to my espresso machine. I make us two cappuccinos while he goes and gets us some breakfast sandwiches from the deli down the street.

We are slipping into a comfortable territory that is terrifying but I'm enjoying too much to stop. When he gets back, we eat sitting in my backyard patio set in a comfortable silence before Silas clears his throat. "I have to help Nathan tonight at that club. I can come by after, but there's going to be a few hours at night where you will be alone. Are you going to be okay? He can handle it if I cancel". I panic for a second but then remember that tonight is when I'm also going to Siren with Carly.

"You're doing that tonight? I'm going there with Carly. We've been planning it for weeks". I feel slightly embarrassed about how happy I am to not be alone tonight.

He's relieved "Oh, that's tonight? Well,

perfect then. How are you getting there and back? You can ride with me".

I consider the temptation but then remember my plans with the girls. "Thanks, but Carly and Allison are coming over to get ready and then we are all ubering together. I'm not totally sure about how I'm getting back but can I let you know?".

He just nods and goes back to peacefully staring ahead until we go back inside and part for the day. He goes to his place to work and I organize my week's schedule before cleaning and getting ready to host.

CHAPTER 33

Carly and Allison come over at five with bare faces and arms full of face masks, snacks and various alcohol mixers. I already had a charcuterie board and some snacks prepared so I add their contributions to the kitchen table. We get to work quickly: putting on music, opening snacks and making strong pre-game drinks. We're meeting some of the group at Siren, but I'm not entirely sure who's all going.

Around seven, we get food delivered so we can eat while we begin actually getting ready. The first two hours were mostly us relaxing, doing face masks, and each other's hair. It's ten when we finally feel truly ready in my bathroom that barely fits the three of us in there getting ready. When we look in the mirror to double-check, we have clear, drunk smiles on our faces- but I do have to say we look great.

Carly and Allison are wearing short dresses that I would be way too scared to dance in- having accidentally flashed my underwear before. I call the Uber and do a once-over again in my full-length mirror and I love my new outfit that I bought last week just for this. I have a white corset that pushes my breasts up but keeps them secure, tight faux-leather pants that are comfortable enough to dance in, and black strappy heels that give me a few extra inches in height. I'm sure I will be impatient to get my pajamas on later, but I'm also a little excited for Silas to see me looking like this since I usually wear very casual clothes around him.

We meet the others in the line outside of Siren and its Theo (Allison's boyfriend) and Zach. There are a few others as well and even more are on their way. Tonight, I'm noticing the single guys in the group are a lot more cordial with me than before, as if they think I'm in a relationship. I guess the last two times I was around them, they last saw me with Silas. I don't really mind them thinking that I'm taken, since I haven't been interested in anyone in the group.

We are finally towards the front of the line- which is even longer than the last time we were here. It seems like Silas's fan base is pretty intense... and I see some of the women in line are dressed like sexy devils. I hear a Siren employee asking a question as he makes his way down the line. Everyone is so loud, his questioning turns into background noise. Carly taps my arm and when I look at her in question, she motions to the same employee that is now standing next to us. Judging by the alert and excited look on her face, I know it's going to be interesting.

When I make eye contact with the guy, he asks "Hazel? Can I see your ID?". I get nervous, but show him my ID which he looks at thoroughly before blandly telling us to see the guy in the front who also makes us all show our ID's.

When he sees all of them, he points to the door and says "You guys can all go in, you're on the list". They all look at me like I'm the second coming of Christ which feels good, I'm also very confused about what the hell is happening. Since Silas is playing tonight, the only thing I can think of is that he asked them to put me on a list.

When I go inside, I don't see his tall figure anywhere, so I assume he's in the back. The current DJ is playing remixes of top 40 songs and a chorus of cheers rings out whenever people hear their personal favorites. I'm out of touch with current radio hits, so a lot of these songs are unfamiliar to me and I'm left out on a few songs but have fun dancing anyway.

We're on the second round of drinks by the time the now familiar devil-masked DJ comes on and everyone loses their mind. I can see why Silas is becoming a local celebrity. Rather than repetitive beats or quick guilty pleasures, it's an appetizer platter of every extreme. One minute it's a remix of a popular bubble-gum pop song, and then it blends into 90's grunge which blends into Latin rap- it's the most exciting thing I've ever heard. I'm so used to the same 20 songs playing in clubs that hearing a metal song with an EDM beat mix into a love son, with a loud-bass hip hop beat makes me excited for every song change.

Everyone around me is reacting the same way, cheering in excitement whenever the next unpredictable song mix comes on. I try to focus my eyes through the smoke and haze to see what Silas is doing as the crowd loses their mind. But, besides the glowing mask on his face, I can barely see him. His body is standing mostly still, but moving things on the mixing table- I can almost imagine him being bored up there.

I hear a classic pop song fade into a familiar one and stop moving. Out of my peripheral vision, I can see the group staring at me but I'm too distracted to care. Silas is playing our song which was an acoustic, happy love song but he's slowed it down and distorted it to a sensual beat, and I see people starting to grind on one another.

Realizing how weird I must look, I begin to dance again. Pretending that I'm not listening to a song that has broken and fixed my heart over and over. Silas looks at me once, gives a slow nod in my direction, and fades it into a popular rap song. The rest of the songs are fun, dancing hits and remixes until about one in the morning. When they finally announce that he's done, they tell everything that they will still play from the club's playlist until two am.

I'm having enough fun- and drunk enough to not really think about where Silas went. So, I go back to goofing around with some other girls in the group, the couples have already gone in different directions to dance one on one. I hear commotion behind me and when I turn to look, I see the tall, lithe body stalking towards me.

The neon devil mask is still on, over a semi-casual black suit. People are staring, but I'm focused on Silas. He's right in front of me as he pulls off his mask with his left hand, and with his right hand, he hooks it around the back of my neck to slowly pull me in for a kiss. His movement was gentle, but mine was a drunk, energetic kiss that he quickly catches up to. When we pull apart, I hear distant whooping and hollering as Silas grabs my hand and guides me to a back corner that gives us a little privacy.

Most people have lost interest now so it's easier to focus on it just being the two of us. He rotates us so that his back is against the wall, rotating me to face him. He seems so confident, but still asks "Was that okay?" in my ear. I answer by getting on my tiptoes and grazing my nose along his ear lobe, causing his whole body to freeze up "Definitely".

His eyes are sparkling as he observes me "Uh-oh. How drunk are you?".

I take a long second to really think about it "Drunk enough to not overthink. Sober enough to know what I'm doing". His response is just a chuckle as he watches his hands graze down my sides. I remember Carly and alertly look around for her, she's already looking at me like she was seeing if I was okay.

When I smile at her, she has a mischievous smile before going back to dancing with Zach. I turn back to Silas who's been patiently waiting, and I'm about to start dancing again when he gets a concentrated face. Then, he grabs me by my hips, giving us distance to analyze my outfit and he moves me around so he can look at the back. "Jesus Christ" I hear him say before he turns me back around. It's pretty innocent at first, but I turn around so my back is against his chest.

Putting my weight on him that he more than accepts, with his hands on my hips guiding me even closer to him. He still has his mask in the grip of his left hand and based on his movements behind me, I think he forgot all about that. I'm surprised that he's not embarrassed to be so intimate where he works here, but my thoughts quickly stop when I feel him crouch over me to have his face in the side of my neck. I can feel his breath on my neck and his breath smells like tequila. I turn my face to kiss him and confirm- yup, definitely tequila.

I can't imagine my breath smells much different after the amount of shots I've taken tonight. I feel for his neck and put my hands on it as I slide down his body... which I begin to feel he really, really likes. His hands begin to explore more as I feel them rhythmically taking swipes over my hips and inner thighs that are soon going higher and higher until our rhythmic moves feel less like dancing and more like a promise of what's to come. From behind me, he grabs my chin, rotating my ear to his mouth "I've missed this".

I make sure none of the people we know are watching us before turning around to face him. We haven't stopped dancing but our knees are now interlocked as his hands are on my hips. On my tiptoes, I say into his ear "Your dancing has improved" and when I look at him, he gets a smile that tells me he's up to nothing good.

Quickly, he moves out of the way so I'm now facing the wall he was just against and he's behind me, still dancing. I put my hands against the wall to slightly bend over and he doesn't miss a beat, just continues his rhythmic pressure against me while his hands continue to roam. "I've been thinking there's probably a few things we've both improved at".

He says it so close to my ear that he doesn't have to project his voice- I can hear him perfectly. We are all but dry humping at this point, so I blame my drunk brain when I move to be perfectly aligned against him. I ask "Did you think about it when you touched yourself here?" as my finger trails along the zipper of his pants.

"Fuck." he swears quickly "yes- many, many times" he almost sounds in pain now so I decide to make it worse.

I turn around to face him again and smile before he bends down to hear me "Maybe I can show you what you've been missing out on the last three years" and I move to walk away from him. He grabs my wrist and when I see his face… he looks hungry- his eyes are dilated and heavy-lidded. So much so, that I look surprised at the animalistic look on his face.

He pulls me by my wrist to say "There's no way you're saying something like that to me and then walking away".

I shake my head "Relax… I'm just telling Carly 'bye'".

His intensity changes into a winning smile "Thank God. I'll go get the car warmed up and wait out front. Tell them bye for me". He grabs my chin to give me a quick kiss before quickly walking off. I look him up and down as he walks out; admiring his tall, muscular frame and the way it fills out his outfit. I notice a few others doing the same. Some look like they've been watching us and some look surprised by the acclaimed DJ who basically had sex in front of them.

Before I even get a chance to say anything to Carly when I walk over to her, she's dancing with Zach and shouts "Have fun, babe! Let's catch up next week" with a twinkle in her eyes. We quickly make plans to hang out within the next few days and I say bye to everyone else who is trying to not look surprised before walking out, into Silas's car. Once I'm in, Silas buckles me up and drives quickly to my house.

"Are you drunk?" I ask him, only now realizing that he could be just as drunk as me.

He makes a little scoffing noise "I had a few tequilas. It would take me a couple bottles to be as drunk as you are".

His hand is on my leather-clad thigh and I put my hand on his, our fingers intertwining. I lean the seat back and stare out the slightly-open window with a smile on my face and wind in my hair. I'm almost asleep by the time Silas parks in his spot, so I clumsily unlock the door and try to step out. When my feet touch the ground, I lose my balance-swaying sideways. Before I can fully fall, Silas has already come over and picked me up to carry me inside.

When we get inside, he carries me to my bathroom and sets me down on the counter. I'm absolutely useless, I just focus on staying upright on the counter so I don't fall but I'm like a corpse in every other way, with closed eyes and lazy posture. He asks me where my makeup remover is, so I give him step-by-step instructions of where he can find what he needs and how to do it.

I could probably have just done this myself after sleeping it off for a few hours, but I'm having fun watching him apply the cleansing oil, massaging my face, and wiping it off with a gentle cloth. Once my makeup is gone and my face is cleaned, I brush my teeth and go to my room to change.

He follows me and sits in the edge of my bad and asks if I need help as well. "I think I got it" as I reach for the back of the corset to loosen the string, giving up after a minute and walking over to him as I gesture to my back. While he's undoing the strings and loosening them up to take off, I lift my foot up to undo the straps and take my heels off.

I make a small noise of contentment when I feel my bare feet on the soft rug in my room and help him pull my top off. I unzip the side of my pants and take those off as well and walk over to my dresser and slide on a small satin slip. When I make my way over, he says in a throaty voice "Come here"

I lean into his body, moving in between his thighs while he looks me over and says "I don't think I've ever seen a hotter thing than you in leather pants… besides you in whatever this is". I go to kiss him but he kisses my cheek and says "I can't get all worked up again when you're this drunk" he says it with such finality that I don't try to argue.

Silas helps me into bed but then quickly goes downstairs to grab my water bottle, some pain reliever and an electrolyte vitamin. He sits on the edge of the bed, watching me to make sure I take what he gave me and once I'm done, I lay down "Can you turn the lights off?".

He turns them off and then asks "Do you want me to help you get sleepy?". I think about it but I know I don't need help, I feel like I could sleep for years.

"Honestly, I think I'm fine just like this. I haven't felt this comfortable in… a very long time".

He nods and gets up to leave, but I stop him. "Silas… can you sleep here tonight?".

"Of course, Haze. I'll be right downstairs if you need anything".

As he nears the doorway I clarify "I mean in here… with me". There's a nervous pause, but he slowly walks over and I stop him. "Wait. Don't wear your dirty club clothes in my bed. Take those off and then come here". He stands there observing me and I don't know how to read him, so I add "I won't touch you, I swear".

He chuckles "Thank you for your reassurance" before doing as I instructed and slowly getting into bed. He's keeping his distance, as if he's nervous that I'll get uncomfortable even though I asked him to be here. I move over to lay my cheek on his chest and sleepily sigh "I lied. I'm touching you. Goodnight".

I feel his chest shake a little from a small laugh before he kisses the top of my head "Goodnight, Hazey".

A few short minutes later, and I was right. The comfort alone was enough to make me fall asleep and this time, I don't have any nightmares. I don't fully wake up again throughout the night. Throughout the night, we rearrange sleeping positions together. Once in awhile, I feel a kiss on my cheek or shoulder or forehead, before being pulled in even closer to him.

CHAPTER 34

Since my new doorbell gets delivered tomorrow, Silas has agreed to spend the night on my couch again. I slept so good in the bed with him last night, but I don't want sleeping together to become a habit until we have established what we're doing. As Silas is leaving in the morning to work over at his house, he asks me my plans for the day. "I have to finish up an order for that bookstore in downtown, then drop them off tonight before getting dinner delivered".

It's only two dozen branded travel-mugs, but I'm still excited to be branching out locally. We both agreed on ordering dinner delivery from a five-star Mexican restaurant in town. "I can go with you to the bookstore. I have a few books on a list I've been wanting to check out and I'm sure you could use a little help carrying the boxes in". We agree on a time and I spend the next few hours in my garage finishing up the order and packing it all up. The trip to the bookstore goes by quickly- Silas and I knew the books we wanted so we didn't have to wander around long.

On the way back, we order the food and he goes to his place to grab some more things. Our time together is comfortable- sometimes we are laughing or flirting, but even the contented silence is nice. While alone, I change into soft leggings and a crop top for another comfortable night, and I start to get the couch set up for Silas to sleep in again before bringing in the food.

Silas comes over shortly after, in some dark gray lounge shorts and a thin white tee that offsets his tattoos and shows his muscles. As he's washing and then drying his hands, he catches me staring at him- his hands, his muscles, his hair. His face breaks out in a dimpled smile as he slowly takes a few steps towards me, placing his hands on my shoulders and staring at me adoringly like I'm a cute puppy. I just smile back at him innocently and try to back away but he quickly wraps me in a tight hug.

With his chin on top of my head and with a struggling voice, he says "How can you look so hot but cute at the same time" and lightly shakes me before releasing me.

I chuckle "I guess that's why I can't ever truly get a man out of my life" and turn so I can begin plating our food. I notice the silence and look up at Silas who almost looks a little... sad? One thing about me that has definitely changed in the last three years is my adoption of dark humor.

I think I killed the moment but he starts speaking "Hazel, I hope I don't need to say this- but just in case... Once Brandon is gone -however that may be- if you don't want me around, you can just tell me and I'll be gone. Don't get me wrong, I'd be crushed because I'd love nothing more than to be around you, but I'm not going to ever make you fear me".

I'm taking in his words but he starts to look at his arms as he gets a sheepish look on his face "I guess the tattoos aren't exactly helping my case of not being a creep". I take a moment to enjoy the tattoos that I can see from his bicep down to his fingers.

Without stopping myself, I say "I think those are the hottest things about you" he laughs and we grab our food, taking it to the couch. Silas sits in what is becoming his usual spot, and I sit over on the love seat still trying to give as much friendly space as possible. He looks confused like I lost my mind and pats the spot right next to him. His face is so vulnerable that I move to the same couch but I still give a foot of distance, which disappears when he closes the distance and sits shoulder-to-shoulder with me as if we've done this every night for years. Which puts the thoughts- and questions- in my mind and I can't hold in my wondering any longer.

"Do you think if you never left, we would be arguing about something right now? Like an old married couple?".

To his credit, he actually takes a second to think about it for a moment before answering "Maybe…? But then we would get to make up after".

I feel my eyebrows go up an inch and he adds "Why do you think I loved pushing your buttons so much before?". My mouth drops and I slowly move my head to the TV as I ignore his self-satisfied grin. I always wondered why he would smirk sometimes when we had a pointless argument.

After an hour of watching our show, we agree to read our new books, so we turn on some relaxing lo-fi music in the background. The soft music is the only noise in my house right now besides the sounds of our pages turning, and soft sipping noises of our drinks. I'm sure there is, but I currently can't think of anything better than having my legs intertwined with Silas's as we face each other on my couch, our backs against its arms. No matter how these ends, I hope I never forget the feeling of looking up once in awhile, only to see Silas already looking at me- refusing to look away until I do.

Also, the occasional quick foot rubs that I've been getting don't hurt either. After a few chapters, I feel my eyes get heavy and look at Silas who looks like he's feeling the same way "Want to brush our teeth and get ready for sleep?".

He looks over sleepily like he's high and says "I thought you'd never ask", I laugh as we make our way to my bathroom upstairs and he has his toiletry bag in hand.

After we brush our teeth and wash our face in a comfortable silence, he begins looking sad "I can't believe I've been missing out on this for three years".

Now that I know it wasn't his fault, I begin to feel sad for our lost years and say "I do have to admit that I'm happy we're doing this now...I think it was worth the wait".

We're talking through our mirror's reflections and I see his face light up a little "So does that mean you don't hate me anymore?". I smile "No... I don't think I do...".

Part of me is still reserved with Silas, I still can't fully let go around him. But I can't deny that my life feels like it has more colors in it ever since we've reunited. Despite him sleeping in my bed last night, I'm grateful he doesn't assume tonight will be the same way. We are standing at my bedroom door, saying goodnight when he goes to kiss my cheek. I turn at the last second so our lips touch, his pleased laugh changing into a quiet grunt as our kissing doesn't stop, only escalating.

We are fully making out when his hands move to my ass, lifting me up to wrap my legs around his waist. The new pressure only makes me hungrier and I start to move against him. He uses his hands to pull me closer, helping me add pressure, before too-quickly setting me down, out of breath. He keeps his forehead against mine gruffly saying "Get into your bed right now and go to sleep before I join you in there and neither of us sleep" and he gives me a chaste kiss and walks out, getting downstairs at an inhuman pace.

We yell goodnight to each other from different levels and I lay down and try to get my thoughts and heart rate to a normal place. I can't stop imagining what it would be like if he did stay here and followed through with his threats. I get a text and quickly go to check, but in my confusion, it's… from Silas.

"Please think other thoughts. I can feel your energy- not just the amount. You're killing me".

I reply quickly, ashamed *"That would have been good to know awhile ago"*.

I hear him chuckle and I fall asleep thinking about work, Brandon, running- anything but Silas.

Sometime later, I'm in my bed and it's dark

and quiet… except for a quiet thumping noise. I realize they're footsteps. Slow, intentionally quiet footsteps. For whatever reason, I know they belong to Brandon- and I know Brandon is in my house.

I'm frozen in fear listening to the slow, sneaky steps creeping up the stairs, towards my room. They stop at the top of the floor for a brief second, and then they continue to my door. I try to quietly roll over to face the door but my noises feel too loud.

The door quietly creaks open and I see a silhouette of Brandon… watching me. I gasp awake. Reminding myself it's a dream, I'm safe- and Silas is downstairs. My heart is beating fast and hard and my whole body feels cold, so I focus on getting my breathing to slow down. The house is so silent that every noise I make sounds unbelievably loud.

I begin to hear the same noise I just woke up from. I sit in concentration and listen as I hear the similar pattern of quiet feet slowly going up the stairs. The steps are quieter, too graceful and too focused. I try to focus on the noise and distance, but my heart is beating too loudly to locate what's happening. The footsteps are now outside my door, and there is now only silence on the other side.

My thoughts are scrambled and illogical and I can't tell reality from what was just happening in my mind a minute ago. More terrified of the silence, I start to slowly get out of bed and face the door and I hear another shuffle right outside. In a panic, I fearfully yell "Silas?".

"It's me" the door swings open and it's Silas. And right after the relief fades, the anger sets in.

Before he can say anything, I rush out "Jesus Christ! You scared the shit out of me". With a hand on my chest, I hope that it'll somehow calm my nervous system down. He's dramatically looking up at the ceiling before stepping into the room.

"YOU scared ME. I couldn't tell what was happening up here. I just heard movement and you gasping for air!".

I take a few seconds to breathe "Well, you didn't have to creep up the stairs".

I lay back down in bed since I hope to be able to sleep soon. He walks in closer, now in front of the bed, "Sorry, I was hoping to just check on you if you were having a nightmare". I ignore the little chuckle in his voice as he sits on my bed. With my blanket now covering me, I explain "Well, I had a dream that Brandon was downstairs, creeping up the stairs and waiting outside my door. So, then I woke up, and heard the same exact thing- I think that took a few years off my life".

He leans over to give me a hug, and not fighting it, I sit up so I can hug him back for a full, comforting embrace. He sways a little back and forth and I kind of feel like a baby being rocked to sleep but it's so comforting I don't say anything to ruin or stop it. With my face still pressed against his chest and my words muffled I ask "Can you sleep in here for the rest of the night?".

With a gentle forehead kiss, he stands up to get into bed, slipping under the covers. Leaving it up to me, he's on his back with his arm open at his side as he looks at me. "Come here, I'll be good" and it takes me no time to move over and lay with my head on his chest and my leg on top of his. His arm wraps around me and even though I still feel adrenaline, I savor the warmth and safety that surrounds me.

My heart is beating fast still and I try to get it to slow down but give up and finally give in: "Silas?".

"Hm…?" It takes me a second to think of how to say it before giving up on subtlety "Can you put me to sleep?". I hear him take a small breath and then I'm quickly drifting off to the feeling of him making gentle lines with his fingertips along my leg that's over him.

I wake up early in the morning, and Silas is already gone from my bed. I hear the sounds of him on his computer working, so after a few minutes of checking my phone and emails, I brush my teeth and head downstairs. He's sitting on the couch and closes the laptop when I come downstairs, asking with a satisfied smirk "How'd you sleep?".

I walk into the kitchen and say as casually as possible "Pretty good…" and I hear him laugh as he gets up to follow me in.

His walk looks more like a prowl as he closes the distance "Maybe one of these nights I can really put you to sleep since it sounds like what I did last night wasn't good enough".

He's right in front of me now, my back against the counter and there's no mistaking his tone, but I play along "Wouldn't you be so lucky?".

He intertwines our hands "Yes… yes, I would be. That sexual energy has been pouring out of you more and more lately". He says it in a lighthearted way but his face looks too intense to laugh at.

Backing away towards the fridge, I look away so he doesn't see my blushing face and say "Hm… your sensors must be off. Too bad you can't get that checked out". I grab the milk and start to make us some coffees. My phone pings and I quickly go to check it, but it's just a notification that my doorbell is in transit to be delivered today.

When I tell Silas, there's no mistaking the brief disappointment in his eyes before he puts on fake enthusiasm "Sounds good, I can install it for you when it gets here".

Feeling the same way as it seems like he does, like he'd be going too soon, I say "Honestly, I wouldn't mind if you stayed one more night on the couch. It's kind of nice having a guard dog by the door".

He laughs for a moment and says "Fair enough, but you know what to do if you can't sleep upstairs" before putting a few pieces of bread in the toaster and cutting some fruit. Leaning against the counter, I realize how grateful I am to have him here. Not just for keeping me safe, or making me feel safe- but for giving me something else to focus on. I know he's busy but he's never made me feel like I'm taking too much of his time or that he's not getting anything out of this.

"Thank you for staying here, Silas. I officially no longer hate you"- he almost chokes on his coffee before going to sit down at the counter's bar stool. I join him with our plate of fruit and buttered toast as we grab small bites with our fingers.

He shakes his head, suddenly serious "I can't believe you're in this situation, Hazey. After what I did, you deserved an amazing man".

I try to not react defensively but fail "It's not like I knew he was like that. He was sweet when I met him... it just went downhill pretty quickly".

He thinks for a second but gently asks "How so?" so I tell him. I start at the beginning of meeting a "nice" guy, the man who "worried" when I was away from him, the "passionate" man who just cared so much. Silas actually looks guilty as I talk through the timeline of events with Brandon but keeps intensely listening. After a few minutes I get up with our empty dishes and walk to the sink, Silas meets me on the other side and grabs them from me, setting them in the sink.

"Keep talking, I'll take care of these".

"There's not much else to say" I say, wiping off the counter. He moves to stand in front of me, and in a quick movement he picks me up by my hips to sit me on the counter.

"I'm sure you'll think of something" he says with a quick smile before returning to the sink.

Wanting to change the subject, I spit out "I'm surprised you like coffee... also does caffeine even help you?".

He welcomes the change in topic and looks at me with a huge smile "You're right, the caffeine doesn't do much. But it's kind of a morning routine. But as far as enjoying, it tastes the same as before. If something tasted good before, it tastes just as good now". There's no mistaking the look in his eye and what track of mind he's in now.

He's done washing the dishes, so he dries his hands and walks a few steps until he's right in front of me and the mood in the room has shifted. "Can you affect moods at all?" I ask, maybe hoping he will say yes but he tilts his head in confusion before the gleam in his eye takes over. He looks down at my knees before gently prying them open with his hands.

I hold in my gasp as he steps in between them to be as close as possible to me, but I don't fight him. I want to see where this goes as his hands fall to either side of me, leaning on the counter. "Nope… any emotions you felt are all you. How do you feel?" he's a few inches from my face, letting his eyes flicker in between mine.

"Well apparently you can tell… why don't you tell me?" I'm slightly leaning back, but he just leans forward to slightly hover over me with our lips almost touching.

"You feel…" he quickly presses a kiss on my lips before continuing "intoxicating." and his lips are back on mine, lightly biting my bottom lip. A small moan escapes my throat and he takes it as the signal it is and suddenly our tongues and lips are moving, together. I feel his hands back on my hips to give leverage so our bodies can be closely aligned. When my hands go in his hair and pull handfuls, he breaks away, breathing hard. He moves back to the counter across from me and sits on it as well to face me as I calm my heavy breathing and try not to look too confused about why he just moved away so quickly.

Suddenly, he looks exhausted with dark, dilated eyes, and an aged expression. We stare at each other for another moment before he quietly says "I don't want to be a rebound, Haze". There's a quiet pause before I ruin it with a short obnoxious bark of a laugh.

"How would you be a rebound if you were my first?". I'm trying to keep the laughter out of my voice but it's not working very well and he looks a little hurt.

"I know but… if we start to go down this road I want it to be because of us and not because of this shitty situation. I don't want to be your distraction".

I think for a few seconds and reply "Well I don't even know what 'us' is right now… I don't think I could give you a certain answer about that for awhile".

He tousles his hand through his hair for a few seconds "I know that I shouldn't talk about your relationship with Brandon… I just wish I was there and I'm mad at myself".

I put a hand on his arm to comfort him but before I can say anything, he adds "But when he's out of the picture, I'm going to do whatever I can to have a fresh start with you".

I try to imagine what that would be like "A fresh start like we just met here as neighbors, not as exes?".

He nods "Exactly. I don't want to be living as ghosts from the past, I want to be current Hazel and Silas. We can't help having our memories together but I don't want to be living in them". I couldn't agree more.

I hop off the counter and cross the two steps over to him "Okay, when that time comes, we can see where it goes. In the meantime, if you change your mind about that boundary that you just set- you know where to find me".

I smile and turn, walking to my couch in the living room. "Yeah? So, if it's up to you…?" he's intrigued and waiting for an answer with full concentration. I turn to face him- he's still on the counter and I'm over by my couch so we have some distance now.

I shrug, "I'm just saying, I respect you wanting it to mean something because you want this to go somewhere… but I'm fine being casual just in case this has nowhere to go".

Slightly faster than human speed, he hops off the counter and slows down to cross the distance to me. He's looking down at me, saying "We both know this has somewhere to go, it will always have somewhere to go". He's back to being too close for me to think, I don't have anything to say but the twinkle in his eye has returned enough for him to quietly say "And when it does… I'm going to remind you just how well we fit together".

I feel my eyebrows quirk in surprise, but I'm cut short of a reply. Because now he's talking in my ear while his hands innocently trace my body. "We've both changed a lot, but I'm willing to bet that all your favorite spots to be kissed… licked…. bit are all the same". I hear my small inhale of breath, and try to think of anything to prove him wrong.

I trace the button on his jeans, noticing the hitch in his breath and say "Only one way to find out… too bad you have your little timeline".

He grabs my hand before I can pull away and his mood has changed, because now he says with gravity "I am serious though. I will take care of this Brandon situation because we both know he won't stop".

I give up on pulling my hand away from his gentle but firm grip "What do you mean by 'take care of him'?".

He quickly answers "I mean: I'm not going to track him down but I know he's going to come back here and when he does, I'm going to be here too".

"Okay… well the best possible scenario is he gets arrested and put in prison for a long time".

He rolls his eyes "Yeah because that always works out…Whenever he's gone, however that may be, you and I are going to have this conversation again". He looks at me intensely until I nod my head and then he releases my hand and gives me a hug. Silas goes back to his house to spend the day there, promising he will be back when the doorbell is delivered to install it and sleep on my couch again. I get back to normal life for a few hours, thoughts of him distracting me throughout the day. I consider my options, but also mentally smack myself for even thinking of that at all.

I still get random texts and calls from unknown numbers and know that I shouldn't even be thinking about Silas right now. And I can't help but to feel that whatever is going to happen with Brandon, I just want it to happen and get it over with. Whatever needs to happen to get Brandon out of my life forever, I'm ready for.

CHAPTER 35

Silas comes over in the evening, and immediately gets to work installing the doorbell. Once we confirm that it's working, we make a pasta dish, drink some wine that Silas brought over, and listen to the soft music playing in the background. I've asked a million questions about his new "condition" and somehow, I still haven't run out- I wonder if I ever will.

"Do nights like this at my house drain your energy faster? Do you need groups of people to sustain yourself?".

He shakes his head while swallowing his bite, explaining, "The nights I DJ give me enough 'fuel', if you will, to last me weeks. That's why it's worth it for me to do it. I don't even get paid for it. Nate always offers because he feels bad but he just can't comprehend how much I'm really getting out of it".

"Does he know?" I ask, a contemplative look comes on his face.

"Nobody knows besides my parents… and you. I think I'd judge someone if they believed me right away- I know I wouldn't believe it" he ruefully laughs and goes back to eating.

When we finish eating, both of us get up to wash and dry the dishes without discussing it, like we have done it a million times. It's a comfortable silence when Silas clears his throat and says "What are you doing tomorrow?". I think it over and just to make sure, I dry my hands and go over to my planner to make sure I have no plans before confirming to him that I'm free all day.

He looks surprisingly on-guard, asking "Can I take you on a date tomorrow? Nothing is expected but I'd like to show you around a few spots. And maybe we can feel out what a fresh start could be like". I stare at him for a second before I feel a genuine, slow smile across my face.

I try to subdue it with a nod "Okay. It's a date, then".

I can see gratitude wash over his face before he dries his hands and comes over to kiss my forehead. He picks me up and carries me over to the couch. We turn on the TV and I hear my phone ping, so I check it while Silas looks for a movie for us to watch. I've been talking to Abby on and off all day about the book series we are reading at the same time, so I'm not even expecting Brandon when I see the text from a random number.

"I mess you"

Ping.

"miss you"

Ping.

"srry, drunk"

Ping.

"Why dn't you ever answwer?"

Silas hears the alerts going off on my phone

and looks like he's trying to not stare or ask about it. "It's Brandon" I say, because I know he's wondering and I show him the texts.

"Should I block him? I almost want to know what he is thinking in case he's in the area again". I don't want to be caught off guard by him. Before he can answer, my phone starts ringing and it's the unknown number that's been texting me, so I let it go to voicemail. Suddenly, I'm very grateful that my voicemail inbox is full so I won't have to hear whatever nonsense he's going to say.

Ping.

"rlly?"

Silas slowly grabs my phone, giving me time to object and then turns my phone on silent and gingerly sets it on the ottoman. "I think that's the only thing to really do right now, Haze. He's already off-kilter and if he's drinking, I don't think anything good can come from entertaining him".

I nod, then sigh before scooting to sit as close as possible to Silas, forgetting about my least favorite ex… as my favorite one puts his arm around me. I try to relax, but it's a little hard when I'm wondering what else is going on with my phone. Silas doesn't react when I go up to my room to get into my "stash"- grabbing a joint and lighter. He turns his head as I come down the stairs and I see the quick flash of his eyes getting big before I say "Want to join me outside?" he pauses the movie and follows me out.

I light it and take a few quick puffs before handing it to him, not saying anything as I cough a few times. "I knew I smelled something coming from here every so often" he chuckles as he takes a big draw, I notice he doesn't cough as he hands it back to me.

Once we finish, we go back inside and this time, we lie down along my couch in a spooning position and continue the movie. I can tell Silas barely feels anything but I'm feeling as good as I can despite the situation, and my thoughts have finally quieted as much as they possibly can.

Later, I wake up to a dark screen asking if I'm still watching the TV and Silas's arm on my waist. I can tell from his breathing that he's peacefully asleep so I turn the TV off, and gently lift his arm off of me as I get up and head upstairs. Not looking back to see if he's awake, and not taking my phone with me because I want it as far away from me as possible.

When I get to my bed, I feel wide awake again. Trying different sleeping positions and breathing techniques eventually gets me to drift into a light, on and off sleep that only makes me irritated. After two hours, I give up and angrily get up and go back downstairs.

As quietly as possible, I walk back over to the couch to see if there is a way for me to lay around him without having to acknowledge that I wasn't able to sleep alone. While standing there, thinking, Silas raises his arm up with one eye cracked open, as an opening to come back to the same position we were in. I crawl over him until I am nestled into his chest with his arm around me.

He whispers "took you long enough" before he kisses my forehead. I know that I'm too awake right now, so I grab the remote from the ottoman and turn on a silly adult cartoon that helps me sleep. It takes me a few minutes to get my heart and breathing slow enough to feel tired, but I slowly start drifting back off to sleep as I see the beginning of dawn.

A few hours later, I wake up at a normal hour and look up to see Silas, wide awake and watching TV. "How long have you been awake?" I croak out, trying to keep my mouth (and morning breath) away from him.

"Since you got back" he says breezily, like he's not annoyed that I woke him up.

I feel my eyes get big and cover my mouth "Oh! I'm sorry if I kept you from sleeping".

He's quick to reassure me "Don't be- you didn't. I only need to sleep for a few hours a night, if that. So, this is normal for me".

A small smile is on his lips as he adds on "Usually, I try to be more productive... but I've been enjoying this". I smile into his chest as he kisses the top of my head, murmuring "But I better go to get ready for a date I have today". I sit up as he gets up and I brush my messy hair with my fingers in hopes that it doesn't look too crazy despite all of my tossing and turning. He's already grabbed his things "How much time do you need to get ready for the day?".

I tell him to come back in two hours and with a quick kiss on the lips he heads over to his house. I don't really need a full two hours getting ready but I hate feeling rushed, so I made sure I have a lot of time to get ready as slowly as I want.

I'd like to say I'm not nervous- especially with other matters at hand- but I admit to myself that I am. It's mostly excitement though, I built "old" Silas up so much in my head that I can't believe that I like his current self even more.

His confidence in himself and the world around him has grown so much despite it not always going his way, that it makes me feel more confident about today. I'm so excited, that I don't even look at my phone notifications, I just swipe them away for another time.

CHAPTER 36

Two hours later, and Silas is back at my door- right on time. I have no idea what he has planned but I wore a vintage mini dress with tights and combat boots. I also have a tote bag carrying a nice outfit in case we end up somewhere fancy. When I open the front door, Silas is wearing a white t-shirt, black boot cut jeans with boots…. and a backwards baseball hat. I know he remembers how irresistible I found him with a backwards hat and I realize he's going to make it very hard to reject him today.

He has an unreadable expression as he examines me walking towards him. When I get close, he turns me to see every angle of my outfit. "How many men are you trying to make me fight off?" he asks as his hands roam my body with a deep concentration. We hop in his sports car that I still don't know the make or model of- just that it's nice and shiny- and drive off.

Once we get on the main road, I ask "Where to first?".

His hand goes on my thigh like it's the most normal thing in the world before answering, "I figured we would need breakfast and coffee first".

15 minutes later, he pulls into a big- yet, packed- parking lot, and I see that it's a farmer's market. I look at him with excitement and he just

gives me a self-satisfied nod and smile before getting out and opening my car door for me. Walking, he's quick to gently grab my hand to hold as we make our way to the entrance. I give in and enjoy the familiarity as I hear him say "I know time changes everything, but I figured I still know exactly what you like".

"Free samples?" I ask.

"Free samples." he confirms, as our footsteps pick up the pace just a little. Within an hour, I've had too many free samples, while Silas bought us coffee, a farm-fresh bouquet of dahlias, artisanal beaded earrings… and a tote bag of many other things that he insisted on buying me. I fought him every time he paid, but he would either beat me to it or tell the people working the stands to not accept my card- which they always listened to.

Always the type to enjoy contact, Silas always found a way to keep our bodies close- whether it was by holding hands or having his arm around me. "Making up for lost time" he said with a wink, the first time he put his arm around my waist as we meandered through the crowd. He held our shared bag as we slowly walked and I actually saw a few clients that I've made items for. I chatted with them while Silas patiently waited. He had to take a few business calls and when he was finally distracted, I bought myself a nice bottle of wine to open when I officially finish the huge order with Silas.

When he noticed, he looked annoyed before he turned back to buy two. I laughed and rolled my eyes at his pettiness but it put a satisfied smile on his face so I got over it. Once our bags were full of goodies, Silas led me a few blocks over to a modern-looking breakfast place with outdoor seating and a perfect spot in the shade. Pulling out my chair, I'm surprised when he sits right next to me rather than across from me. I look at him in confusion but he doesn't indulge, he just says "Order whatever you want".

We used to sit next to each other at restaurants all the time but I feel a little embarrassed to look this cheesy in my mid-twenties.

"I'm paying for myself" I say proudly. At his hurt expression, I add "You bought me enough at the farmer's market. Thank you for that, by the way".

His arm is on the back of my chair and he leans in so others don't hear him "I don't want to sound like a huge ass…. But let me pay for today. I promise I can afford it".

At my puzzled look he smiles and adds "I've actually been saving money living in this small house, I was living somewhere much more expensive before… don't worry about my financials. Please".

He looks so serious and almost annoyed that I accept but then add "I just don't want you to spend all this effort and money on me… or risk making you mad if I end up not wanting to be something together. And… I don't want to feel like I owe you when you've been so sweet to me" he leans away to look at me straight on with the most disgusted, yet somehow, handsome face.

He quietly says "Ew- what kind of guys have

you been dating? 'Owe me'? Even if you don't want to date me, please don't ever date a guy like that" he shivers and looks at his menu for what he wants. I let out a small laugh and think about how I've never even thought about how weird that is. The waitress comes by a minute later and we order quickly, handing her the menus and thanking her. He looks back over to me "Thank you, Haze. Let's have fun today- you've got enough going on. I want to enjoy our first date".

He looks at me with an expression of waiting for me to agree, which I do, before giving a huge smile and changing topics. We talk for awhile before the food comes and once it does, we fixate on eating the delicious food, taking turns trying each other's orders. I wonder to myself if we would always be able to at least be friends and… I think we could.

I know that he would probably always want more and I think I would too- but if our past is too hard to get over, I hope he will always be in my life one way or another. After a few minutes, I remember a question I've been meaning to ask.

"Hey, Silas?", he looks up at me and swallows his food "Yeah?".

"How DID you end up being my neighbor? I'm assuming this isn't a coincidence" I used my finger to gesture in between the two of us. We've kind of talked about it before, but today I want a real, thorough answer.

His forest-green eyes take me in for a moment, a soft expression on his face when he answers "My dad saw you and him… he said there was a bruise". I see the muscle in his jaw twitch "I looked into Brandon and he has previous records of that type of history with other woman so this was the only thing I could think of".

I raise one eyebrow and he adds "Well… I'm sure I could have thought of other options- but I may have had a selfish reason to get this involved".

All of a sudden, his grin looks rather devious. I reply "So, your parents knew you were alive? And they didn't think to tell me?".

His face turns contemplative as he answers "I asked them not to because we all agreed it's probably best… but once my dad saw the bruises, the plan changed. They loved you Hazel, and they still do. They weren't going to watch while something happened to you".

"So… there was no motivated seller?".

"Oh, there was a very motivated seller- me." he looks way too proud of himself.

"And Sebastian?" I ask.

"He's a very good friend and business partner…" he answers before looking down at his watch.

Looking back at me, he says "You can ask as many question as you want, but we have an appointment in 2 hours. Do you want to wander around a bit before then? There are some stores nearby that you'll like". I don't even question the appointment- Silas quickly pays and we leave and go around the corner.

When I walk hand-in-hand with Silas the two blocks over to the next stop, I realize I've been missing a lot by not checking this area out sooner.

It's a big downtown area- full of different shops and restaurants that could occupy me for days. We meander through a bakery for some treats, a small vintage thrift store and a secondhand bookstore. I see even more stores on the other side of the street that I make a mental note to come back for.

After almost two hours, we head back to Silas's car to drive to the appointment he mentioned. I gave up on questioning him on what it is, wanting to enjoy a good surprise for once. When we park, I see the sign "Downtown Day Spa" and look over at him with skeptical eyes. He puts his hand on my knee, using a soothing voice "I know you need a massage, Haze. And I want one too, don't be selfish and deprive me of this".

I roll my eyes, unable to hold in my smile as he stops me to run around the car and open the door for me. When I get in, the manager greets us and walks us over to a room with two tables and I quickly give Silas a look that says "Really?" and he smiles and shrugs. The manager lets us set our items down and takes us to the men and women's areas for showers, giving us robes and slippers. We are given 20 minutes to individually shower and get settled in the room. When I get in, Silas is already done and face down on the table. He is clearly naked with a sheet covering his bottom half.

Since he's not looking, I take a second to myself to enjoy his defined muscles on his back that lead up to the definition in his arms and the veins in his tattooed hands. His tattoos cover most of what is visible to me, and I think I could spend all day admiring the art… and apparently the canvas, too. I hate myself for the jealousy I instantly feel when I imagine our massage therapist liking what she feels and, but I try to push that feeling down as much as possible.

I go over to my table and begin to slip my robe off, loudly whispering "Don't look".

He keeps his head in the same place but mumbles "I'm keeping my head down... but I noticed your ass got bigger and you can't stop me from imagining it. I don't even think I can stop that". I quietly gasp in horror at his apparent observational skills... he acts so innocent and unaware that I wonder what else he's been thinking.

As I get under the covers, I briefly wonder what else on him has a changed and gotten bigger. I immediately try to get that thought out of my head and am grateful that the massage therapists choose right then to knock and enter the room. The next hour goes by entirely too fast and I make the mental decision to make massages a monthly priority. Silas is right, I really did need this. When we leave, I think that I genuinely feel relaxed for the first time in years. I also know that part of it is because I feel safe... and that's all because of Silas.

He grabs my hand and takes me to a fun bar nearby, and we each pick a drink that looks like it belongs on social media. I quickly text Carly to ask if she wants to come here sometime- I already know she would love something like this. We're sitting at a high-top table and I look down at my feet, seeing them interlocked like zippers with Silas's.

He's apologizing before looking back at his phone, replying to a business email really quick before setting it down and forgetting about it. As our drinks empty, he leans in with a serious face and says quietly "Today… I want you to pretend we just met. I don't want you to like this date because of our past, but as if you just met me and because we are actually currently hitting it off. Okay?".

I nod and ask "So how am I doing then? Is this a good first date?".

I hear the joy in my voice that I've grown to miss before he answers with complete sincerity "I would be completely satisfied doing this for the rest of my life. I think this is the best day I've ever had".

I raise my eyebrows in surprise and he just stares back in earnestness. "I agree that this is a great day, but…" his eyes widen a little at whatever I'm about to say. Which is: "I'm kind of getting hungry". I'm not sure if I should be embarrassed since we ate (a lot) about four hours ago, but I don't really care.

He chuckles and says "We have one more stop and then we are getting dinner, don't get grumpy yet". We end up at a furniture store.

Since he didn't explain anything, I just look at him, confused, until he explains "Please pick out a new patio set. You never look comfortable on that other one and it stresses me out". I laugh but since he's offering, I walk off towards the area with outdoor signage and sit on different chairs to see what's more comfortable. Less than an hour later, we are walking out with a with a delivery date set for a week later, and the cost being more than any of my furniture. Combined.

I picked out a comfortable set that a small

group could sit at, but the chairs also lean back for when I'm alone, reading. "Are you just trying to flex, or are you really this comfortable financially? This seems like a pretty big gift for a 'first date'". I hear the suspicion in my voice but can't help it. I don't know how to openly accept this much from someone.

He was always generous, but in college we barely had any money so it was nothing compared to what this is like. He gets more annoyed every time I ask. Silas sighs and answers "If it will make you ask less, let me just say it like this: If you knew how comfortable I was, you wouldn't hesitate letting me pay for everything". He opens the car door open for me and as I get in, I say "Well jeez, no need to brag". He barks out a laugh and walks around to get in the driver's seat.

When he's in, he says "You can even order soda at the restaurant if you want" before driving out of the parking lot. I ask him if we can stop at a gas station on the way there so I can change into an outfit I brought for dinner and he finds one on the way. I change into heels, with a navy mini skirt and a matching navy blazer that both reach the same length on my upper-thigh, and a black mock-neck top.

Silas wet his hair to get rid of his hat-hair and is now donning the perfectly tousled hair. I get in the car and when I look at him, he looks at me like we aren't going to make it to the restaurant. His hand traces my bare thigh as he's staring at it, in concentration with his now-familiar dilated eyes. I make a throat-clearing noise to bring him back to the real world and he snaps his head back up to look at me.

He just mutters "I like your outfit" before driving off, a little dazed. I feel a small smile on my face as I know he really likes my outfit, and isn't just flattering me. We pull up to a very fancy looking sushi restaurant, with the valet taking Silas's car as we walk inside. Before he lets go of my hand, he squeezes twice it just like he did when we were in college. I remember he told me that his mom always did that when he was a little kid and I smile that the habit hasn't died.

The exterior was minimal and modern looking, but the inside has a warmer vibe with tones of red, dim lights. Out of habit, I immediately look at the menu for prices but then decide if he's not worried about the cost of food then neither am I… also the menu doesn't have prices so that made it easy. Our waiter comes by to give us some waters and take drink orders. We both order cocktails before Silas orders a few appetizers to share. I look at the menu memorizing my order to tell the waiter, when I try to covertly spy at Silas- only to see that he's already staring at me.

We stare at each other for a few seconds and I watch as his face slips into a smile, and feel my own face match. I lose the staring contest, like always, and shyly look down at the menu to get my thoughts in order. I set the menu on the table just as the waiter comes back with our drinks and appetizers, then takes our food orders and menus. Silas seems content to keep looking at me and in my nervousness of being watched, I blurt out the first thing that comes to mind.

"So… I noticed your canine teeth are now slightly longer than the rest. Does that go along with the other changes?". His tongue dashes out to feel along his teeth and canines- I try not to react at how sexy that sight is- before he answers "I guess so… I haven't really noticed to be honest".

"You haven't noticed that biting things got easier?" I start to laugh at my own dumb joke but stop when he grabs my finger. I watch in shock as he presses my finger lightly to his canine and looks at me with a questioning look.

"Ow!" I pull my hand back and look for blood and see a little dot. Like a needle made the prick of blood. Faster than I can react, he grabs my hand again and licks the blood before I jerk my hand back in shock, while he wears a satisfied smile and his eyes look almost black.

I try to grab his hand but he moves too quick and I whisper-yell "Give me your hand!" turning into a 5-year-old and wanting my finger-biting revenge.

He laughs and whispers back "So vengeful! I'll put my fingers in your mouth later- the waiter's coming back over".

I think he's just saying that to get me to stop but then the waiter is right there with our food. When he leaves, I just say "I'm changing the subject, but you owe me blood. What are we doing after this?".

He says in a very business-like tone "Well… we have to get dessert obviously" and I quickly confirm "Obviously".

Then, I wait for him to add "and after that... is up to you- we can keep entertaining ourselves or we can go to my place or yours and relax… find a movie, whatever you want."

"I like the way you think" I smile at him before looking at our plates with Christmas-morning joy.

It looks like something from a magazine. Fresh cuts of different fishes with mixes of sauces and fruits or other additions mixed throughout. I have to stifle an embarrassing reaction when I take a bite- It's absolutely the best thing I've ever eaten.

Silas watches me carefully before seemingly being pleased by my reaction and taking a few bites himself. I don't want to make him feel too confident, but this is the best date I've ever been on. It feels like the newness of our early dates but the comfort of knowing someone a long time.

I love that he's still the most attentive date and always finds a way to either have our feet or hands touching and doesn't seem like he wants to be anywhere else.

As our plates are being cleared, Silas goes to the bathroom to wash his hands. I jump at the sound of my phone ringing. When I take my phone out of my purse to look, I see it's from an unknown number.

Brandon.

CHAPTER 37

Once the ringing has finally stopped, I receive a text: "*Hazel, I'm here*". I look around in a panic before realizing he probably means my house, so when he calls again, I answer.

"Hello?" I ask in a cautious voice, wanting him to lead the conversation. He's full of energy, using a loud, quick voice "Hey, It's me. I'm here and I wanna talk to you". At the same time, I get a notification from my ring app that confirms he is in front of my door, but I don't tell him that.

My car is out front, so he obviously thinks I'm home, but I can't tell him that I'm out with someone, or on a date.

"Brandon, I'm not home right now- I don't feel comfortable talking to you in person, can you please leave before I call the cops?".

He sighs impatiently "Don't call the fucking cops, I want to talk to YOU. Wherever you're at- come back to your house so we can talk in person".

His speech pattern sounds a little different and I realize he's most likely not sober. "You broke into my house, you can't be coming over. I'm sorry but if you want to talk, we can't do it in person".

I am immediately annoyed with myself for apologizing but I'm doing whatever I can to keep him calm. I realize Silas is walking over and he sits down with full attention on my conversation, with a face in concentration. I make a move to stand up, but Silas shakes his head and I sit back down- he wants to listen. I'm tired of doing this on my own, so I stay where I am. I missed a few seconds of Brandon's tirade- I must have missed something because now he's yelling "WHERE ARE YOU?".

I try to calm him down but I can hear him banging on my front door in the background. "Brandon, I'm calling the cops. You need to leave right now, they already have a case opened".

He's silent for a second- besides his loud panting- but then he says "You're threatening ME?". I watch as Silas gets up with his phone to his ear and steps a few feet away. I can barely hear him talking to the police, telling them of Brandon being at my house and being very aggressive.

Brandon is screaming something but I can't even make out what he's trying to say, so I interject "I'm out at dinner right now, the cops are on the way and you need to hang up, Okay?".

I realize I'm talking to him like a little kid. Silas is off the phone with the cops before he walks over to me, calmly and quietly saying "Hand me the phone".

I know that won't go well so I whisper "What? No!" hoping this situation can de-escalate before my neighbors hate me for this trashy scene.

"Who are you talking to?" Brandon sounds very sober now which is even more terrifying. "Oh. So that's what's going on. A date?" -suddenly, my phone is now out of my hands and in Silas's.

Too quickly, he grabbed my phone and brought it to his ear- I give him a shocked but angry look because I know this won't make it better. Luckily, the waiter is busy and no one seems like they can hear us- we are talking very quiet but I still feel embarrassed. I'm clearly upset at this and he doesn't seem like he's enjoying this anymore than me, but he continues to listen as Brandon still thinks he's telling me off.

After a moment of listening and looking more and more angry, I can tell he is trying to keep his voice down as he says "Hey, Brandon. It's time to hang up- and you really need to stop scaring Hazel". A few seconds go by of me trying to listening to Brandon say something and Silas clearly answering a question. "It's none of your business, and it's time for this conversation to end because the cops are on the way. Just leave".

Brandon hangs up and I quickly grab my phone back to check the camera. He angrily hits my door several times before walking and stumbling off angrily. I look up at Silas "What the fuck? Was that supposed to help? He's even more pissed". Silas, however, is too calm for my liking and I want to yell at him until he apologizes, which he doesn't.

"He was only faking his pleasantness in the beginning to sweeten you up- don't fall for that shit". He puts his hand out across the table in hopes that I will hold it, but I keep mine under the table. He has the nerve to look surprised and then a little hurt.

"Well, whatever he was going to do, he's definitely going to do it now. Thanks for the help,

Silas". I start looking at the restaurant's exit to gauge if I could and should just get up and go figure out a ride home.

Silas gets my attention by saying my name and then says "If you really think I'd let anything happen to you then you aren't thinking clearly enough to get a ride home". He's only making me more annoyed so I look at my phone to check the cameras for anything but since there's nothing happening, I turn the ringer on my phone up. If Brandon is feeling brave and crazy, then I want to know what he's thinking if he calls.

"You shouldn't have grabbed my phone or talked to him, I wasn't thinking clearly and now I have an entirely new problem".

Silas gets a dark look on his face but takes a second to calm himself before saying "You're right. I'm sorry for involving myself and I won't ever grab your phone from you again. But, how can this situation get worse?". He leans in a bit to talk even quieter "He's already been showing up at your house with guns- knowing there is another man around will at least show him that you're not completely alone".

I think it over and Silas has a point so I just take a deep breath to calm myself. I hear the apology in Silas's voice when he leans in to hold my hand "Don't let that jackass ruin anything- we are having a great time and I will keep you safe. The rest doesn't matter right now... but I did call the cops so we should probably start heading there soon". We flag our waiter down to get the check and he quickly walks to the back to get that for us.

As we wait, Silas tries to reassure me since I'm obviously stressed. "It will be fine, nothing is going to happen that wasn't going to anyways".

He's right, but I still say "I know, I know. Thank you for trying to help but I also don't want to feel weak, hiding behind one guy just to get away from another".

He thinks about it for a moment and says "I get that… but there's also way too many men that don't stop their shit until there is another man to worry about'.

'Take advantage of the fact that there's a very hard to kill man living next to you and protecting you" he ends with a small grin… I guess he's right.

"Okay, fine. But just so we are clear I am not defenseless". His eyebrows go up in response.

"Oh, without a doubt, Haze. I have no doubt you can handle this entire situation on your own. But if he focuses his crazy eyes on me instead of you now- so be it".

My eyes start to water at the reassurance, so I focus on the waiter who is making his way back- empty handed. I look at Silas, who is also staring at the waiter in confusion. "Sir, my boss recognized you and insists the meal is on the house". Silas stares at him for another second before nodding and thanking the man who wanders back off.

Now I'm staring at Silas, waiting for an answer as he turns to me and shrugs "The owner is a commercial client of mine, he's been wanting me to check this place out but I didn't have a date. Thank you, Hazey". We get up to leave and when I look back at the table to make sure I didn't forget anything, Silas already put enough cash down as a tip that's at least double the cost of our meal.

When we get the car on the highway, I get a notification on my phone of a motion alert so I go to check- it's the police. We told them we weren't home so they are looking into the windows and the backyard to make sure Brandon is absolutely gone. I have enough proof of harassment to get a restraining order so I put in my notes app to do that first thing Monday morning.

About twenty minutes after they leave, I get another motion alert and at this point I'm more annoyed than anything. I look and it's Brandon- he's more like a mosquito than a man at this point. He must have noticed the cops left. He's quicker and more purposeful this time, unlocking my door and getting into my house like it's the easiest thing in the world. We are still ten minutes away so I call the cops again and tell him that he's back and now officially inside my house so they send out a squad car.

My hands get too shaky to hold my phone by the time we hang up. I notice with hazy vision that Silas is pulling his car over to the side of the road. My phone still has the live feed of my camera going, so Silas very gently asks "Can I hold this so we can watch?". I don't have a voice right now so I quickly nod. After less than five minutes total, Brandon is back out and quickly walking to his car, driving off. The cops get there a few minutes later when he's already gone. I realize that I'm having trouble breathing.

So, without really thinking, I'm urgently feeling for the door handle to get out. "Hazel, what are you do-". Before he can finish asking, I fling the door open and get out, quickly walking to the tree line for privacy. In the few steps it takes to get there, I hold my panic attack in as much as possible until I can get into the cover of the foliage before I completely shatter. Space, I just need some space for a few minutes to get my breath under control. Then, I'll be fine.

Once I confirm that no one can see me from the road, I put my hands on my knees and bend over to hyperventilate and focus on getting breathes in a steady rhythm. I begin to cry as I go into a kneeling position with my face in my hands. After a few moments, I hear slow steps coming from behind me.

Silas didn't know me when I had panic attacks- they came shortly after he left, so I can tell he's trying to figure out what to do. I don't have them often but I know I usually just need space and to focus on my breathing, so that's what I concentrate on. I hear him crouch down next to me and put a soft hand on my back, moving it up and down.

I try to focus on that sensation and feel my crying getting under control. When he starts saying comforting words "You're okay", "Just breathe in and out" I turn and push him with all of the pent-up energy in my body. He falls backwards on his hands- a shocked and hurt look on his face that switches to confusion after a second.

"This is YOUR fault! You just had to

intervene. Look what a good job of 'protecting' you've done!" I scream.

Silas calmly gets up and says "I'm sorry. When we get back, I'll go in first but all that matters is that you weren't home. Because you were safe with me".

He starts to step towards me so I push him again "Get away from me!". He doesn't budge but I keep pushing him and swearing at him- I've officially lost my mind, I don't feel in control of myself at all.

He looks at me with hurt and confusion before swearing and rushing me in a hug which I try to fight off. "Breathe, Hazel. Breathe in and out slowly". I stop yelling and fighting him, my hands reaching around him and fisting his jacket while I sob into his shirt until my breathing regulates. I keep thinking about what would have happened if I was at my house like Brandon thought I was and what he could have done.

I'm also seeing his escalation first-hand, and him crossing boundaries I wasn't as worried about before. Even if Silas is my neighbor, at the end of the day, I'm alone. When I calm down, I notice Silas is gently swaying back and forth kissing the top of my head. He's humming our song, so I take a few extra minutes to just let what he's doing work and enjoy the calming moment. "It really is going to be okay, Hazel. I don't care if I need to be attached to your hip until he's gone."

I just nod and quietly say "I'm sorry" into his chest.

"No you're not. Because you don't need to

be. Let's get back in the car and get warmed up, okay?". Before I can answer, he picks me up and carries me to the car, setting me on the passenger side and buckling me in. I've never felt more like a toddler than I have in the last 20 minutes but this completes it.

As Silas gets on the highway, he breaks the silence "Was this your first panic attack?".

"No, but they don't happen often" I can hear the exhaustion in my voice.

"When did they start?" he asks. I notice rain starting to patter on his windshield before he turns his wipers on. Waiting a moment, I debate on telling him something less pathetic before I end up sighing and just telling him the truth.

"When we were looking for you".

The silence drags for a moment before I hear Silas say "I should've just taken you with me". It sounds like he was saying it more to himself than me so I just let the statement go, but I think about what it could have been like.

CHAPTER 38

When we get back to my house, it doesn't look like anything happened. We talk to the remaining cop that is at my house, confirming that nothing looks out of place and that no one is in the house. I show them the video and they finally believe that this situation is as big of a deal as I've been thinking it was. They tell me to call them if I see or hear from him again as he will definitely be arrested.

When they leave, Silas does another check throughout the house and confirms nothing and no one is inside my house. He suggests I put on some comfy clothes and when I come back downstairs in sweats, he has a hot cup of tea and an edible waiting for me. He has a sheepish smile when I raise my eyebrows at the random assortment.

"I couldn't think of anything else to help relax you" I chuckle at that, and take the tea but leave the edible- I don't want to risk any anxious thoughts tonight. I look at him in hopes that he can feel my sincerity as I say "Sorry the date ended so badly, you put so much thought into it and it really was amazing".

Silas guides me over to the couch and says as we get settled in "No apologies, you were an awesome date. I hope you know that no matter what either of us did, he was going to find a reason to freak out".

I think about it and agree with a sigh "You're probably right… but let's stop talking about him, he's had enough airtime for one day". He just smiles as he puts his arm around me, pulling me in with a kiss on the cheek "Remember that time when we were on that road trip and my tire went out?".

I feel the smile on my face recalling the memory and add "and then I changed the tire on the side of the road because you didn't know how?". Afterward, His dad swore that he taught him how to, but Silas insists he never did.

He sighs "You were wearing this cute sundress and sandals, changing a tire on the side of some road in the middle of nowhere. And then the most intimidating biker shows up out of nowhere, asking if you need help".

I remember the look on Silas's face as he saw Rod saunter over "Yeah and you looked so embarrassed that I said 'no' just to save us both". I can't stop laughing at this memory of us that's embarrassing for the both of us.

Silas looks serious again "I know how to change a tire now. Why didn't you tell me it's so easy?".

I quickly reply "Well you could have watched me!". He's looking off in thought "I was honestly too embarrassed to watch you, I just wanted it over as soon as possible, I went home that night and spent an hour online making sure that it would never happen to me again".

"I'm sure that you felt like an absolute moronic, useless, beta-".

Silas barks out a loud laugh "Jesus! It sounds like you thought that. I'm comfortable with my masculinity, thank you".

I laugh at his offense and reply "Anyways…. It made me feel really good at my own skills. But I am happy you know how to change your tires now. If you need me to install any shelving into your house, let me know".

He barks out a laugh, and then says "I need you to get to know matured, experienced Silas. Do you think this house was like this when I bought it?". I'm shocked by the idea that he worked on this house before I got it… and that he did it for me.

"You did work on it?".

"Well… Okay I had a team work on the bigger projects like making the bathrooms and patios better, but the security features were me".

It all makes sense now, and I hear the surprise in my voice "Wow… I didn't realize. I just thought the past owner were security nuts".

His focus moves away in thought as he remembers "No… They also had dumb landscaping so I had that redone as well. BUT, just so you know… If you need shelving added I can absolutely do that all by myself" he finishes with a proud wink. I start thinking about that balcony outside of my room that looked newer than the house and look at him with skeptical eyes "My bedroom balcony…." he just looks at me, waiting for me to get it out.

"Was that your addition?" I ask.

"Of course, Haze. I don't know why you were always so fixated on a second story balcony- you never even talked about getting a house, but always talked about a bedroom balcony. So, I figured if that didn't get you, then nothing would".

I can feel myself staring at him in awe before looking down for a minute so that I don't say anything stupid or hand him my heart on a platter. Instead, I tell him what I want to do with the ever-so-important balcony. The furniture I want to get to make it cozy, ending the day with a book and the view of the sunset, and maybe even filling it with plants.

He gives me some advice and promises to help me make my "balcony dreams come true". And I can't wait... I might even share the space with him sometimes. The next hour flies by with Silas showing me pictures of what the house looked like before he worked on it and it looks like a totally different house. The old carpet is gone, the old wood cabinets have been replaced, even the ugly-colored walls have been painted over.

I don't feel like acknowledging it, but he basically gave me this house for free- or the least amount possible before I would consider it too suspicious. "Well, if real estate doesn't work out for you, I think you have a knack for interior design".

I get quiet when I see his awkward expression so I ask "What?".

After a second of staring at me, Silas says "Your Pinterest board is public. Everything else was just filling in the gaps, or seeing related posts". The sentence just hangs there as I stare at him with an open mouth.

I try to remember my other boards and if I've shared anything else that could potentially be extremely embarrassing. He leans in with barely concealed laughter "Way to toot your own horn". Later that night, Silas and I are both on edge as we get settled for the night. He's made several laps outside and around the front street just to make sure that nothing seems odd. He also goes around the house and double checks the doors and windows before telling me we are fine. I've been checking my phone every couple of minutes, wondering if Brandon will try to confront me again. Almost hoping for it so that I can know where he is.

When Silas finally sits down in the armchair, I can see the frustration in his eyes. I'm standing a few feet away when he asks "Do you want me to get you a hotel for a bit? I can stay here to keep on eye on things but maybe that will help you feel better". I need to face this head on or he's always going to be following me somewhere. I take the few steps over to him to sit on his lap and look up at him.

I notice the brief second of surprise but don't mention it "I already moved states. I'm not going to stay in a hotel too… but thank you".

I cuddle into his chest, inhaling his scent that's somehow always calmed me down as he puts his arm around me. After a few minutes of a relaxed silence, I ask "Can we fall sleep to a dumb cartoon in my bed?". Instead of answering, he gets up with me in his arms- and carries me up to my bed. He drops me there and goes around the house to turn of lights and check on things one last time.

When he's back upstairs, we go to the bathroom to get ready for bed together. I tell him I need to change so he exits the bathroom to do the same and I hear him lay down on my bed. Silas said he didn't want to be a rebound… but would he believe me if I said he wasn't? I know I wouldn't be using him to get over Brandon, I've been over him before I even knew Silas was still alive. And where we are at right now isn't because of our past. If I met a completely new man who was this sweet, patient and I had this chemistry with- I would want to do the same things to him.

If Brandon never called me today, I don't have any doubts where we would have ended up tonight. I don't want to let a crazy narcissist ruin our mood for the evening… and I don't think I'm going to. I go to the cabinet in my bathroom that has a small bag with a new outfit I bought.

I picked it out because it's not so over-the-top that it will make me feel embarrassed to walk out in, but it's still very sexy. Tiny, loose satin shorts and a matching loose-cropped tank, both in light pink and white lace. The outfit is still pretty tame that if Silas did reject me, I could still wear it to sleep… but I don't think he will. Because I happen to know that light pink is his favorite color on me.

When I walk out, Silas has changed into soft shorts and a loose tank top that shows off his oblique muscles, while donning a relaxed look that goes hungry in an instant. He must have suspected what I was up to because he wasn't laying down for sleep, but sitting on the bed and facing the bathroom, leaning back on his hands. His feet are on the ground and he opens his legs as I walk over to him to step in between them.

A raspy voice that I haven't heard in awhile comes out of my mouth "How can I prove to you that you're not a rebound?".

He's looking at his hand as he trails the back of his tattooed knuckle from the bottom of my torso upwards "You're doing a pretty good job of it right now". When he finally looks up and I see his dilated pupils, he says "I hope you remember our conversation. This isn't a hook up to me, so I'm understanding this as us actually trying for something real". His eyes flash back and forth between mine waiting for an answer.

When I nod, his control snaps and his hand is on my ass in an instant, lifting me up to crawl backwards on the bad until he's flat on his back, and I'm above him- straddling him. He's strong enough to make moving me look effortless- like I'm a doll. It only takes me a second to get readjusted to our new position. He looks at me in awe as I look over him but before I get carried away, I say "Thank you for the date, it felt like an amazing start to a new beginning".

He looks away, towards my body to slide his hands up my thighs until they rest at my hips. "Except for the loser ex part, that's the best time I've had in three years. I should be thanking you". He gently squeezes and I look down at the contrast of our bodies, his almost completely covered, and mine almost completely bare. He sits up and our torsos are aligned as I trail kisses up his neck to whisper "Do you have a condom?".

He leans back a little to get a better look at my face "No… I can go to the store? I do want to let you know that I'm clean".

Our noses are barely touching and I say "I am too… and I'm on birth control".

He gets a little more serious "If you want me to stop or slow anything down… you know you can just tell me, right? I'm more than happy to stop anything you don't like".

I just nod again- I think we're both beyond talking anymore at this point so I lean into him and we begin to kiss. He's being slow and gentle and I wonder if he's worried about hurting me, so I go along with the speed he sets. I want to be a passenger- an observer to him and what he does- and what he wants to do. I know I trust him, and I know how good he was when we were younger, so I can only imagine what he's capable of making me feel like now.

My body begins to move with a mind of its own, little slow movements to guarantee more friction and pressure between us. I hear a groan in the back of his throat has he uses his hands on my hips to add even more pressure. I feel how hard he is but I try to concentrate on his tongue and lips as they go from mirroring my movements to gently biting. I suck on his tongue, enjoying the loud noise that he makes before he uses an arm to hold me as we flip over, leaving him on top.

He looks feral… and I'm intimidated in the best way. I forgot how good it feels to be nervous with someone I trust, knowing that I'll be okay but that I'll still enjoy the journey. He leans back down to kiss me much more aggressively as we take turns kissing each other's necks, lips and ears- and I feel a quick pain on the side of my neck. He must have accidentally bit a little too hard and draws a prick of blood, and when he looks at me, his eyes are almost black and glazed over.

Propped on his elbows, trailing his nose down my throat, I'm in awe as he goes back to licking the same spot that was just bleeding for a second and he seems… vacant. He's so entranced that I now understand what he means by it being a high- he's in complete, calm bliss. As he moves his lips back and forth over my neck, humming, I get a brief flash of fear that he will take a life-changing bite. I give into the thought… maybe that wouldn't be so bad.

I can hear the moans I'm making but I don't have the focus to be embarrassed about it, or about rocking against his thigh that's interlocked with my own. He moves his head to look down at my movements, and I see that my shorts are completely soaked through- and I know he does too, because he gently starts to trace a finger along the inseam. His rugged hands against the soft pink satin is one of the sexiest things I've ever seen.

He looks back up at me and he looks lucid again, but there's a wolfish look in his eyes that tell me I'm about to be devoured. Silas sits up, removing the pressure and puts both of his hands on my hips, his thumbs going into the indents of my hips that I've always loved. He observes me with a slightly tilted head as he moves my left leg to his side so that he's in between both thighs. He leans over me to take off my tank top and I help him take it off along with his next.

Silas suddenly gets a wicked look in his eyes and picks me up, carrying me over and placing me in front of my full-length mirror. I'm confused why, until he stands behind me as we look at ourselves in the mirror, him towering over me. He pushes my shorts down and bends me over so my hands are propped against the wall on either side of the mirror before he kneels down behind me. I watch in the mirror as his large, tattooed hands grab my ankles and gently pulls my right ankle farther apart, separating my legs.

Then, his hands are on my hips to shove his face in between my thighs from the back, licking and kissing everywhere his tongue can reach, focusing on my pussy. I have nothing to do but stare at myself in the mirror, seeing what my face looks like in complete pleasure, but before I can climax- he stops. Too quickly, he stands back up behind me.

Our eyes lock as he kisses me neck, reaching his right hand around to press two fingers into me and slowly begins to slide in and out. I'm completely bare, but I'm in too much ecstasy to care or to over-analyze the sight. I notice a smirk on his face as I let out a loud gasp that morphs into a groan as he uses his thumb on my clit.

My patience has run out so I reach around to pull his shorts down, watching as they fall on the floor in the mirror. I feel his dick spring up and nudges up against me and I try to maneuver in an effort to push it inside me. He just shakes his head in a scolding gesture. I can't believe it… but every body part grew, not just his height. It was already big before so I want nothing more than to feel it inside me. As I feel myself close to an orgasm again, he spins me around and picks me up. Oh… he's edging me on purpose.

He stalks back over to the bed and throws me down on my back, and I look up at him expectantly. The familiar man before me looks like a full-on predator now and as he climbs over to me, it feels like I'm being hunted. His face is focused and serious, like he's in his own little world and enjoying every minute of it. I watch as he grabs my thighs and spreads them as wide as possible, getting into position so our cores are almost aligned.

He grabs his thick length in his hands and gently presses against my entrance. As wet as I am, it's still going to take a second to adjust- I've never been with anyone this big before and his width is the most delicious pain I could imagine. I grab his forearms for more stability as he begins to create a rhythm of slowly pushing in and then sliding out, adding a little more every time until he's all the way in.

As I begin moving my body to match his pace, Silas uses one arm to steady himself and one arm to lift my ass up, making me gasp for air as he starts going faster. His eyes flash from my face, to all over my body, like he can't decide where to look first. He moves his hand that's holding me up, to stick his middle finger in my mouth which I hungrily accept and begin to suck on. He takes it out too soon and goes back to lifting my ass up, but now I feel the same finger shoving into my ass. I pull him down so I can bite his neck as I feel the pressure mounting. Hearing him moan too makes me finally erupt in a wave of pleasure so intense, I feel like I'm blacking out.

He keeps a slow rhythm until I'm back down, pulling his finger out. I quickly recover while he covers me in kisses and his pace slows down. Biting my shoulder, I can swear he's bitten hard enough to break skin, so I ease the pressure by digging my nails into his back. My nails don't seem to bother him even though I think they are also breaking skin. That might be because now he's slowly licking my shoulder while keeping the same rapid pace. He already told me that he would have to bite HARD for it to risk changing me, so I enjoy the tingling pain without worries.

I hear him whisper "Fuck" before he aggressively bites the mattress, needing something to really sink his teeth into- before I push to turn us over so I can be on top. He quickly helps me, so I set the pace as he watches and covers my breasts with his hands, softly touching them. He sits up, sucking on my nipples until I feel myself on the verge again. He slightly picks up the pace and I can tell he's close too. I notice a little vein in his neck when he asks "Do you want me to pull out?".

I speed up my pace and say "Not at all" and that makes us both lose control. He grabs my hips and uses his strength to add more pressure, before we are both over the edge, moaning into each other's necks.

We sit in that position for a couple of minutes, breathing heavy, before he picks me up and carries me to the bathroom so we can clean up. We take a quick shower and fall back into bed, cuddling with a new intensity.

A few hours later, I woke up in the middle of the night to Silas's arms around me, feeling like something was off. I don't know what it is, but I put on a pair of underwear and a shirt Silas left here a few days ago. Using the bathroom, I walk back to my bed but stop at the porch door to look out over the back yard- everything is still and quiet.

Once I am closer to the bed, I can tell Silas is awake but he's just quietly watching me with a small smile when he notices his shirt on me. Without saying anything, he wraps me in his arms and cuddles his face into my neck and I fall asleep a few minutes later.

CHAPTER 39

I wake up to Silas trying to disentangle himself from our entwined sleeping position. When we make eye contact and he has confirmation that I'm also awake, he smiles softly. Kissing my forehead, he whispers "I'll be back in 10 minutes with some coffees".

I just make a sleepy agreeing mumble that he chuckles at before getting dressed and quietly walking out. It looks to be pretty early, I guess around 8am, but I don't feel like checking my phone so I just nestle more into bed to wait until he gets back. My thoughts go back and forth about last night- wondering if we made a mistake and moved to soon, but also being too curious and excited to stop. It feels so good having genuine excitement again and I want to savor it as much as possible but I don't want to ruin anything before it actually begins by getting too excited.

Right now, it's impossible for me to feel any sort of regret about last night, or the date. He's made it clear that he feels like he missed out on me just as much as I felt I missed out on him these last few years. I feel the unstoppable smile on my face thinking about all of the ways he's made me feel like he's taking "us" seriously. I put my worries to the side. I've dreamed about him coming back for so long- now that it's coming true, I don't want to waste it.

He only left five minutes ago, so I'm surprised when I hear a noise. Before I realize its coming from my back door. Not knowing why he would be in my backyard, I get out of bed so I can head downstairs. And that's when I hear glass breaking. I know that something is wrong- very, very wrong. I grab my phone and call Silas, but just as he answers, I hear scuffling downstairs so I stop to listen. I don't want Brandon to hear me on the phone and know where I am so I don't say anything to Silas when he picks up.

I hear him asking 'Hello?' and saying my name with increasing panic in his voice, but I leave the phone on the bed as I slowly walk to my bedroom door. Silas swears and I assume he's on the way even though he doesn't hang up.

In the meantime, I'm concentrating so hard on the noises downstairs, that I hear my own blood pumping. I'm panicking too hard to try to use a gun right now but I grab it anyways, and I grab a small hunting knife I had by my bed for this exact scenario. I turn the lock on my bedroom door quietly but when I step back, the floorboard underneath my foot squeaks- and the noises downstairs stop.

Now, they are walking with purpose, across the living room and up my stairs. Without even trying the handle, Brandon rams his shoulder into the door, causing it to smash open. Pieces of wood go flying, and I jerk back in shock from the small explosion. He looks absolutely crazy, and I can tell he hasn't been taking care of himself. His eyes are dark and bugged out and I can smell him from across the room.

When we lock eyes, he just looks determined. "I'm guessing I don't have much time before your dog gets here, let's make it quick" and charges over to me. I take the safety off the gun and point, but when I go to shoot, its empty.

He stands in front of me and looks at me like I'm an idiot "Obviously I took the bullets out when I was here". I realize that's what he was doing when he was in my house but before the horror can sink in, he's lunging at me, trying to grab the gun.

He can't see my knife because it's folded and in my palm while I try to hold the gun away from him. Despite it having no bullets, I still don't want him to have it- especially if he has the ones he took out of it in his pockets. He manages to yank it out of my hands, and I flinch as he brings it down-hard- on my head.

My vision flashes black for a moment as I try to stay standing. Taking advantage of my loss of balance and near unconsciousness, he hits me again just as hard which makes me black out for a moment, and I'm barely fighting back.

I don't have the knife in my hand anymore and I silently pray that he didn't see it fall out of my hand. I'm focusing so hard on blocking any potential hits to my head, that I don't realize I'm already out of my bedroom.

He's standing over me as he grabs a fistful of my hair and begins to pull me by it, down the stairs. My head is in excruciating pain all over, but I try to use my legs to kick up into him. It connects a few times but it's annoying him more than anything so instead, I just focus on getting his hands off my hair.

Each stair feels like a mile, as I hear him call me every foul name he can- and then I hear him say "cheating whore". Even though I'm fighting to stay conscious, I fully realize the absurdity of Brandon's thought process and I know that he's too far gone.

Once we are at the bottom of the stairs on my wood floor, he crouches over me and slaps me in the face. He's yelling something, but I don't listen as I take advantage of his distraction and kick my foot out in hopes it could trip him or anything to get a moment to get him away from me.

All it does is piss him off more.

He's back on top of me, so I try to throw my hands up to protect my face, making him grab my hands and hold me down while saying in my ear "I've been waiting a block away all morning for that creep to finally leave, but once he comes back, I'm shooting him in the head".

He stands back up and continues "and once you're done watching that, you're next". I try to scream but he hits me in the jaw and I feel like I can only take one more before blacking out completely. Brandon has only been in the house for maybe three minutes and he's already succeeded in almost killing me. I almost want to laugh that I thought I could just move away from him and be done with this. Brandon stops what he's doing, and I hear the bullets being loaded into the gun. Just as I start spiraling into darkness, I hear my front door crash open.

Before I can even look to see what's happening, I hear a gun go off twice. Brandon makes a surprised grunting noise and suddenly, he's off of me.

I can't do anything but lie there and worry that Silas is getting hurt, but I can't seem to make anything out right now. I know I heard the gun go off but I didn't feel anything hit me- I also don't know if I would feel anything right now- I'm sure my body is in shock.

In my fading consciousness, I hear a loud thump on the ground, and then there are weird wet, crunching noises along with more repetitive thumping.

I turn to look for the noise, but I hear Silas urgently say "Hazey- don't look over here, okay? Everything's fine".

Normally, I would be annoyed being talked to like a little kid, but hearing Silas so calm helps me to just focus on staying conscious.

A moment later, Silas is crouching over me- and there's blood on him. Despite the situation, his face is in pure awe as he looks me over as he keeps whispering "You're okay" in relief. I want to ask him what's happening but before I can get the words out, I see that he's on the phone.

Silas gently instructs me "Stay awake, okay?" and I nod and lay there, trying to open my eyes wide to help me stay awake, because I can feel my brain trying to shut down.

I hear him wrap up the call with 911 before he hangs up and spends the rest of the time trying to keep me awake until the ambulance gets there. I can feel him doing that thing he did weeks ago, giving me energy as I feel my body healing itself. I make it until I hear the medics coming in, finally allowing myself to drift off...

After endless scans and prodding when I first get to the hospital, the doctors are amazed by how little trauma my skull shows despite the amount of blood all over me. My best theory is that my body used the energy from Silas to heal the worst of the injuries rather than focusing on keeping me awake.

When I ask if I can talk to Silas, they tell me that he will be here tomorrow morning, and that I just need to focus on resting for the rest of today and tonight. With an odd expression that I can't understand, they assure me that Silas is doing fine and I have no need to worry about him.

As soon as they let me rest, I'm able to sleep the rest of the day and night- waking once in awhile after the horrible flashing nightmares of what I just went through. The next morning, I am checked in on again.

Despite some pretty gnarly bruises, I don't have any damage beyond that. Just as I think I'm done and on the way out, the nurse lets me know that two police officers are here to ask me some questions. I figured that was going to happen so I wait for them, eager to get this part over with and ask what happened to Brandon.

A male officer comes in and he looks to be around my dad's age, while the female officer next to him is probably in her mid-thirties. I know that before I ask them anything, they will want all of their questions answered first, so I try to be patient as they go through their list. I tell them the truth and everything I know: Brandon broke in after watching the house and beat me with a gun several times. Fortunately, there was an ongoing record with Brandon so they believe me.

I try my best to repeat everything that happened yesterday, along with everything Brandon said to me. I also tell them how I heard Silas come in and before I knew it, he was next to me, comforting me. Once they seem satisfied, I ask my only question: "Where's Silas?".

The officers exchange a look before the older male officer tells me that he should be at the hospital by now, waiting to pick me up. They explain that he acted in self-defense and they aren't going to investigate the situation. When I ask what they mean by "situation" they look at each other briefly before the female officer says "Brandon died yesterday, ma'am".

I look at them in shock, not believing that he could truly, really be gone. The very first feeling is relief, and oddly enough, grief is soon to follow. I can't help but feel sad for his family, I've met them a few times and everyone was so sweet. After a few moments of silence, I ask "How?".

The male answers, in a surprisingly uncomfortable tone "He was, uh… repeatedly hit in the face to the point of no recognition. To be quite frank with you, we had to check his wallet to confirm his identity". I feel myself staring at him with my mouth in an 'O' shape- is that what those noises I heard were?

I cringe at the memory of the wet, crunching noises. Unsure of what to ask next, the female cop adds "Like we said, we know that this was done in self-defense so we aren't pursuing Silas in Brandon's death but, Hazel. Please be careful. I didn't even think damage like that was possible-".

The male interrupts her "We don't want to give you too many visuals. But what she is trying to say is, strength like that isn't something any of us have seen and even though it's nice when it's in your defense, don't go from one violent guy to another".

My first reaction is defensiveness but I also understand what they mean so I just nod my head and thank them as they head out. I could sit there and ask them questions all day but I think Silas would have more answers anyway. Once the cops are gone, a nurse comes in with an outfit from home and says my ride is here and that whenever I am able to, I can go down and check out. I slowly stand up, evaluating every pain in my body to make sure nothing is too damaged.

Then, I change, and make my way down to the front desk. Silas picked out a pair of leggings and a loose shirt, I can tell he was concerned about my comfort and I'm not complaining. Once I get to the front, I see Silas, standing and clearly waiting for me… with a bouquet of white dahlias. I'm grateful for the flowers- and so, so grateful he chose white ones instead of red. I've had enough of that color for awhile.

When our eyes meet, he happily- and

cautiously- eyes me over like he's assessing all of my damage. My face has a few bruises but it is still looks surprisingly healed for what happened to me yesterday. I have a smile that I can't hide as I walk up and he doesn't say anything, he just hugs me in a too-gentle hold and I can feel his face in my neck, breathing into my hair.

We stay like that for a few moments before we pull away and he says "Thank God you're okay. Let's get you home and you can talk about it when you're ready". He holds out his hand, which I take as we walk down to his car. He puts the bouquet in the backseat, and gingerly helps me into the passenger side, acting as though I'm made of glass.

Once we are in, I turn to him and say "I have a million questions" he lets out a little laugh and starts driving us home.

He says "Fire away- I'll try to keep up".

I take a deep breath and just ask without thinking "Are YOU okay? What happened to Brandon? Why am I mostly healed? What happened to you after I left? Why don't your hands look that bad if you punched him?". I get a little dizzy and remind myself I need to take it easy.

I clamp my lips together while I wait for a fraction of the answers that I am going to ask today. He looks at me quickly, checking if I'm done for now and then tries his best to answer just as quickly. "Yes, I'm completely fine. Brandon- I killed him. I just kept punching until his face was gone". I cringe and gag a little at the visual- and the noises I remember.

"You're mostly healed because I did as

much as I could without making anyone suspicious-energy can heal you if I focus on it. I was questioned by the police but had to convince them I didn't need to go to the hospital as well and just waited by my phone all night to possibly hear from you. As for my hands" he quickly flexes his fingers "I told you it takes a lot to hurt me". I'm quiet, absorbing all of his answers, making sure I am actually retaining them before I have more questions.

As far as I know, Silas has never hurt anyone so I can't imagine him hitting someone over and over to the point of killing them. "That's it? No more questions?" he looks at me in surprise before looking back at the road.

I think for a second before I quietly ask "…Have you ever done anything like that before?".

He looks a little disappointed but answers anyway "Never. But I would do that to him all over again, if I could. Not because it was fun, but because I kept imaging what he would have done if I wasn't there".

When we get to the house, Silas runs to my door to help me out. Once we are both standing, he softly cups my face in his hands and lightly kisses me on the lips. I'm savoring the breeze around us and the smell of freshly-cut grass when he interrupts my trance. "I had the night to clean up everything but if I missed anything, just let me know. Okay?".

I know that neither of us want to see reminders so I nod and he follows up with "Also… don't force yourself to stay here. Even if it's just for a night you know that you can always stay at my place for as long as you want".

I smile and kiss him "Thank you, Silas. You're the best neighbor ever" and his eyes go wide in shock and amusement.

"Neighbor? Once you're fully healed, I'm going to show you exactly how neighborly I can be" I feel him playfully nip at my ear. We walk inside and everything looks clean and new- minus the smell of chemicals- and I notice a few additions to my house.

"Is that a Ficus?" I point to the front window that now has a cute fig tree in front of it.

He shrugs "I had extra time last night so I started stress shopping".

I laugh and look at the several boxes of healing supplies- heating pad, ice pouches, pain relievers. I don't know what stores around here are open or that deliver that fast but I don't even get a chance to ask before Silas grabs my hand and says "Can I show you something else?". He looks so nervous that I don't question him, I just nod and I don't miss the gratitude on his face when he smiles and gently pulls me to a wrapped present on the kitchen counter that I didn't notice.

It feels like a canvas, so I look at him suspiciously before gently pulling the wrapping paper away. He's watching me with excitement, and I understand why when I look down. "You've had it this whole time?" He's proudly nodding as he grabs the wrapping paper and puts it in my recycling bin. It's the splattered canvas from our first date.

He asked to keep it a few months in and gave it to me as a gift for our first anniversary. On our second anniversary, I gave it back to him, wrapped with a bow- like it was just now. I immediately ask him to hang it for me in my bedroom, so we grab a hammer and nail and put it on the wall over my reading chair.

We head back down the stairs hand-in-hand and I stop as soon as we get to the bottom. My eyes go wide as I remember something "I heard the gun go off! Twice! The cops didn't mention anything about a shooting… did I hallucinate that?".

Silas points to a healed scar on his collar bone "No, that asshole shot me twice… but it'll will be perfectly healed in a day or so".

I look for the second wound and he points to his skull and says "My head too" with a laugh and a shrug.

When he sees the alarmed look on my face he just says "See? I told you I'm hard to kill…. I do have to give him credit for good aim though, because I move fast". I look closely and run my fingers through his hair, along his scalp but nothing feels abnormal.

My confusion is obvious so Silas supplies "It didn't go through or anything… you know better than anyone how hard headed I am". I can't help but to laugh at his lightheartedness during such a serious situation. I am also so, so grateful for it because I've had enough seriousness for awhile. I guess that's just another new side effect of Silas's new body. I'm done asking questions and spend the rest of the day at home, relaxing with Silas by my side.

CHAPTER 40

I make the very smart and very adult decision to never tell my parents the full story. I decide that I will tell them I had a restraining order and that he's left me alone. Normally, I tell my parents everything but I don't see the need since the situation is now gone. I'm annoyed with myself that I actually feel sad he's dead but grief is not linear- this was completely avoidable and that's exactly what I was trying to do. I remember how sweet his mom was and feel bad mostly for her.

She doesn't know her son was like this and I hope she doesn't find out the extent of it because the tragedy in itself is hard enough. He was also close with his siblings so I know that they will be crushed by the news, I debate on telling them but I don't think it's my place and I don't want to risk rubbing salt in the wound.

The same night I return home, I'm eating dinner with Silas when he gets up to wash dishes. Once he's done, I notice him guardedly staring at me so I just look at him questioningly. He leans against the counter and sighs before saying "I know that Brandon didn't give you space and I don't want you to feel any pressure with me- I want to take our time getting back to knowing each other. So now that you're officially safe, I want to let you know that I can go back over to my place at any time, including right now if that's your preference".

I stand up and walk around the kitchen counter to give him a hug, before I step back to look at him. I know he feels vulnerable and he's trying to make the best decision for us. "Silas?".

Alarm takes over his face as he quickly scans me for sign of injury. "What is it? Does something hurt?" but I put his fears to rest with a half-smile before replying "You don't have to, but I was sort of hoping you'd stay the night tonight. Can you make that little speech again tomorrow night instead?".

He takes a step forward so his face is over my own as I look up at him and I feel his gentle hands in my hair "I'd love to. But I won't let you take advantage of me again. You need to heal a little longer".

He smiles and he looks so much like his old self when he smiles like that, I can't help but feel like my old self- careless, excited. I don't know if it's the meds, or if he's using his "gift" while I'm still healing, but I have the most amazing, long sleep I've ever had. I wake up the next morning to Silas behind me, with arms wrapped around me in a spooning position. I can tell he's awake, so I turn around to face him. He's analyzing me, seeing how I feel after having him sleeping over for the first time without needing to. I just smile at him without saying anything which he smiles back to, looking relieved.

I don't say it, but I don't regret a single second I've spent with him, and last night was one of the best nights of my life. To have zero stress, and to finally be able to really and truly have each other was an amazing thing to spend a whole night knowing.

With a kiss on my forehead, he gets up and pulls me with him to the bathroom. We brush our teeth together, smiling at each other through the mirror- before heading downstairs for some tea. I know we need to have a real conversation about what we are doing together but I'm not sure if it's too soon since a man was just killed in my house…by Silas. But then I look at him and I just don't care.

Since we are sitting at the island counter, I turn to face him as he looks over at me in confusion. "So… you mentioned wanting to take it slow?" he's staring deeply at me while I ask this and then he gets a little smile on his face in relief.

He replies "Well first, let me ask you this: Do you want to try?" and now, it's my turn to smile "Yes. but slowly, I'd like to work up to that".

He likes my answer but lets his eyes flicker in between mine for a few seconds before thinking out loud. "Alright… well, I know I've already spent a few nights in your bed but let's go back a few steps" he pulls my chair closer so that my legs are on either side of his chair.

"I'd like to take you out on a few dates… spend more time getting to know 'new Hazel' and then…".

"-then what?" I interrupt at the mischievousness on his face but he boldly continues.

"Then, when I earn your trust back fully and

I prove to you that we are better than before, I'm going to spend the night again. And this time I'm fucking your brains out".

My mouth drops a little at his sudden confidence. He helps close it with a kiss before chuckling and getting up to rinse the mugs out.

Later that day, when Silas is standing by my door saying goodbye for the night, I ask him "Silas, is your favorite food still enchiladas?".

His face lights up and without any hesitation, he answers "Yes. I haven't been able to eat them in three years, Hazel. Please tell me you're asking because you're thinking about making them". I laugh and kiss him goodbye before going back inside to make my grocery list for the next day: everything I'll need to make enchiladas.

EPILOGUE

1 MONTH LATER

It took a few weeks to feel "back to normal". Once the frequent headaches started wearing off, I focused on getting back to my routine and going on walks again. Silas and I agreed to take a few weeks to focus on ourselves- he understood that I emotionally needed some time to process and talk everything out with my therapist. We still saw each other more often than I'm proud to admit for thinking I was just focusing on myself but being with him just feels… right.

We haven't slept together again, and we've both taken turns stopping our kissing before it gets too far. As much as I want to, like really, really want to, I think we could both use some time just getting to really know each other without the stress we had around us when Brandon was around. Although, I am very aware of how much I'm ready for that to change… soon.

Silas has taken me on three dates that were just as thoughtful and wonderful as the first one. He's worried about me "overdoing it", so they haven't been all-day ones- mostly nice dinners. Even though I wish we hadn't had the last few years taken from us, not many couples get a second chance after a few years of maturing, so I want to do everything the best way possible. We still have just as much fun together, but there is now a comfort between us that came from going through the worst things together and coming out on the other side.

Since Carly knew a little of what was going on with Brandon, I gave her a quick summary and let her know I will need to be a couch potato for a few weeks. I invited her over for a few relaxing nights watching reality TV- thinking she would be bored the entire time. But she's insisted that she's been needing some lazy nights since Zach has been keeping her so busy.

More than a few times, I've fallen asleep only to wake up some time later, to a very clean house. Of course, she denies doing anything but I still plan on buying her quite a few coffees. Now that I'm better, we have a few calendar dates set up to have some fun like before… this time, some of them are double dates.

Abigail obviously was a rock. She's the only person I've told everything to, since she's been there since the beginning. Like me, it took her awhile to believe and process everything she was being told- but she got there eventually. As always, she's been there for long conversations as I processed everything, and to update me with her life. We are planning a summer girls' trip and I can't wait to have another memory with her. I lucked out with some awesome friends who didn't need to, but continuously proved themselves again and again.

For the last two weeks, I started going on my long walks again and even started jogging a little. Sometimes my head begins to hurt if my heart beats fast so I'm content taking it slow. Silas has slowly been struggling more and more at keeping his distance, so lately he's come up with silly excuses to come over (like forgetting his phone charger). Somehow, he ends up staying to cook or generally fuss over me. I told him no, but he always has gifts he brings over or things for my house that he somehow knows I need.

At first, I was worried that Silas would leave again. Part of my time in therapy is how to accept past hurt without it controlling my present life, and Silas makes it easy. He's never giving me a reason to think he doesn't want to be around me as long as possible. The more conversations we have about the past, the more I know how badly it hurt him to leave. As much as I hate Brandon for how he treated me, I'm grateful that it brought Silas and I back together. I'm getting ready for a slow day with some of my favorite older music playing when I hear a knock at my door.

Knowing the familiar pattern, a small smile creeps on my face as I go to answer it.

It's Silas.

But rather than his usual outfits of casual tees and jeans, he's wearing black dress pants and a black button up shirt with the sleeves rolled to his elbows. I'm too busy taking in his randomly fancy outfit to notice his semi-nervous face- until I hear his chuckle and he pulls a bouquet of flowers from behind has back- dahlias.

With a lop-sided smile, he hands me the flowers "Happy Birthday, Hazel!" he says with a huge grin and open arms, pulling me in for a hug and a quick kiss.

I quickly pull back "What?!" there's no way I forgot that.

He laughs "You forgot your own birthday? Look at the date on your phone". I look at him suspiciously before doing exactly that- he's right. It is my birthday. I haven't heard from my parents, but I realize it's still very early in the morning so I turn my ringtone up to hear it later.

He kisses me again and says "I can tell you're feeling better because you're listening to music again". I think how annoying it will be if he can always hear everything I'm doing but decide that for now, it's been a good thing- so I step aside to invite him in which he happily accepts.

Silas saunters into my house, turning abruptly to look at me "You don't have plans today? Normally you plan your birthdays months in advance".

I'm still in shock, so I just reply "No! I can't believe I forgot!". I know this year wasn't normal, but I still can't believe I haven't even thought about my own birthday.

Silas interrupts my thoughts when he steps closer and says "Well that's good news, then. I have my house all set up for a two-person birthday party". He finishes his sentence with tucking my hair behind my ear and nudging my chin up slightly to look at him, gauging my response.

My face breaks out in a smile "Birthday party, huh? That's pretty hard to say no to on my birthday".

He leans down to give me a quick kiss "Good- that was the plan". He slowly walks back to my door "Have a peaceful morning, food and coffee will be delivered in a few minutes. When you get your food, take a bubble bath and relax. Once you're ready, come over to my place around twelve".

I agree before we kiss and Silas leaves, leaving me to put my flowers in a vase and receiving a breakfast delivery shortly after. After a long and peaceful bubble bath with a coffee and huge breakfast, I take my time getting ready and enjoying the texts and calls from my loved ones wishing me a happy birthday.

My parents surprised me with a round-trip flight to visit them next month and I can't wait, I've missed them so much. They've offered to visit me soon, but I need to figure out how to handle Silas being back in my life and how to explain what I can to them.

Once it's twelve, I lock my door and excitedly head over to his house. I gave myself a blowout and have on a new, black mock-neck mini dress with tights and knee-length leather boots. His door is slightly ajar, so I slowly push it open in anticipation, and my jaw drops. He's at the counter opening delivery containers from a restaurant we both love, but that's not what my eyes keep going to. There's several more bouquets throughout the room, with candles and music playing.

I see a few wrapped presents in the corner, along with bottles of wine and my favorite snacks… oh and a huge delicious looking cake- when I look back at him, he has a smile like it's his birthday too. At first, all I can say is "Oh… my god!" but he only smiles more until I step fully inside, set my stuff down and shut the door behind me. As I'm taking off my shoes, he walks over and grabs my hand, leading me to the barstool at the kitchen counter.

We are both sitting, facing one another and I say "You did way too much!" and look around again in excitement and curiosity.

He gets a slightly more serious look on his face "No… I didn't, Hazey. This is your birthday and I want you to enjoy it. I have the day planned so just get in the receiving mood today, okay?".

I just smile and nod while looking at the cake, hearing him chuckle. He gets up and brings over two wine glasses and a bottle of prosecco, pouring both halfway full and adding a few sliced strawberries, holding his glass up for a 'cheers'. I tap his glass with my own before taking a sip.

"So," I hear Silas start, and know that he's about to say something that makes him slightly nervous so I set the glass down to face him again. "I know that we lost some time, but I wanted to remind you that we're still young. We're only 25- well 26 now, Hazel." I take in his words and nod, knowing there's more.

"But I still don't want to waste any more time. You've had a little bit of space and time to clear your head… but I love you and I can't wait any longer to say it". That's his first time saying that to me in years, and I try to focus on what he goes on to say.

"I see the way you look at me, even when you're trying not to, and I think you feel something similar" I interrupt him to softly confirm "I do". He gently holds my face in his hands before giving me a gentle kiss on the lips "Not to make your birthday about me…" then he kisses my forehead, and then both apples of my cheeks "but will you be my girlfriend?".

I go to give him a big hug- with him sitting on the stool, I'm finally his height when I stand. After kissing him a few times I whisper "of course" and we kiss some more. He gently guides me back on the stool with his hands to say something else. "I want your birthday to still just be that, so I was thinking we can still celebrate on our old date if you want, but we don't have to".

Knowing he's waiting for my response, I say "That's perfect… thank you, Silas. Not just for this- but for everything" he just smiles and nods at me. "We have a few long conversations ahead of us" I say, causing Silas to wait for me to elaborate, so I do. "You're… different now. And I want to know what it would be like if I joined you in that before we plan a future together". His face makes me stop talking because I can tell he needs to say something.

I wait as he slides forward and gently grabs my hand "We can absolutely discuss all of this, but I think we can enjoy today and save that conversation for tomorrow or any other day. That's a big discussion and it's a topic that I'm unfortunately also missing a lot of information on".

I nod, knowing we have a lot to go over and will most likely need to find out if there's others like Silas, and where they are. We make plans to sit down and go over everything we need to know tomorrow, and if we can find any information on the man that bit Silas in the first place.

Even with the little information I have, I would be happy to join Silas in this journey and I wouldn't need much convincing to let him change me as well. I would be happy to be unified with him in every way possible, and if he asked me three years ago, I would have said the same thing.

I lean in so our faces aren't far apart and say "I love you too" because I need to say those words out loud before I burst like a balloon. And his huge smile is instant and grateful. He holds my head in his hands and leans in to say something that I assume will be very romantic because he has a certain look in his eyes but he asks "Are you hungry?". I laugh- but, I am- so I also nod.

After a lunch of imported pasta, Silas begins to bring over the cake with a candle and lighter in hand. The cake is pink and heart-shaped with "Happy 26th birthday, Hazel!" written on it in white frosting. Setting the cake in front of me, he moves back to stand behind me as he lights the candle. I feel him kiss my temple and say quietly in my ear "Make a wish".

I take a few seconds before I smile and say it to myself, before blowing the candle out. I wish for the next year to be the best one yet... and I have a good feeling about it. Silas takes the candle out and holds it a few inches from my mouth so I can lick the frosting off before he sets it down. Silas tilts my head backward to kiss me, walking back over to the other side of the counter to grab a cake knife and two plates with forks.

After slicing mine, he forks a small bite and puts it up to my mouth so I can taste it- and it's delicious. Its vanilla buttercream with strawberry jam in between the layers- I can't believe he remembered all of my favorites. I do the same- lifting the fork up to his lips, watching his perfect mouth take the bite as he makes a soft groan and swallows. We share a few long, sweet kisses as we take turns feeding each other bites of cake.

Being together like this, freely, makes me want to skip the entire celebration and go upstairs to his room. I tell myself to just make it a few more hours of enjoying my own birthday before I ask my boyfriend to make my day even more special. Once we finish our cake, Silas stands and leans over me, looking at me tenderly and playing with my hair. "I'm so glad you were born, Hazey" and before I can say anything, he asks the second-best question of the afternoon: "Now… are you ready for presents?".

THE END

ACKNOWLEDGMENTS

I remember making a book in third grade and writing an acknowledgement section... funny how sometimes your interests never change!

This is my first book, and I am anonymously self-publishing this so if you are reading this, then thank YOU. I am endlessly grateful that there is a way for awkward introverts to send their random daydreams into the universe, but that would not be possible if there were not people willing to read those daydreams. I'm also thankful for a support system of my husband, family and friends who have always made me feel like I need to follow my dreams and if they crash and burn, then I have people to catch me.

THANK YOU!

ABOUT THE AUTHOR

JESS J. BLOOMS

Jess J. Blooms is a lifelong reader, obsessed with romance, passion and realistic dialogue.

When she's not at her full-time job, you can find her going outside as often as possible... usually stress walking somewhere.

Or she may just be trying to convince her husband to get another pet besides their cat and tortoise.

Did you like it?
Did you hate it?
Did you love it?
Do you want to make fun of it with your friends?

Either way… Please review!

Honest reviews on Goodreads and Amazon keep books and authors going 😊

From Before

www.ingramcontent.com/pod-product-compliance
Lightning Source LLC
Chambersburg PA
CBHW070517310726
48976CB00002BA/461